Praise for Elizabeth Hickey's Captivating Historical Novels

THE WAYWARD MUSE

"Well-realized."

—*The Seattle Post-Intelligencer*

"Hickey exhibits a keen gift for period detail and character development . . . bringing all the characters, even peripheral ones, to life."

—*The Portland Tribune*

"[Hickey's] full-blooded characters move through the pages with verve and passion for life and their art."

—*Romantic Times*

"Elizabeth Hickey conjures up the fascinating love story behind an artist's vision and brings it to life with richly imagined characters and historical detail. It is an enchanting novel."

—Tova Mirvis, author of *The Ladies Auxiliary* and *The Outside World*

"Elizabeth Hickey's rendering of the pre-Raphaelite movement in English poetry and art is evocative and enchanting. Jane Burden is a heroine worthy of the Brontë sisters."

—Brenda Rickman Vantrease, author of *The Illuminator* and *The Mercy Seller*

"With sumptuous and persuasive detail, the novel unveils for us the intoxications and burdens of always being someone's muse."

—Jim Shepard, author of *Project X* and *Love and Hydrogen*

THE PAINTED KISS

"An expressively written debut. . . . Hickey's language is sensual, lush, and unhurried, and the prose wears its author's research gracefully."

—*Publishers Weekly*

"A graceful imagining of the joined lives of a rising, soon-to-be-famous artist and a young woman in fin-de-siecle Vienna . . . evocative . . . lovely."

—*Kirkus Reviews*

"In Elizabeth Hickey's compelling novel of tempestuous lives amid the tawdry bohemia of artists' studios and the glittering innuendo of Viennese café society, longing pulses from the page. . . . Vivid, atmospheric, engaging, and very, very real."

—Susan Vreeland, author of *Luncheon of the Boating Party* and *Girl in Hyacinth Blue*

"Richly atmospheric and haunting."

—Lauren Belfer, author of *City of Light*

"A multi-colored, breathtaking read."

—msn.com

"The lovers are well-crafted and the atmosphere and ambience of the European art world is conveyed beautifully."

—*Romantic Times*

"Full of unexpected pleasures . . . a beautiful novel."

—*The Sunday Oregonian*

"A richly crafted, atmospheric narrative."

—*Tucson Citizen*

"A resonant debut novel."

—*The Seattle Post-Intelligencer*

ALSO BY ELIZABETH HICKEY

The Painted Kiss

The
Wayward Muse

Elizabeth Hickey

WASHINGTON SQUARE PRESS
New York London Toronto Sydney

Washington Square Press
A Division of Simon & Schuster, Inc.
1230 Avenue of the Americas
New York, NY 10020

First Washington Square Press trade paperback edition July 2008

WASHINGTON SQUARE PRESS and colophon are registered trademarks
of Simon & Schuster, Inc.

For information about special discounts for bulk purchases,
please contact Simon & Schuster Special Sales at 1-800-456-6798
or business@simonandschuster.com.

Manufactured in the United States of America

1   3   5   7   9   10   8   6   4   2

ISBN-13: 978-0-7432-7319-0
ISBN-10:   0-7432-7319-2

For Jonathan

Acknowledgments

Many thanks to Kim Witherspoon, Greer Hendricks, Catherine Drayton, Rosemary Ahern, Suzanne O'Neill, Eleanor Jackson, Lori Andiman, Hannah Morrill, and Meryl Moss. I am indebted to Jasper Selwood and, as always, to my husband, Jonathan Selwood.

The Wayward Muse

One

JANE Burden was considered the plainest girl on Holywell Street, and that Oxford slum was home to many worthy contenders for the title. Mary Porter, who was afflicted with a lazy eye and copious freckles, lived there, just across the street from Alice Cunningham, who had crooked, discolored teeth and thinning hair. Number 142 was the residence of Catherine Blair, whose neck and ear had been horribly burned when she was a baby, and whose left leg was somewhat shorter than the right. But even she was considered marginally better looking than Jane.

Though Jane had no discernible deformities, her neighbors had their reasons for attributing to her a surpassing ugliness. First of all, she was tall. There were, perhaps, young women who could carry this height gracefully, but Jane was not one of them. Self-conscious, she stooped. Her limbs were ungainly and she often stumbled, or knocked into tables, or hit her head on something. Her neck was very long, and in spite of her dressmaking skill, her sleeves were always too short and her bumpy, bony wrists stuck out awkwardly.

She was also too skinny. She had no breasts to speak of, though she was already seventeen, and no hips. The old ladies shook their heads and told her mother that she would not have children. When she was reproached with this, she thought to herself that it was terribly unfair to be blamed for something that was not her fault. She couldn't help it that her father and her brother claimed the largest share of the thin vegetable stews and coarse loaves of bread that were all they had. Of course, somehow her sixteen-year-old sister, Bessie, who had as little to eat as she did, still managed to have rounded cheeks and a respectable bosom.

Jane's hair was as coarse as a bristle brush and curly. Occasionally she used a hot iron in an attempt to create orderly waves, and she regularly stole from the stable the oil used to shine the horses' coats, but neither iron nor oil worked as well as she would have liked.

But it was her expression that truly made Jane Burden plain. For she seldom smiled, and her green eyes, which might have been considered striking on another girl, were empty. They weren't sad; sadness could be fetching. They were not grave and serious or soft and pleading or tearful and melancholy. They were blank. Jane's eyes told everyone who met her of her misery and her despair. They told of a girl who had ceased to hope for anything, who had gone deep inside herself to withstand her lot. It made the others uneasy.

Jane fretted about her ugliness, of course. A poor girl's looks were all she had, and without them she could never hope to marry. Without marriage her life would be even worse than it was now. If she was lucky, she could work in the kitchens at one of the big estates. If she wasn't lucky, she'd be a scullery maid in a household one step above her own.

But brooding only made the situation worse. It put a wrinkle of worry between her thick, dark brows and twisted her bow-shaped lips into a grimace.

On this day, however, her lack of beauty was not foremost among her worries as she descended the vertiginous cellar stairs. Her primary concern was supper. Her mother would expect the meal to be ready when she stumbled home from an afternoon of gin and neighborhood gossip, and Jane wasn't sure she could fashion a stew out of the little they had. Were there any carrots left at the bottom of the bin? Were there any onions that weren't rotten, or any potatoes that weren't black and bitter? Perhaps she could send Bessie out to look for some mushrooms.

It wasn't until she reached the third step that the stench of fermenting urine and excrement enveloped her. She gasped and nearly fell, gripping the rickety banister for support.

"Bessie!" she shouted back up the stairs. "It's happened again!"

Their house always stank of waste, of course; it was next to the Holywell Street privy. Jane had grown accustomed to it. But the strength and power of the foul odor was so strong she gagged and retched into her apron. When she was finished she untied it and tossed the soiled garment over the banister. Then she forced herself down the steps and into the cellar. She held her candle high and scanned the walls.

Her shoes slopped in mud. She followed the wretched stream to its origin, a crack in the mortar of the south wall, two feet from the floor. Human feces was oozing through and dripping down the stonework.

Jane heard her sister at the top of the stairs.

"Is it the privy?" Bessie cried.

"Of course it's the privy," snapped Jane. "Bring me the mop and bucket."

"Why does this always happen to us?" Bessie whined. "Why are we so unlucky?"

"Luck has nothing to do with it," said Jane grimly. "Now, hurry. And bring me a rag, too. We need something to stuff in the crack."

"We need a new house," muttered Bessie, but she did as she was told.

Bite your tongue, thought Jane. They had lived in four houses in three years, each more terrible than the last. Though she could not imagine what could be worse than living next to the privy. There was the smell, of course, and the periodic flooding, but what Jane hated the most was the fact that everyone on the street walked by their house to use it, stopping to peer in the windows and make rude comments.

The house was hardly more than a cottage, with one room for eating and cooking and another where the five of them slept on straw pallets. It had been made, as many of the street's houses had, from river rock that had been broken into brick-size pieces, but it had not been made well. The entire structure listed to the left, and the windows and doors weren't true. It looked as if it might collapse at any moment. In fact, one of the street's houses had collapsed a few years before, killing a woman and three children, "and some very good laying hens," as Jane's mother had put it.

No, she couldn't imagine anything worse. Even to live out in the open, in the rain and snow, might be uncomfortable, but at least there would be fresh air.

Bessie appeared at the top of the stairs.

"How did it happen?" she asked, holding out the mop, bucket, and rag.

"The night soil men must not have come," said Jane. "Or there's a hole in the container."

"Well, I'm not going to mop up that filth," Bessie announced. She sat down on the top step and smoothed her skirt as if she were attending a luncheon party.

"Do you know how furious Mrs. Burden will be if she comes home and finds the cellar flooded with this?" said Jane.

"Mrs. Burden will be too drunk to notice," said Bessie. To each other, they never called their mother Mum or Mummy, but only Mrs. Burden.

"She'll notice when there's no dinner, and all the vegetables are ruined," said Jane. But Bessie would not be moved.

"You know there wasn't anything down there worth eating, even before it was submerged in filth." She pulled her needle and thread out of her apron pocket. "I've got sewing to do. There's a tear in my blue tarlatan, and I wanted to wear it to the theater tomorrow night."

With a sigh Jane went back into the muck of the cellar. The fetid sludge had risen to her ankles. She was concerned that the pressure on the wall might bring the whole thing down. Jane could only pray that stuffing the crack would hold it until someone, her father or the neighborhood mason, could patch it.

Jane filled the bucket and carried it upstairs and out into the street. She didn't want to dump it back into the leaking privy, so she used the drainage ditch next to the Gibbons's house. Bessie held her nose daintily each time Jane passed. After fifteen trips the leak in the wall had slowed to a trickle but the dirt floor was still a morass. Jane went to the ash pit and filled her bucket with ashes. She threw them down on the cellar floor. The smell was still horrific, but there was nothing to be done about that.

Jane heard shouting from upstairs. "Why is the fire out? Where's the supper? Jane? Bessie?"

Their mother was home.

Jane trudged up the stairs. Her shoes and the hem of her skirt were soaked with brown liquid. Her blouse was gray with ash, and her face and hair were streaked with ash and sweat.

Ann Burden stood rather unsteadily in the doorway. She'd been a farm girl once, and had the freckles and the lines around her eyes to prove it. Never a beauty, the years of hard work, first in the fields and then in Oxford's most squalid neighborhood, had taken their toll. One of her hips was higher than the other and rolled when she walked, or rather, limped. Everything about her was hard: her eyes, her jaw, her sinewy body. Only when she was drunk did her features soften into maudlin self-pity.

When she caught sight of Jane, she screamed with fury. Jane reflected that, in a way, she was lucky because she was too disgusting to be hit. To hit her, her mother would have to touch her.

"What have you done?" Mrs. Burden hissed.

"The privy overflowed again," said Bessie helpfully.

"So you thought you'd go swimming in it?" her mother said sarcastically.

"I was trying—"

Mrs. Burden cut her off. "Trying to track that filth all over the house? Trying to disgust me more than you already do?"

"I was trying to clean up the mess," Jane said. She felt like crying, but that would only enrage her mother further.

"Useless girl," said Mrs. Burden. "What did I ever do to deserve a daughter like you? Ugly as an old shoe, you are, and twice as worthless."

Jane said nothing to her mother because what was there to say? The only thing to do was to let the tirade run its course.

"I told her we should wait until you got home, but Jane never listens to me," said Bessie.

"Shut up, Bessie," said Mrs. Burden, "and start the supper. I want to speak to Jane alone."

"What will I use for vegetables?" whined Bessie.

"Go down to the cellar, find something that looks usable, bring it up, and wash it off," said Mrs. Burden, not looking at her. Bessie hesitated.

"But—" she began.

"Go!" shouted Mrs. Burden. With a little squeak Bessie ducked her head, as if to ward off a blow, and was gone.

Mrs. Burden beckoned Jane into the kitchen. She lumbered over to the rocking chair and lowered herself onto it with a groan, but Jane knew better than to sit. She stood in front of her mother and waited.

"I met Mrs. Barnstable tonight," said Mrs. Burden. "You are to walk with her son Tom this Sunday after church." She smiled slyly as she waited for Jane's reaction.

Jane's throat closed. Her collar was choking her. Tom Barnstable was a tall, gangly youth of twenty with a walleye and a face erupting in pustules. His name was ridiculously appropriate, as he and his father both worked at the stable with her father.

"Think you're too good for him, don't you?" said Mrs. Burden, watching her face. "Well, let me tell you something. With your looks you'd be lucky if Tom Barnstable would have you. And believe me, I'm going to do everything I can to make it happen. You'll not be hanging around here, a millstone around my neck until the day I die, if I can help it."

"I won't go," said Jane faintly. "Tom is a bully. He hits his little sisters; I've seen the bruises."

"An ear boxing or two would do you good," said Mrs. Burden. "I've spoiled you, letting you go to that school, letting that Miss Wheeler lend you books. You've gotten above yourself. I have a feeling Tom will keep you in line."

"Please," whispered Jane.

"You're going to walk with Tom on Sunday. You're going to wear Bessie's pink bonnet, which doesn't help much but at least gives your face a little color, and you're going to be as charming as you can possibly be," said Mrs. Burden. "Now get out of my sight."

Jane ran out the door and into the street. It was not yet dark and she hoped that she would not meet anyone. Her clothes were still damp and the wind chilled her. She ran down the street toward town.

Jane sometimes imagined that she lived far away from Oxford. Usually she pretended that she lived in the Balearic Islands, which she had read about in a geography book. It was warm there, she knew. You could live in a raffia hut lapped by the sea and eat lobster stew by the bowlful. This time she tried to imagine that she lived in London, in a brick town house on a fashionable street. She would have a cook who would make lamb stew, piping hot and fragrant with rosemary, and rolls dripping with butter. For dessert, she would eat sponge cake with caramel sauce, and strawberry trifle. Jane would wear goat's-hair shawls from India and fine silk dresses from China.

Sometimes Jane's daydreams comforted her, but not today. She could not escape the fact that she was cold and dirty. She couldn't pretend that she was pretty. She was ugly and she must marry Tom Barnstable or no one.

Jane finally stopped at the end of Holywell Street; she couldn't go on into town covered in filth. She tried to think of somewhere else to go, but there was nowhere else, so she turned and started back.

Halfway home she heard a cat yowling and she quietly stepped into a doorway, hoping not to be seen. A tortoiseshell cat hobbled pathetically by her, dripping blood from its ear. Then she heard pounding footsteps and Tom Barnstable ran by, a stone in his hand, an expression of glee on his face. He did not see her.

My future husband, she thought, and then she did cry, sliding to the hard stone step and burying her face in her stinking skirt.

Two

HE next day Jane tried to forget about her mother, and the cellar, and Tom Barnstable. Instead she focused on the play that she and Bessie were to see. Going to the theater was a rare treat for them. Their tickets had come from a friend of Bessie's whose mother had taken ill. And it wasn't a third-rate local troupe either, but the touring company of the Theater Royal Drury Lane, from London.

"What should I wear?" Jane asked Bessie as they scoured the pans.

"The yellow dress is the only one you have that isn't too short," Bessie said, "though it does make you look terribly sallow. I've repaired the blue tarlatan. It's sadly faded but Mrs. Burden said I can't have another dress until spring, no matter how much I grow."

"Maybe if I wore the black velvet collar," Jane considered. "At least then the yellow wouldn't be near my face."

"Oh, I was going to wear it," pouted Bessie. "Peter Gourley is going to be there, and you know he's an apprentice at the haberdasher's now. He's very particular about how a girl's turned out."

Jane wondered how Tom Barnstable felt about how a girl was dressed.

"You can borrow some of my rosewater, though, if you like," said Bessie. "Peter gave it to me. It was fearfully expensive, so mind you just use the tiniest bit."

"Thank you," sighed Jane. She did not like to admit that she disliked Bessie, not since their older sister, Mary Ann, had died of tuberculosis six years before.

In the evening Mr. Burden came home from the stable and Jane's brother, Jamey, returned from his job as a messenger. Without a word to anyone, they sat down at the table and waited for their supper. When Jane and Bessie placed a bowl of boiled turnips and a plate of brown bread on the table, their brother grabbed them immediately and emptied them onto his plate.

Bessie shrieked in dismay. "But there's no more—," she began.

Jamey mumbled something, but his mouth was full and no one could understand it.

"Something wrong, girl?" asked Mr. Burden, reaching over to take a turnip from Jamey's plate. He didn't shout, or thump the table, or raise his arm, but even Bessie knew better than to challenge him when he used that particular tone.

"No, sir," Bessie said, shaking her head.

They ate the rest of their meal without speaking. The only sound was Mr. Burden's grunts as he mopped his plate with the bread. Mrs. Burden and Bessie and Jane had only boiled potatoes. As soon as Mr. Burden's plate was empty, he clapped Jamey on the shoulder and they left the house without a backward glance. They would spend the evening at the pub and return after the women were already in bed.

After washing up, Jane and Bessie went to the bedroom to get ready for the theater. Jane's yellow dress was made of the cheapest wool available, and had been worn so many times that the once gold-colored fabric was dull and pilled. At least the style suited her figure, thought Jane. Mrs. Burden might be illiterate, but she was widely known to be the best dressmaker on Holywell Street, and she had imparted her only useful skill to her daughter. Jane had altered the one pattern they owned, so that her dress had dolman sleeves and lowered armholes. For the thousandth time she thought how nice it would be to have braided or fringed dress trim and an amber brooch.

Anxiously she studied the hem of her skirt. "I think it is too short," she said. "Can you see the tops of my boots?"

Bessie had decided that the hair ribbon she had planned to wear wasn't fit to be seen and tossed it to the floor. Now she turned to look at Jane. "Yes, you can," she said. "I think you are going to be a giantess, Jane. Isn't there any way to let it out?"

"There's no more hem left," said Jane.

"Look in the fabric bag," said Bessie. "Maybe you can cut out a quick band and sew it on. How do you like my hair?"

Jane found a piece of cloth that would do for the hem of her skirt. She took off the dress and laid it on her pallet. Then she set to work, clad only in her chemise. She had to hurry if she was going to be ready in time.

The blue cotton she had found was left over from making Bessie's dress and would look very odd, but it was better than being indecent. In a very short time, the task was done and she put the dress back on.

Jane tied Bessie's sash so that each loop of the bow was the exact size and shape of the other, and vigorously brushed the lint and dirt from the back of Bessie's skirt. She straightened Bessie's velvet collar and curled her front hair with hot tongs. Bessie glanced at her reflection in the window and, with a satisfied toss of her head, pronounced herself ready.

"What about me?" said Jane. Bessie turned and looked at her sister. She clapped her hand to her mouth and tried to stifle her giggles, but couldn't.

"Oh, Jane, you look terrible!" she said.

"What's wrong?" asked Jane in alarm.

Bessie showed her the large spot of mud on the front of her dress. "I don't know how you missed seeing this. Your collar is crooked, your skirt is twisted, and two of your buttons have popped off."

Just then Mrs. Burden barreled into the room.

"Look at the two of you," she said. Her eyes were still sleepy with drink but her voice was sharp. "I often wonder where I went wrong," she continued, "one daughter so ugly as to be deformed, the other as silly as a Punch and Judy show. I suppose it was marrying your father, though he was handsome enough then."

"I think I look very nice," said Bessie stoutly.

Mrs. Burden laughed mirthlessly. "Oh, you'll get a husband, I'm sure. Mind he doesn't send you back when he finds out how lazy and rude you are. But at least you've got proper carriage. Not like this one. Look at how she slouches. Another girl would be walking about with books on her head, but she just stands there with rolled shoulders."

Jane thought to herself that if there were any books in the house, she would gladly practice, but she said nothing.

Her mother smacked her on the side of the head. "I know what you're thinking," she said. "Ungrateful girl." Then she collapsed onto the pallet she shared with Mr. Burden and began to sob.

"Why did I lose my boys?" she wept. "Mrs. Allen has four strapping sons, all a credit to her. I've only got Jamey, now that John and Francis and Michael . . ."

Jane stood quietly, thinking of her dead brothers while Bessie sewed her buttons on with trembling fingers. They had only been babies, all killed by cholera. She supposed that was why their mother hated them, because they should have been the ones to die.

Bessie blotted the stain on Jane's skirt with vinegar water, and most of it came out. Jane pinched Bessie's cheeks to make them pink, and they shared a spritz of the rosewater. Then, having no mirror, they examined each other from top to bottom to make sure everything was in order. Having satisfied themselves that it was, they left Mrs. Burden weeping on the straw mattress. Soon she would suspend her tears long enough to lumber into the kitchen and pour herself more rotgut gin. By the time they got home from the theater, she would most likely be asleep.

Jane and Bessie set off down Holywell Street, toward town.

On the way they passed Tom Barnstable. Suddenly he was everywhere, thought Jane. Why couldn't he join the army or fall down a well? He wore a sullen expression as he kicked a pebble down the street, but when he saw them he nodded and smiled, revealing a mouthful of gray, dead teeth. It seemed to Jane that he looked particularly at her. When they had passed, Bessie nudged Jane in the side.

"Don't say anything," said Jane, her jaw clenched.

It was a short walk to Oriel Street. A throng was gathered at the entrance to the modest auditorium where the colleges held their debating competitions and less popular musical concerts.

Bessie gripped Jane's arm. "Everyone's so well dressed," she whispered.

"Yes," agreed Jane, trying not to notice that several people had stared pityingly at her skirt. "I see Dr. Holman and his wife. She looks very pleased with her fox tippet."

They joined the line waiting to pick up tickets.

"Do you see Peter?" Bessie asked. "He promised me he would be here."

Jane scanned the crowd of theatergoers, so different from the people she usually saw. "There he is," she announced when she caught sight of a freckled young man waving frantically at her sister from the back of the line.

"Save my place," said Bessie, and was gone.

A man was selling lemonade at a booth across the lobby, and Jane was just wishing she had money to buy some when she felt that someone was staring at her. She looked around and her gaze locked with that of a young man slouched against the wall next to the lemonade booth, sipping a glass of beer. He had large, expressive eyes, dark as coal oil, deeply set in a face as smooth and chiseled as honey-colored Italian marble. A small, sardonic smile played across his full lips when his eyes met hers. He turned to whisper something to his companion, who squinted in Jane's direction. Quickly she turned around. Her heart was pounding but she told herself that the young man must be ridiculing her poor dress or laughing at her ugliness. What other reason could he have for staring?

When she turned back to look, they had gone, and Bessie was beside her again, holding the playbill Peter Gourley had bought her. Jane said nothing to her sister, knowing that even if she could explain what she had felt when the dark young man stared at her, Bessie would tell her she was imagining things.

Their seats were all the way in front and on the extreme left side of the theater, so that they could see into the orchestra pit and the wings. It was excruciating to stare at the musicians pulling their instruments out of their cases and not be able to turn around and look for the young man and his friend. Jane tried to pay attention to the things Bessie read to her from the playbill, but the cushion on her seat was ripped and as she fidgeted she fervently hoped that the springs poking her uncomfortably did not tear her skirt.

"Did you see two young men in the crowd?" asked Jane finally, despite herself. "One tall with gold whiskers, the other dark?"

"Where?" said Bessie, swiveling around.

Jane grabbed her by the sleeve. "Don't," she hissed.

"Were they handsome?" inquired Bessie. "Why didn't you mention it before? Now they're putting out the lanterns and I can't see."

"Shh," Jane said as the curtain was cranked open. "The play is starting."

The play was the musical comedy *Ben Bolt*, and there was lots of tripping over chairs and mistaken identity. Jane tried to follow the plot, but she was distracted. She kept thinking about the dark gentleman. She was surprised she had never seen him before. He was too old to be a student, so she supposed he must be a tutor at one of the colleges.

"Let's go and stand by the lemonade booth," she said to Bessie at intermission.

"Why?" asked Bessie. "We can't buy any. Though maybe if we find Peter, he will buy me one and we can share it."

"Just come," said Jane. She pulled her sister to the place where the two young men had stood, and waited.

"Are you hoping to see the gentlemen you were talking about? Because I don't think—" She broke off with a squeal of fright when she saw that the gentlemen in question were right in front of them.

"Good evening." The one with the dark hair bowed. Bessie squeezed Jane's hand, evidently expecting her to handle the situation. Jane nodded her head. She reflected that though this was an extraordinary event and she should be alarmed, she was not.

"My name is Dante Gabriel Rossetti," the young man continued. "You may have heard of me." Jane shook her head uncomprehendingly. She tried to think how she might have heard that name. Was he an actor or a circus performer? Had he committed some spectacular crime?

"This is my friend Edward Burne-Jones. We've come to paint the new Debating Hall of the Oxford Union." Burne-Jones was very young, almost as young as Jane, and his silly handlebar mustache did nothing to hide the fact. He flushed pink when his friend said his name, and nodded at Jane without meeting her eyes.

"I had not heard that the Debating Hall was being painted," said Jane. Though Burne-Jones was modestly dressed in a suit that Jane knew would later draw scathing condemnation from Bessie, Rossetti's clothes were obviously very expensive. Though why a painter would be attired so sumptuously she could not imagine. She was uncomfortably aware that he might be looking at her dress, with its patched hem and worn fabric.

"There are several of us, up from London, but Rossetti here is our leader. He's a very famous painter," said Burne-Jones. He spoke very softly and Jane had to strain to hear him over the crowd in the hall.

"I suppose I'm well-known in some circles," said Rossetti modestly.

Jane thought this was very strange. "You've come all the way from London?" she asked. "Could they not hire local men to do it?"

"I think you misunderstand what kind of painting we do," said Rossetti. "We're artists." He waited for the light of recognition. "Picture painters."

Jane felt very foolish. Beside her, Bessie shook with nervous laughter, which she tried to disguise as a coughing fit. The blond young man handed her a handkerchief.

"I'm sorry," Jane said. "It's just that I've never met any picture painters."

"I suppose you must be very rich," giggled Bessie.

Rossetti ignored this and turned to Jane. "May I ask your name?"

"I'm Jane Burden and this is my sister, Bessie," she said. "Why do you want to know?"

"I was wondering if you would be interested in being an artist's model."

Jane stared at him, incredulous.

"A fine gentleman like you, from London, has to come all the way to Oxford to make sport of a poor girl like me?" Jane was very angry.

Rossetti turned pale and his face looked more like a marble bust than before. "I assure you that is the furthest thing from my mind. Forgive my freedom in speaking to you, but I never stand on ceremony where beauty is concerned."

"Beauty?" Jane thought that she must have misheard him. Or misunderstood in some way.

"You must know that you are very beautiful," Rossetti said. Jane glared at him but could not detect any sarcasm in his tone.

"I do not enjoy being teased or ridiculed," she said, and turned away.

"It's completely proper and ladylike," continued Rossetti to Bessie, who was nearly in hysterics now. "Young ladies in London, young ladies of good family, sit for me all the time. I'm looking for someone to pose as Guinevere, you see. You know the tale of King Arthur and Launcelot?"

"I have read it," said Jane, turning back to him despite herself at the mention of one of her favorite stories. Her school had quite a good copy, and Jane had read it many times and pored over the engravings. Jane was sure, though, that Guinevere had golden hair and pink cheeks.

"I apologize again for my boldness," said Rossetti, "but I must tell you that you're the most beautiful girl in Oxford. Maybe in all of England. I have to put you in my painting."

Now Jane began to wonder if instead of playing a joke, he was completely mad. She looked at Burne-Jones to gauge his expression. He was nodding vigorously and with apparent sincerity.

"We all think Jane quite ugly," said Bessie, collecting herself.

"You are wrong," said Rossetti, looking at her so sternly that she shrank, frightened, into the velvet curtain behind her. "You are as wrong as it is possible to be."

"We must go," lied Jane. "Our friends are waiting for us."

"Will you come to the studio?" Rossetti begged. "I can't finish my painting without you."

"I have a lot of chores to do," Jane said. She had still not made up her mind as to whether or not he was to be taken seriously.

"I'll come," Bessie said. She had recovered from Rossetti's earlier rebuff.

"But it's your sister I want!" said Rossetti callously. "Can't you convince her to sit for me?" He stepped close to Bessie and it seemed for a moment he was going kneel before her. She drew back pettishly.

"You can't convince Jane of anything she doesn't want to do. She's like an old mule," Bessie replied.

"A mule!" said Rossetti. "More like a Greek goddess, or a Byzantine princess, or a Roman empress. A pagan queen. I could paint you as all of those things, and more. A biblical heroine! Judith, or Sarah, or Mary Magdalene!"

Rossetti was practically shouting. Jane thought that the people filing past them to return to their seats must be staring in horror.

"I will find you after the play is over," said Rossetti, "and I will persuade you!"

He must be mad. The most beautiful girl in England! Jane gave up trying to follow the play and mulled over Rossetti's words. It was, of course, a ridiculous thing to say. I suppose he could be a poor artist, she thought. But the one called Burne-Jones said he was very famous in London. Perhaps he specialized in painting ugly or deformed individuals. But was there any chance, even the smallest chance, that he knew something the people of Oxford didn't? Did she dare to hope that he was right?

Of course not. She was the ugliest girl in Holywell Street. But still she could not get his words out of her mind.

After the performance she found him waiting in the same place. He was so handsome and so beseeching, she almost smiled.

"All right," she said. "I'll model for you."

He laughed and she saw that his teeth were straight and white. She did not see him reach for her hand until it was enveloped in his.

Time froze. She couldn't hear the crowd, her sister's voice, or her own heart, which seemed to have stopped. She couldn't see Mr. Burne-Jones or Mr. Rossetti. She couldn't feel her own body in space. All she could feel was the paralyzing lightning strike of Rossetti's skin against her own.

The instant he removed his hand from hers, her reason was restored and she stepped back, aghast. She glanced furtively around to make sure no one had seen. Theatergoers were rushing by, hurrying home, not paying the least bit of attention. Her heart was thundering, as if to make up for the beats it had lost, and she thought Rossetti must be able to hear it. She stared into his dark eyes and tried to think what to do. Should she rebuke him for taking such a liberty? Or pretend that it had not happened?

Burne-Jones was handing her a card. Without thinking she reached out and took it with her left hand, as if the one Rossetti had held was injured.

"Don't dress up, don't change your hair, don't do anything to yourself," said Rossetti, bowing. "Just come."

After the two men had walked away, Jane looked at the card. It had a university address, the next day's date, and eleven o'clock written on it. She showed it to Bessie.

Bessie tossed her hair. "I wouldn't go if I were you. That Italian one isn't right in the head."

As they walked home Jane could still feel the place on her hand where Rossetti had touched it. What kind of man would take a strange girl's hand? What kind of girl would allow him to do it? What was she getting herself into?

Their mother had fallen asleep at the kitchen table but woke up when they opened the door. Neither Jamey nor their father was home yet, which was to be expected. Sometime the following morning they were likely to stumble in, bruised, perhaps bleeding, covered with mud. In a foul temper and with a violent headache, Mr. Burden would yell at each of them, choose one to whip, and then sleep through his one day off from the stable.

"How'suh theeter?" Mrs. Burden said sleepily.

"Jane met a gentleman," said Bessie. Jane immediately wished that she had sworn Bessie to secrecy. She had thought her sister would show more discretion, or at least more common sense.

"What?" said Mrs. Burden, fully awake in an instant.

"He wants to paint her. He says she's beautiful."

In a single stride Mrs. Burden was in front of Jane, and slapped her hard.

"Foolish girl, he wants to make a whore of you," she said.

Jane tried not to cry, but the blow made her eyes water. "It's for the university," she choked. "I'm to be Guinevere." She held out the card to her mother, who took it and ripped it in two without looking at it.

"You'll be nobody, which is who you are," said Mrs. Burden. "You'll not go to meet this gentleman, whoever he is."

"He's an Italian," said Bessie helpfully.

"An Italian!" her mother roared. "Stupid, stupid child. Flattered you, did he? And why'd you believe him?"

The next day Jane woke up at dawn and crept into the kitchen. Her mother was asleep on the floor by the fire. She found a stub of pencil and a scrap of paper in the kitchen and scribbled a note of apology to Rossetti.

Dear Sir, she wrote. She tried to remember the most elegant forms she had been taught in school.

> *I regret to inform you that I have been unavoidably detained.*
> *I send you my most heartfelt apologies for any inconvenience I*
> *may have caused you.*
> *Your humble servant,*
> *Jane Burden*

When she was finished she looked it over and sighed. It looked poor and shoddy, not at all what she wished it could be. Still, her handwriting was very good and she thought it sounded well. She folded it carefully and placed it at the bottom of her brother's messenger bag. She could only hope that he wouldn't notice it until it had been mixed in with his mail for the day. She doubted he would abet her in sending a note to a man if he knew. Quietly she stole back into the bedroom. Bessie had not stirred.

Jane went to the window and stared out at the gray dawn. As she caught her own reflection, she saw the swollen mark on her face. I couldn't model even if I was allowed to, she thought sadly.

She went about her day's chores and tried not to think about it. When the appointed time came, she hoped to be able to slip out to the chicken coop and comfort herself by petting the birds, but her mother evidently thought she might try to sneak away, and made her sit close beside her and shell beans for two hours.

Well, she could think about Rossetti. Her mother could not take that away, at least. She recalled his amused expression when his eyes had met hers across the theater lobby. Amused, but not mocking. She felt that he had taken her measure, that in some way he knew her. But how was that possible? She was barely educated, she had never left Oxford, she had nothing, while he was a sophisticated and cultured London artist. Yet she could not shake the feeling that in his eyes she saw sympathy and understanding, and an invitation to join him in his wry detachment. It was an offer she burned to accept.

She wondered if she might run into Rossetti and Burne-Jones on the street and if she did what they might say to her. She was excruciatingly aware of having disappointed them. Even if her note was delivered, even if their day of work wasn't ruined, as she feared, it would not change the fact that she had given her word and then broken it.

That night she dreamed about him. He pointed a brush at her and talked to her very seriously in what she supposed was Italian, but she couldn't understand any of it. Then he dipped his brush in mud and painted the front of her house in thick, black strokes. Jane tried to stop him, but she was frozen in place. She shouted, but no sound came out. Then, exhausted with the effort, she woke up.

On Sunday, just as Bessie had predicted, Tom Barnstable found her after church and asked if he could walk her home. And though she wanted to say no, her mother's eyes on her made her say, "That would be very nice," instead.

As they walked she waited for him to begin a conversation, but he said nothing. After a few awkward moments, she pretended to look in the shop windows.

"The cowslips are pretty," he finally said.

Since they were on High Street and there were never any cowslips there, even in the spring, she did not quite know what to say. "Yes," she said. And then, "But I prefer roses. Though neither will bloom for several months yet."

Tom had evidently exhausted all of his knowledge of flowers with his cowslip comment, and seemed stumped by the idea of roses. He began to tell Jane about a horse at the stable that had a peculiar boil on his forelock. Though she wasn't especially fond of horses, Jane thought with relief that at least when Tom was talking, it wasn't so uncomfortable. She could nod and smile intermittently, her mind far away with Rossetti, and all was well.

At her doorstep he paused in his story, and began to squirm. Jane thought with dread that he was going to ask to see her again.

"My parents," he said, "would like to call on your parents. Would that be all right with you?"

"Of course," said Jane with difficulty. "I shall enjoy meeting them."

"Would Tuesday next be all right?"

"That would be fine. They can come for tea."

"Then it's settled," he said, and smiled, horribly, Jane thought.

"Yes," she said. She watched him saunter away and, when she was sure he was gone, ran as fast as she could toward the woods where she and Bessie liked to go and gather walnuts. She could not face her family just yet. Her mother would be sure to make suggestive comments and Jane did not think she could stand to listen to her.

She returned in late afternoon with three mushrooms, which mollified her mother somewhat. Still, all through dinner Mrs. Burden made references to "Jane's beau" until Jane wanted to run to the well and drown herself in it.

That evening they were surprised by a knock at the door. Jane thought perhaps Tom Barnstable had come back, and her heart began to beat wildly. She did not allow herself to hope that it could be Rossetti. She looked at Bessie in a panic, hoping she would see her alarm and answer it, but Bessie was very nearsighted and her lap was full of mending. She made no move to get up. Mrs. Burden looked at Jane.

"You expecting a guest?" she asked.

Jane shook her head.

"Must be someone selling something. Not a very smart salesperson, to come here. I'll get rid of them. Knowing you, you'd feel sorry for him and take out every penny of the egg money for his books or his shoe polish or his cutlery." With a groan Mrs. Burden rose and went to the door.

"Pardon me," said a voice Jane thought she recognized. "Might I speak with Mrs. Burden?"

Jane leaped from her seat and went to the door, but Mrs. Burden was blocking it with her body. Over her mother's shoulder Jane could see Burne-Jones, looking gangly and uncomfortable.

"I'm Mrs. Burden," her mother said, keeping the door open just a crack. "What's this about?"

"It's about your daughter Jane," he said, giving Jane, or at least the part of her that was not blocked by Mrs. Burden, a small smile. Mrs. Burden's tone became belligerent.

"Are you the Italian? She's not a prostitute, if that's what you're thinking," Mrs. Burden said. "She may be ugly, she may be the laziest girl in Oxford, and the most disrespectful, but she won't sell herself for money, not while I have anything to say about it."

Burne-Jones blushed. His expression was pained, and even Mrs. Burden could tell that she had greatly embarrassed him.

"No, Mrs. Burden, I'm not"—he choked on the words a little— "the Italian. I'm Edward Burne-Jones, lately of Oxford. I had the pleasure of making Miss Burden's acquaintance at the theater the other night, along with my friend Mr. Rossetti."

"Rossetti!" shrieked Mrs. Burden. "I don't want to hear any more about him. Treacherous people, the Italians."

"Mr. Rossetti is as English as you or I," said Burne-Jones emphatically. "He was born and has lived his whole life in London, where his father is a respected professor of languages."

"I don't care who his father is. It's obvious he's a libertine and a rogue. You look well enough, but the fact that you're associating with him and conversing with my daughter without an introduction—well, I'd say your morals are suspect as well."

Burne-Jones withstood this quietly.

"If you speak with a Professor Lowell at the college, you will find that Mr. Rossetti and I are exactly whom we purport to be: artists from London who are in Oxford to paint the Debating Hall."

"If you are an artist, you must be a bad one, to want to paint her," said Mrs. Burden, echoing Jane's thoughts of the night before. She jerked her shoulder back toward Jane. "I never saw an uglier girl."

Burne-Jones was too polite to contradict her directly. "Nevertheless," he said. Then he brought out his best argument. He pulled several shillings out of his pocket and handed them to Jane's mother. "This is how much she'll make for a day of sitting. I'll see to it that she's paid at the end of every day, if you let her come."

Mrs. Burden seized the money and Jane knew Burne-Jones was about to triumph. "Are you sure it's Jane you want?" said Mrs. Burden curiously after she had counted the coins carefully and put them in her pocket. "Are you sure it's not Bessie?"

"Mr. Rossetti was quite clear," Burne-Jones said.

"Well, there's no accounting for taste," said Mrs. Burden. She opened the door all the way and allowed him to come in.

There were particulars to be worked out. "She can only come two days a week," said Mrs. Burden. "I can't spare her more than that. And her brother will come pick her up. There'll be no standing around and flirting. I know about artists. My uncle was a sign painter. You can't imagine how many women he had."

Burne-Jones kept a straight face with great effort. "Of course," he said.

Three

$\mathcal{J}$ ANE hurried through her morning chores as fast as she could. The moment they were finished, she skipped out the door, ignoring her mother's shouts to mind herself. For a glorious moment she forgot that she was ugly and poor, and thought only of Rossetti. He was everywhere and in everything. The bright sun was the blinding flash of his smile, the limpid eyes of an adorable urchin were his eyes. The soaring college spires reminded her of his graceful carriage. Passing the tailor she recalled his lovely clothes, and crossing the steps of the Bodleian Library made her think of his poetic speech.

Despite living in Oxford all of her life, Jane had never been inside any of the colleges. She had never been invited before. It was a world that had always been closed to her, as a girl, and a poor one. Even her brother was stopped just inside the gates. He had seen the open courtyards with their flowering trees, but he had never seen the private chapels, or the classrooms, or the living quarters. Still, Jamey's limited access was more than she could ever hope for. Until now.

Jane knew the guard at the gate to the Oxford Union. He gazed at her curiously and asked what her business was in a suggestive tone Jane disliked, but when she gave Rossetti's name, he let her through.

The Oxford Union was a debating society open to all Oxford students. It had been established more than thirty years before, but only now had the money been found to build a hall. Jane followed a brick path planted on either side with very young oak trees that one day would provide majesty and shade but that looked a little bit pathetic now with their spindly trunks and leafless branches. The redbrick building with sandstone mullions and cornices was similar in design to many of the other buildings in town but, unmarked by moss or soot or time, it seemed callow and garish.

The courtyard was full of young men in billowing college robes. They nodded to her as they passed and she saw in face after face an unmarked beauty, the softness of an easier life, an innocence and obliviousness that touched her and angered her at the same time. The young men were glamorous, and beautiful, and utterly stupid in their privilege. She hated them, all of them, all except Rossetti. Somehow he was different. Every now and then a tutor would pass, gray haired and stern looking. She thought they glared at her, wondering what a girl was doing here. Any minute one was going to stop and question her. She would try to explain, but they wouldn't listen to her and would throw her out. Rossetti would be disappointed again, and angry. He would wash his hands of the stupid local girl who could not manage to appear at the appointed time.

At last she was at the door. Too intimidated at first to push the door open and step inside, she rapped on it lightly. There was no answer. She waited a few moments and then knocked again. Nothing happened. She had just about decided that she must be brave and push her way in, when the door opened.

It was Rossetti. He wore the look of amusement she remembered. Jane found that she was overcome with self-consciousness and could hardly look him in the face. He was so beautiful she had trouble catching her breath.

"My lovely," he said. "I heard a scratching at the door but I thought it was a cat. Come in."

He led her into an enormous, high-ceilinged room that she

realized was suddenly, unnaturally quiet. She counted seven other young men in the room. They were all staring at her.

"Eyes on your work!" Rossetti commanded. "Let Miss Burden become accustomed to our environment. You'll scare her half to death." Someone threw a pencil in their direction but the young men obeyed Rossetti. Now the only eyes on her were his.

"Thank you for your note," he said. "I felt as if I was in a fairy story, receiving a missive from a captive princess."

"I'm so very sorry—," she began, but he raised his hand.

"Nonsense," he said. "It is I who should apologize. I had no idea that my innocent invitation would cause you so much trouble. But now everything is arranged and you are here! Let me take your coat. You wander around. See what you think."

The Debating Hall was composed of one great room, oval in shape. It was quite bare except for the scaffolding on the walls and the artists' equipment. Each young man had his own easel and his own table for supplies. At first she stood still and watched the young men timidly, but they had obeyed Rossetti and were hard at work again, paying no attention to her. When she was sure they would not notice, she walked quietly around the room and peeked over the shoulder of each one to see what he was working on. They all seemed to be doing something different. One was copying a bust, another a still life of apples on a silver tray. One seemed to be working entirely from memory. Two of the young men were dressed in doublet and hose and stood stiff and frozen while Burne-Jones sketched them.

"That expression is nothing like noble thoughtfulness, Morris," complained Burne-Jones. "You look like you just sucked on a lemon."

"My neck is stiff," growled the model named Morris, a plump, curly-haired young man holding a sword straight out in front of him. "And my arms are tired. How long does it take you to make a sketch?"

He looked so ridiculous in his costume and so awkward in his pose that Jane felt a little less uncomfortable.

"Poor Topsy," said the other model, as slight and blond as Morris was solid and dark. "Should Ned give you some chocolate to sweeten your temper?"

Morris dropped the sword with a loud crash and Jane nearly jumped out of her skin. "Find someone else for your Launcelot, I'm through." Jane couldn't tell if he was really angry or not. He grabbed the other model by his collar and attempted to wrestle him to the ground.

"Morris," cried Burne-Jones, "I'm nearly finished. Ten more minutes."

"I was only teasing," cried the pummeled model.

"Serves you right, Faulkner," said Rossetti. The models returned to their places, red faced and breathless. Burne-Jones returned to his drawing.

"The artistic temperament," Rossetti said, smiling at Jane. "We can't do anything with either of them. But they're harmless."

Jane knew that she should say something, but when Rossetti was near, her mind was a blank.

"So many gentlemen," she finally said, and immediately cursed herself for being stupid.

"Don't worry," said Rossetti. "Miss Lipscombe is coming to sit a little bit later, so you won't be completely outnumbered." He smiled sympathetically, as if he knew how she felt.

As she surveyed the room, she finally thought of something to say.

"Why is the scaffolding still here?" she asked. "I thought this building was completed months ago."

"Look up, Miss Burden," Rossetti said, and she obediently lifted her head. Above her was a walkway that ran all the way around the hall. The walls were divided by arches into ten bays. Above that was a brick dome.

"That is where we are to do our work," he said. "Each of those ten spaces has to be filled. I'm to do three of them."

She still wasn't sure how this would be accomplished. Would she be asked to model up there? Jane was afraid of heights and hoped this would not be the case. But she smiled and nodded in what she hoped was a confident way. Rossetti immediately understood that it was all a mystery to her and very kindly explained what they were doing.

They were to paint murals on the walls. It had been Rossetti's idea to make it a series illustrating the tales of King Arthur and the Knights of the Round Table. The legends had nothing whatever to do with debating, but that was what Rossetti wanted to paint, and he had used his powers of persuasion to convince the architect to let him do it, and to choose the other artists who were to join him. They were only being paid housing and expenses, but Morris and Burne-Jones were young and inexperienced and saw it as a great opportunity to have their work on display.

Rossetti carried his well-worn copy of Malory's *Le Morte D'Arthur* with him everywhere and knew the story by heart, and his favorite part was the quest for the Holy Grail. He knew what scenes he wanted to paint—Launcelot's vision of the Holy Grail, the knights Galahad, Bors, and Percival receiving the Holy Grail, and Sir Launcelot in the queen's chamber. He had begun to sketch the first two already, but it was the third scene for which he needed Jane.

"I wish I could paint Launcelot and Guinevere in the chamber bed together," said Rossetti, "but of course that's impossible. The union would never allow it and it would be a horrible scandal." Jane blushed when she thought of modeling for such a picture, and was glad that Rossetti had thought better of it.

"So it is to be afterward, when Launcelot and Guinevere were besieged by Mordred and his men. Launcelot of course has been caught unawares and has no armor, and they are both sure that they are going to be slain, that this is the end. What an anguished moment! The difficulty is how to portray all of the emotion, especially of the queen."

Jane must have looked worried, for Rossetti laughed and touched her arm in a way that was meant to be reassuring. Instead it shocked all the breath from her body. She tried not to gape like a fish.

"It's all in how I organize the composition," he said. "You won't have to do anything but pose how I tell you, and if I've set things up right, the tension will all be there."

They had come to Rossetti's work space, where he had taped sketches of the first mural painting to the walls. Each showed a knight asleep in the right-hand corner of the paper and a statuesque woman leaning over him with an upraised arm. Jane could not see any difference between the sketches and she wondered why he had to do so many.

Rossetti watched her looking at the drawings. "Now that you're here, I may rework the messenger. I'm not quite satisfied with her proportions. Miss Lipscombe is not the stunner you are. Yes, I think I will redo it."

Then Rossetti led her around the room and introduced her to each young man. Mr. Dixon, Mr. Price, Mr. Faulkner, Mr. Prinsep. Their names and faces were a blur. They looked much like the undergraduates she had passed in the courtyard—young, blond, prosperous looking.

Morris appeared to be the youngest, the shortest, and the most unkempt. He had changed into his regular clothes, but when he took her hand Jane could not help but remember how thick his legs had looked in hose. Her face grew hot at the memory. Perhaps he realized what she was thinking because he gave her the briefest of glances before turning away.

"Topsy is shy," whispered Rossetti to her. "But I assure you he is first-rate. Not quite an artist yet—he's just started. But he works tremendously hard. He's my most promising protégé." Morris had turned back to his table and was running his hands through his hair as he stared at the paper he had taped to his easel.

"Don't let his appearance alarm you," Rossetti said. "He pays no attention to his grooming when he's working." Jane nodded and hoped he could not hear them.

"How long do you think you will need me?" she asked bashfully. "Altogether, I mean?"

Rossetti gazed at his drawings and thought for a moment.

"A few weeks at least. Perhaps months. It will take some time to finish the entire series of sketches. When the time comes to paint, we'll cover up the windows and whitewash the walls and the ceiling. Then we'll paint directly onto it as the Italian masters did. When I'm actually painting the frescoes, I won't need you unless I've made a mistake that I need to correct, or I change my mind about how I want to do things, but that could easily happen, mercurial as I am." He took her hand and squeezed it. "I hope that isn't too much trouble for you."

"Oh no," gasped Jane. Her heart sang at the thought of perhaps three months with Rossetti. She prayed it was long enough to make him fall in love with her.

Four

JANE found posing very difficult. She felt awkward as a foal, all legs and very stiff, and she watched enviously as Miss Lipscombe, with only a few terse instructions, expertly folded herself into the positions the artists wanted. Her form was as pliable as bread dough and she didn't seem to mind when Burne-Jones or Rossetti put a hand on her back to bend and twist her. If Rossetti tried to gently move Jane, her muscles tightened and locked. If he spoke to her, she could understand the words but her brain could not make her body understand. Rossetti was very patient with her, which embarrassed Jane even more. He was quick to praise her if she inadvertently found a tilt of the head or a curve to her back that pleased him. Still, Jane was convinced that she would be told at the end of the day not to come back.

When she was finally in position, there was nothing to do but watch Rossetti. He was absorbed in planning out his sketches and Jane was able to scrutinize him without fear that he would catch her staring.

He carried himself like someone who had been thought beautiful from a very young age; his grace was slightly studied, as if he was used to being looked at, and his confidence seemed unerring, though he was no longer slender and his hairline was beginning to recede. Jane guessed he must be around thirty. There were shadows under his eyes that suggested he kept late hours, and a rosiness to his complexion that spoke of drink. Somehow, though, these imperfections only added to his appeal.

As for his work, she was ignorant of painting and it was hard for her to know whether it was good or not. She had a vague sense that other painters painted portraits, or landscapes; they did not illustrate fairy tales. Beyond that, as to style, or composition, she had no idea.

As he worked Rossetti began to recite a poem:

The blessed damozel leaned out
From the gold bar of Heaven;
Her eyes were deeper than the depth
Of waters stilled at even;
She had three lilies in her hand,
And the stars in her hair were seven.

Her robe, ungirt from clasp to hem,
No wrought flowers did adorn,
But a white rose of Mary's gift,
For a service meetly worn;
Her hair that lay along her back
Was yellow like ripe corn.

Jane was enchanted. "I have not heard it before," she said. "What is it?"

"It is the beginning of a longer poem called "The Blessed Damozel," by the young poet Dante Gabriel Rossetti," he said.

"You wrote it?" Jane could not believe it. "It's beautiful."

"Yes, I like the first two stanzas very much, but then it gets muddled." He spoke the rest of the poem to her, and though she tried, Jane could find no fault with any of it.

At noon they broke for luncheon and Jane was able to stretch her clenched muscles. Shyly she sat down at a table in the center of the room that had been laid with a cloth. Cups and saucers were stacked in unsteady towers and silverware was heaped in piles. Miss Lipscombe appeared, followed by a boy with a tray.

"The young men come and grab what they like," she said. "Like savages. But you and I shall have a proper meal." She sat down and deftly poured tea from a samovar into two of the cups. "Sugar?" she asked Jane.

Miss Lipscombe's father owned a dry-goods store and she had never spoken to Jane when they passed on the street. Jane was surprised that the girl was being so civil now.

"Thank you," said Jane, wincing as she reached for her cup. She quickly set it down and began to rub her shoulders.

"You're working too hard," advised the other girl. "I've watched you. You won't be able to stand tomorrow if you don't learn how to release."

"How can I, when I have to stay so still?"

"It's as if your skin is a shell," said Miss Lipscombe, after a moment's thought, "but inside that shell everything is soft. Like a chocolate cordial."

Jane had never had a chocolate cordial, but she was grateful for the advice. Rossetti had told her he thought the other girl a very good model.

Miss Lipscombe passed her a plate of bread-and-butter sandwiches, but although Jane had not had breakfast, the proximity to Rossetti made her feel too ill to eat. Instead she gathered her courage and asked her companion a question.

"Is Mr. Rossetti really famous in London?" she ventured.

Miss Lipscombe's eyes blazed. "You don't know?" she asked. Daintily she wiped her lips with a linen napkin and leaned over to whisper in Jane's ear. "He's a scandal," she said.

"What do you mean?"

"Well, he's the leader of a group of artists called the Pre-Raphaelite Brotherhood. They make terribly shocking paintings. The Academy won't have them. They won't exhibit them."

"Why not?" asked Jane, trying to imagine what could be as shocking as that.

"I don't know, exactly," admitted Miss Lipscombe. "All I know is that in London they are notorious, Mr. Rossetti most of all."

"And your father let you come?" asked Jane wonderingly.

"Well, he doesn't know," said Miss Lipscombe with a wink. "I'm supposed to be at my elocution lessons, but what fun is that? I begged Mummy and she agreed that a girl should have a little adventure before she's married."

"You're going to be married?"

Miss Lipscombe smoothed her radiant hair. "Of course," she said. "In twelve months' time. To one of three gentlemen; I just haven't decided which."

"Oh," said Jane.

"If Mr. Rossetti were richer, I might think about marrying him," Miss Lipscombe went on, eyeing her biscuit thoughtfully. "But my father won't let me go to anyone with less than five hundred pounds."

"Mr. Rossetti isn't rich?" asked Jane with a sinking heart.

"Oh no," said Miss Lipscombe. "He's got nothing. His father is a professor or is writing a book or something. His mother takes in language pupils, and so does his sister."

"But his clothes, his manners . . . ," Jane sputtered helplessly.

"I didn't say he wasn't a gentleman," said Miss Lipscombe indignantly. "But Morris pays for everything. He's the rich one."

It was a terrible blow. Jane knew very well that a man without money of his own could not afford to marry her.

The post came at twelve thirty and the artists wandered over to eat biscuits and read their letters.

"One from your mother, Ned," said Rossetti. He handed the letter to Burne-Jones. "I'm sure we'll all be fascinated by the latest account of her rheumatism. One for me from my brother," Rossetti went on. "If it contains a check, we'll end work early and go to the Lamb and Thistle."

A cheer went up from the other young men. Rossetti deftly sliced the envelope with his knife and pulled out a check. "Thirty pounds," he announced.

"A cheer for William Rossetti," said Burne-Jones, "who puts up with your folderol so patiently."

"I won't ask you what you mean by 'folderol,'" said Rossetti, "as I am in too good a mood to argue with you. You, dear Ned, have another, from sweet Georgiana." He held the letter over his head and Burne-Jones, who had his fragile dignity to preserve, waited impatiently until Rossetti got bored with the teasing and handed him the letter.

"They're engaged," Miss Lipscomb said, nodding at Burne-Jones, who was fiery red and smiling a tiny smile as he read his letter. "They can't marry until she's eighteen, and she can't be more than fifteen now."

"Anything from Emma?" inquired Ford Madox Brown. He was older than the others and Jane thought he looked rather severe.

"Not today," said Rossetti. "I suppose that's what we all have to look forward to when we do marry, to be ignored and taken for granted. I wouldn't be in a hurry, Ned, if I were you."

Brown smiled wryly. "I just hope no one is ill," he said.

"Topsy, your only letter is from your mother. I think we should hear that one read aloud; Mrs. Morris is always so entertaining."

Miss Lipscombe rubbed her fingers together and winked at Jane. Rossetti opened the letter and began to read:

" 'Dear Son, I hope you are well, et cetera.'" He paused as he skimmed the letter. "'Weather at home, cook has been sick . . .' it goes on in that vein for some time. Here we are: 'I know that I have no influence over you at all, that you are a stubborn and defiant boy and determined to do as you please, but I must beg you to reconsider this desire to be a painter. If your father were alive, I am sure he would be able to dissuade you, but I am only a feeble old woman.'" Here Rossetti stopped and waited for the laugh.

"Feeble like a circus strongman," roared Faulkner. Morris looked angry but said nothing.

" 'You have your inheritance and you are free to squander it as you like, on paints and degenerate companions.' Yes, she describes us accurately, doesn't she, gentlemen?"

"All right," said Brown, taking the letter from Rossetti. "That's enough. Let poor Topsy read his mother's diatribe in peace."

Rossetti and the others groaned, but they always deferred to Brown on the rare occasions when he checked them.

"Poor fellow," said Brown as he watched Morris exit the room, the letter crushed in his hand.

"Poor fellow?" said Rossetti. "I'd like to be as poor a fellow as Topsy. I'd find great consolation in my bank account after a letter like that."

"He's too young for me, I think," whispered Miss Lipscombe. "How old do you suppose he is—twenty-one or twenty-two? And that hair, like a bristle brush! But you might try for him. He's been watching you, I've seen him."

"He hasn't." Jane did not know where to look. She fiddled with her teacup.

Miss Lipscombe put a hand on hers.

"His father owned a copper mine. Just think of it!"

After luncheon Jane tried to put the suggestions the other girl had given her into practice, and she found that she did not tire as easily. Morris left the hall immediately after the meal to check on some armor he was having forged. The others worked until three. Rossetti seemed pleased with her progress, and when he shook her hand at the end of the day he held it much longer than was polite.

Jane was relieved that her brother was late and not there to see it.

After waiting for twenty minutes with still no sign of Jamey, she began the walk home alone, stopping along the way to look in the shop windows. Her favorite was the pastry shop. She liked to look at the cakes in the window. Today there was a four-layer tower frosted with white buttercream and decorated with gold leaf. Tendrils of icing swirled along the sides. The base was piled with ladyfingers. A wedding cake, she thought. There were rings of pound cake and sheets of gingerbread. There were small custard tarts with whipped cream, apple tarts with caramelized-sugar tops, and lemon tarts adorned with glazed fruit. The coins in her pocket jingled and for a wild moment Jane thought about going in and buying something, a pecan sticky bun or a piece of marzipan cake, but she knew what her mother would say, so after a last longing look, she walked on.

She came to Blackwell's Book Shop. A volume of Spenser was laid open on a stand, revealing a dainty watercolor illustration. How she would love to own it! How she would love to sit in some soft chair in a warm room and turn the fragile pages! The card next to the book said that it was offered for thirty pounds. It almost made her laugh through her tears. Thirty pounds! Her father earned nine pounds a year, her brother six. But now, she reminded herself, she was earning money, too. Though none of it was hers to spend, it meant mutton in their stews and new dresses.

She decided that it wouldn't matter to Rossetti that she hadn't any money. The important thing was the feeling you had for a person, and she knew he understood that:

At the end of the first week, Jane asked her mother to cancel the tea with Tom Barnstable's parents.

"I always knew you were a fool," Mrs. Burden said as Jane stood before her, trying not to look too happy, "but this is the worst yet. You think that because a silver-tongued devil throws a few compliments your way, he wants to marry you? Compliments are free. Marriage costs. Men don't marry women they pay, I can tell you that. He'll need someone with at least two hundred pounds a year, I'd imagine, the way he spends." Mrs. Burden had been asking around town about the young painter and knew how much he owed every merchant on High Street.

"He doesn't need anyone else's money," said Jane. She could not help defending Rossetti. "He makes his own money selling paintings."

Her mother laughed. "It's a lot easier drawing checks from the bank than painting pictures. And your Italian is a lazy one, I can tell."

Jane could not understand her mother's attitude. "I thought you'd want me to marry a gentleman, if I could," she said.

Mrs. Burden snorted. "Rossetti a gentleman? That's a laugh. But it's neither here nor there because he won't marry you, mark my words."

Jane's happiness flickered for a moment. Still, no more was said of Tom Barnstable and his parents. For this, at least, Jane was grateful.

One day Jane arrived at the hall and noticed a stranger standing in front of Rossetti's easel. He was tall and thin and bewhiskered, with sharp features and a falcon's piercing gaze.

"You've failed with this one," he was saying to Rossetti. "It's too schooled, too orderly. Even the brushstrokes seem to all flow in one direction. Think of Tintoret. The earthy exuberance, the seemingly casual composition. Think of Tintoret as you paint, and you will do better."

Jane stole a glance at the painting, and saw the image of the knight asleep that she had seen a sketch of the very first day. Only now it was rendered in clear, bright colors, ruby and lapis and emerald, like the medieval enamel work in the church treasury. She thought it very beautiful and could not understand why the gentle-man complained.

"How can it be too schooled when I've never been to school?" snapped Rossetti. "I'm the original savage, remember?"

"You say that, but I know you study," said the other man, trying to soothe him. "I am saying that you are studying the wrong things."

"I haven't looked at another man's work since I left London," said Rossetti. He saw Jane and tried to smooth the grimace that was contorting his face. "My dear," he said. "I would like you to meet our patron, John Ruskin."

"And friend," said Ruskin quickly. "I am also a friend."

"How do you do," said Jane.

Ruskin studied her.

"She has quite a foreign look, much like the women you see at the port in Marseilles," he said, as though Jane were not there. "She will lend authenticity to your tableaux. She can play a Semite, a Greek, an Italian, any number of characters for whom the usual English rose won't do. Yes, I like her very much."

"So do I," said Rossetti, smiling apologetically at Jane.

Ruskin at last spoke to her. "Are your parents English?" he asked.

"As far as I know." Jane tried to smile, but she felt very uncom-fortable with the question.

"I wouldn't doubt that if you trace your family tree, you will find some Gypsy blood." The thought seemed to excite him. Jane felt a flash of rage. She wanted to tell him that he was very rude, but she was afraid of him, and of offending Rossetti.

"I must get back to work," said Rossetti curtly.

"And I must see what the others are about," said Ruskin. "After all, I want to get my money's worth."

When Ruskin had gone Rossetti flung the offending canvas from the easel. Then he came very close to Jane and drew the curtain of her hair back from her ear. "I am so sorry," he whispered. His breath tickled her throat and Jane forgot to be angry.

"Who is that?" she asked dreamily.

"He's disagreeable, I know," said Rossetti. "But he's very rich. He quite loves the Pre-Raphaelites. Especially me, now that Millais has defected."

Jane did not know Millais, but a defection sounded interesting.

"What happened?" she asked.

"Never mind," said Rossetti, abashed. "Let me arrange you; we're already late, thanks to him." A couch had appeared next to Rossetti's easel and he eased Jane onto it.

"Drape your hand across the back," he said, "like so. And fling your head back over the arm." As he instructed her Rossetti took her arm and then her head in his hands and gently guided them. Jane tried to breathe, but it was if she had put on a corset that was much too tight.

"Close your eyes," he said, his breath on her cheek. She thought he was going to kiss her. She waited, and then felt the cool breeze as he walked away.

"That's perfect," he said from the easel.

I must have him, Jane thought. I don't care what I have to do. She thought she must be transparent, that Rossetti must be able to read her thoughts, but when she peeked at him from under her lowered lids, he was hard at work and seemed to notice nothing.

At tea Jane asked Miss Lipscombe about John Ruskin.

"His books are quite famous," she said. "But all anyone talks about now is his marriage."

"What happened?" asked Jane.

"It was annulled," Miss Lipscombe said. She leaned close to Jane. "On account of impotence!"

Jane would not have imagined the other girl knew such a word. She heard it often enough on Holywell Street, as an epithet shouted by drunk women at their drunker husbands. But it was shocking to hear it of a gentleman.

"They were married for six years and never ... ," said Miss Lipscombe meaningfully.

"She didn't want to?" asked Jane breathlessly.

"It wasn't her, it was him," said Miss Lipscombe. "They say he had imagined that a woman would look like a Greek statue"—here she lowered her voice to a whisper—"*down there*, you know, and was shocked to see that Effie wasn't."

Jane had never seen engravings of Greek statues with their smooth, hairless pudendum, but she nodded as if she understood.

"So he wouldn't," Miss Lipscombe said. "Imagine, she's the prettiest little thing, but he was completely revolted by her. She was a perfect angel about it, but he was just beastly to her, never letting her go out, making her stay with his horrible parents, who just rule his life. No woman could stand it. He took John Everett Millais on a trip to Scotland with them so he could paint his portrait. Millais paint Ruskin, I mean. And Millais and Effie fell in love. She left Ruskin and sued for an annullment. He tried to convince everyone that she was crazy, but no one believed him, of course."

Jane stared at Ruskin, who was standing behind Rossetti and pointing at something in his drawing. Rossetti was scowling and looked ready to fling his easel at the other man.

"How horrible," said Jane. "What became of Effie?"

"She married Millais and they are happy as can be. What's strange is, Ruskin tried to stay friends with Millais, but of course Millais can't stand him, after what happened."

"I should imagine not," said Jane.

After tea the couch was gone.

"Ruskin says you should be standing off to the left," said Rossetti, looking harassed and irritated. "Guinevere is at the window, helplessly watching the advance of Mordred and his men."

"How do I stand?" asked Jane.

"Put your hand up, like this, as if you were pulling back a curtain," said Rossetti. "I'll have a curtain tomorrow, but for now just pretend. Turn a little bit away from me so I can sketch you in three-quarter profile. And tilt your head, as if you were listening intently for the arrival of your doom."

Rossetti mumbled to himself as he worked. Across the room Jane could hear Miss Lipscombe laughing. Jane wished she could say something to Rossetti, that they could laugh and joke easily, but she couldn't think of anything to say that would interest him. She knew nothing about Italian painters, French Gothic cathedrals, or medieval literature. She had not read *The Stones of Venice* and did not subscribe to *Blackwell's Magazine*. She would have liked to ask him more about Ruskin, but such gossip was inappropriate for mixed company. All she could do was watch him watching her.

"This isn't right," Rossetti said after a few minutes. Jane froze in dread. Perhaps all of his compliments were meaningless. Perhaps he was really dissatisfied with her. He was thinking that hiring her had been a mistake. It might be her last day in the studio and she had barely spoken. For the hundredth time she berated herself for being so awkward and stupid.

"The composition is out of balance," he said. "Not to mention that putting Guinevere over in the corner like that hardly does justice to your supreme gorgeousness. Let's change it around." He removed the sketch from his easel and taped up a fresh piece of paper. "Now then," he said, turning to her, "I want you to stand as straight and tall as you can, and then turn that lovely neck of yours up to the sky." She did as he asked, feeling distinctly vulnerable with her throat so exposed. She closed her eyes.

"Genius," said Rossetti. "That curve of your neck, that vulnerability, contrasts perfectly with your impervious air. And with the eyes closed, that's exactly it. It's as if you're saying a last, desperate prayer. But you must turn your face just slightly toward me," Rossetti said. "Let me show you." She heard him coming toward her and then he was gently touching her jaw. Jane thought she might collapse in a faint. She felt him brush the hair away from her face. Then he took both of her hands in his.

"Put them here," he whispered, and brought her hands to her throat. He could have been telling her he loved her, his voice was so soft and gentle. "Keep that serious expression. You look almost anguished, which is exactly right."

Jane knew she was trembling but she hoped Rossetti did not notice. Or if he did, that he would think she was merely cold.

"I'll put your women on the right, in the back, weeping," said Rossetti to himself as he walked back to his easel. "Launcelot will be on the left, guarding the window, his sword at the ready. This is much better."

"I'm ready to begin painting you at last," Rossetti said late in the afternoon. "You'll wear your costume tomorrow."

"My costume?" said Jane, somewhat bewildered. "But I was never fitted for a costume."

"Oh, Topsy takes care of all of those things," said Rossetti carelessly. "He's ingenious in that way. He sketched out your dress ages ago and had a seamstress make it up. He sketched out a helmet and visor, a chain-mail gorget, and a broadsword for Launcelot, too. No one can complain that my figures are implausibly dressed. In the meantime, let's do one last preparatory sketch."

With her eyes closed Jane could not watch Rossetti as he worked. She could only hear the sound of the pencil on the paper and Rossetti's mumblings as he talked himself through, correcting mistakes, adjusting planes, moving things around. Again she tried to think of something to say, but could not. After a few minutes Rossetti broke the silence.

"Tell me about Oxford," he said. "I find it too quiet. I can't sleep without the soothing rattle of carriages on cobblestones and the clatter of commerce outside my window."

Jane thought wryly to herself that he should come to Holywell Street, but she didn't say so. "There's not much to tell, sir," she said.

"Tell me about your family then. Tell me about your mother. I hear she is terrifying. Burne-Jones could not speak for three hours after returning from your house."

Jane laughed, and without thinking found herself telling Rossetti about the privy overflowing. Perhaps it was the fact that she could not look at him as she talked that created a sense of intimacy. She tried to make it a humorous story, omitting her mother's rage and the threat of Tom Barnstable.

"Poor Jane!" he said when she had finished, but he said it merrily, not pityingly. "All that is needed is three wicked stepsisters and a pumpkin coach."

"I didn't mean . . . ," she stammered. She did not want him to think she was looking for sympathy.

"Once when I was growing up in London, I found a family of rats living in our flour bin. I was horrified, of course, and ran shrieking to my mother. Do you know what she told me? Throw them into the frying pan, they're already battered!"

Jane gasped. As low as her family had sunk, they had never eaten rats.

"Did you do it?" she asked.

"Of course she wasn't serious," said Rossetti. Jane wasn't sure if he was telling the truth or not. "No, I dusted them off and tossed them out the back door by their tails."

"You miss London," said Jane, emboldened.

"It is the most wonderful place in the world," agreed Rossetti.

"Tell me all about it," said Jane. "I want to imagine that I am there."

"Before I came here I lived in a place called Red Lion Square, in three rooms on the first floor of a brick town house near Bloomsbury. The courtyard in front is quite wild with climbing roses and ivy-covered plane trees, and when I sit there I imagine I am in the country. I've left that place, though, and Topsy and Burne-Jones are going to live there. I've taken a flat at Chatham Place." Jane had only the vaguest idea of London, and she didn't know where Chatham Place might be.

"It's a big white house," he said, "made of sandstone blocks, with a large back garden in which I keep many pets. So far I have a raccoon, an armadillo, two parrots, three owls, and a woodchuck. I'm hoping to have a kangaroo shipped from Australia when I go back to London. Someday I'll buy a wombat."

"It sounds like a lot of work," said Jane.

"Not really," said Rossetti. "The animals are very independent and mostly take care of themselves. If they get sick my manservant Hobbes looks after them."

"And the inside?" asked Jane.

"Oh, it's wonderfully gloomy, full of heavily carved oak furniture, silk-paneled walls, velvet curtains that I never pull back, fantastic iron candelabra lit with church candles, and tables strewn with curiosities. I have a collection of starfish, a severed hand in formaldehyde, and mounted on the wall the head of a wild boar."

Jane shuddered. "Sounds gruesome."

"Doesn't it?" said Rossetti cheerfully. "I didn't shoot the boar, or cut off the hand, or collect the starfish. I like to visit curiosity shops when I'm out on my daily walks. I find things. I like to visit bookstores, too. I have thousands of books, poetry mostly, Spenser and Dryden, Byron and Shelley." Jane glanced up, startled by the mention of such indecent authors. Rossetti winked. "I beg your pardon," he said, not sounding sorry at all. "I shouldn't even mention the names of such scandalous personages to a young lady."

Jane blushingly lowered her eyes again. "I wish I could read Byron or Shelley," she whispered to herself. But Rossetti had heard.

"When you come to my house in London, you shall read them to your heart's content," he said, and Jane thrilled at the way he assumed that she would come one day.

Jane was taking tea with Miss Lipscombe when Morris approached her, carrying a small bundle.

"Your costume," he said abruptly, and would have walked away, but Miss Lipscombe stopped him.

"How very unfair of the others, to make you their messenger!" She flashed Morris a flirtatious smile. "Don't you think, Jane?"

"I don't mind," said Morris gravely. "I like designing the costumes nearly as much as painting them."

"Dear me, and do you sew them as well?"

"Mr. Rossetti says you have designed the knights' armor," Jane interposed, hoping he was not too offended by Miss Lipscombe's insinuating tone.

"I'd have forged it myself, too," said Morris, eagerly, "but the Oxford Union is not equipped for such an undertaking. I had to go to a blacksmith in town. Though he let me temper the steel and hammer it out, so I was able to learn the process. Next time I'll make my own suit of armor."

Jane thought it was a very odd life, to have even one occasion for making a suit of armor, much less two.

"How do you know what to draw?" she asked. "How do you know what a chain-mail gorget would have looked like?"

"There are illustrations in medieval texts," he answered, looking pleased that she had asked. "I have a good memory for things of that kind."

Miss Lipscombe was bored with the turn of the conversation.

"Let us see the dress, Mr. Morris," she said. She nodded to Jane. "And then I'll show you where to change."

Morris held the package out toward Jane and she reached for it. At the moment of transfer, however, Morris leaped back, as if she were infected with the plague, and the package fell to the floor. Blushing and apologizing, Morris picked it up and set it on the table, then practically ran to the other side of the room and his own easel. Jane unwrapped the package and saw that it held a moss green velvet dress, straight and loose, with gold embroidery on the sleeves, and a cape of peacock feathers, tied with teal silk ribbons.

"It's lovely," said Jane. "Where on earth did he find real peacock feathers?"

"He's clever that way," said Miss Lipscombe. "He might know a gentleman in London who owns a trimmings store, or he might have plucked them from the tails of the birds at his mother's park. Whatever he needs, he figures out a way to get it."

Jane's opinion of Morris rose.

She put on her Guinevere gown and cape in the office that was used as a dressing room. She noticed that the velvet was made of fine silk and that the smocking on the bodice was impeccably done. Morris must have spent a fortune on this dress, Jane thought. Though no measurements had been taken, it fit her perfectly, and she could tell by the eyes on her when she walked to Rossetti's easel that it suited her.

Jane stepped into her place and clasped her hands to her breast. She lifted her face to the ceiling and closed her eyes. She waited for the muttering and the sawing sound of pencil on paper, but there was silence.

"Is something wrong?" called out Jane nervously. She did not see Rossetti turn and catch sight of her, but she heard the intake of his breath.

"My God," he whispered. "It is Guinevere."

Jane opened her eyes and found that Rossetti was staring at her with a terrifying intensity. In his expression she saw admiration, and awe, and a little bit of fear. It said that she was the only woman in the world.

In a moment he had her by the shoulders and was pushing her toward the changing-room door.

"What is it?" asked Jane fearfully. "What are you doing?" Rossetti didn't answer. Jane stumbled backward as she looked around. Was anyone watching? But all eyes in the room seemed to be on their own work.

When they were inside the changing room and the door was shut behind them, Rossetti took her face in both his hands and kissed her, knocking her backward, into the rack of costumes. Fervidly she returned his kiss. Coats and gowns were torn off their hangers and fell to the floor.

"Forgive me, Guinevere," he breathed. He grasped the bodice of the beautiful dress and for a moment she worried that he might tear it. "I've tried to contain it but it will not be contained." He kissed her again and all thought disappeared. His body pressed against hers was solid and insistent.

"This is wrong," he gasped. He pulled away to look at her. He pushed a lock of her dark hair out of her face and held it in his hand.

"I don't care," Jane said. She wound her arms around his neck and kissed him harder. It didn't bother her that he had called her the name of a mythical figure from long ago.

"Rossetti," they heard Faulkner call. "I'm lifting the last scone to my lips, and if you want it you'll have to fight me for it."

As if released from some magical enchantment, they broke apart.

"Wait here," whispered Rossetti. "I'll slip out and in a few minutes you do the same. No one will be the wiser."

"I'm unsheathing my sword," he called to Faulkner, "and I vow on all that is sacred that the scone will be mine!" He kissed Jane once more and then, opening the door just a crack, squeezed through and joined his friends.

Jane waited for her breathing to slow and the beads of sweat on her forehead to evaporate before she left the costume closet and returned to her place in front of Rossetti's easel. If any of the other gentlemen noticed anything, they remained discreetly silent.

Five

THAT afternoon, Mrs. Burden eyed Jane suspiciously as she carefully counted her pay. She might not have been able to read a train schedule, but she never miscalculated by a penny.

"He hasn't taken you out, has he?" she asked sharply. "Mrs. Harris's son is a porter at the union and he told her . . . You haven't gone anywhere with him, to the river, or out the Iffley Road to pick violets, have you?"

Jane shook her head dreamily, imagining lying on the bank of the river with Rossetti, watching the herons and swans glide by in the placid water. Her mother saw her smile and was beside her in a second, her tanned, muscular hand digging into the flesh of Jane's upper arm.

"Mind what you let this gentleman do with you," she said in a low undertone. "There are worse things than marrying someone you don't care for, you know."

"I don't understand you," Jane stammered.

"I think you do," said her mother. "But that's all I'll say about it. Thanks to him we've got extra chickens and a new cooking pot. Another week and Jamey can have a new pair of boots. The old ones are more holes than leather." She had never said thank you, but Jane did not expect her to.

"How does he court you, with all of those other gentlemen

around?" whispered Bessie as they lay in bed that night. "I would think it would be quite awkward."

"He doesn't give me presents, if that's what you mean," said Jane, thinking about the kiss. "And he doesn't flirt."

"Has he ever written you a note, or a poem?" asked Bessie. "Has he ever spoken to you of his feelings?" Jane had to admit that he had not.

"I don't think I'd like it to be just unspoken knowledge," said Bessie. "I wouldn't like to think I'd misjudged."

Jane only laughed. Rossetti knew something that the people of Holywell Street did not. He knew she was a fairy queen. She was a princess taken from her royal position at birth and placed with a lowly family for her protection, he said, and she had almost begun to believe it herself. She basked in the romance of this secret; she gloried in this new idea of herself. Her silence was now called dignity and condescension rather than stupidity. Her height and her skinniness were regal rather than ugly. It was no wonder that Jane glowed, or that her mother suspected she was doing something she shouldn't. Jane felt a little sorry for Bessie now, with her sights set on a very thin, very homely shop assistant.

The next day Jane went to the studio and immediately changed into her costume. When Rossetti came in, though, he did not want to sketch.

"Come with me," he said, taking her hand. "I want to look at the wall where I'm to paint. Plan things out."

"Up there?" asked Jane with alarm. "Are you sure it's quite safe?"

Rossetti laughed. "As safe as being on the ground. Don't worry, I won't let you fall."

So with Rossetti behind her to catch her if she slipped, Jane lifted her encumbering skirt with one hand and held on for dear life with the other. She tried not to look at the hard marble floor below her.

Once on the platform, she felt better. It was penned in by a rough wooden fence and it would have taken some doing to fall over the side. Through the slats she could see the tops of the artists' heads, but they seemed very far away.

"Which part of the wall is yours?" she asked, feeling dizzy. She saw that some of the others had already begun their frescoes.

"Here," Rossetti said, pointing to the white space between stenciled flowers by Morris and a completed scene of Merlin by Burne-Jones. But he did not look at it. Instead he caught her around the waist.

"Kiss me, Guinevere," he said. "My heart's desire."

"Here?" she said between kisses. "Are you sure?"

"Why not?" he said. "No one can see us." He was making alarmingly quick work of the slippery velvet-covered buttons on the front of her dress. She wriggled free of him before he disrobed her entirely.

"Won't they hear us?" she asked, rebuttoning as fast as she could.

"Morris!" Rossetti called to the man below. Morris did not look up. "You see?" he said, crawling toward her once again. But Jane was still uncertain. Her mother's words came to her, unbidden. There are worse things than being married to a man you dislike.

Rossetti had opened her dress again and was sucking at her breast in a way that made Jane gasp. "Mr. Rossetti!" she cried.

"Don't call me that," he said, panting a little. "Call me Launcelot." He pulled her onto the hard wooden planks and pinned her arms above her head.

Jane tried but found she couldn't say it. "Sir," she said instead, "I'm sorry but I cannot do this." She was beginning to be frightened.

Rossetti released her hands and sat up. Jane held the bodice of her dress closed with her hand.

"Of course you can't," he said, looking down at her mournfully. "It's just . . . I thought I would never find you. You're like some kind of miracle, emerging from the mist, from the darkness."

"I know what you mean," said Jane, thinking of Holywell Street.

"You do?" His eyes held her fast. He took her hand. "Well, then. How many people find that? How many people die searching for it? I can't just relinquish it, not if you feel the same. I won't!"

His kiss was gentle this time, beseeching. Before Jane knew what she was doing, she was pulling off Rossetti's waistcoat and tugging at his shirt. His body was cool and smelled of bergamot and anise. She let him fold back her skirt and pull off her petticoat and pull down her knickers, shuddering as he touched her. The pain when he pushed himself into her combined with the fleeting thought that he was taking her virginity, ruining her prospects and perhaps her life. But she could not be sorry. There were worse things than giving yourself to the man you loved.

He moved above her and she watched his face until she, too, was forced to close her eyes. "Yes," they said together. The starlings that had flown in through the transoms and gathered on the ceiling beams startled and wheeled away with a cymbal crash of wings.

Six

JAMEY was waiting for her at the gate, his hands in his pockets, his cap pulled low. His empty messenger bag dangled from his shoulder. As soon as he saw her, he started walking and Jane had to hurry to catch him. Jane felt her heart swelling with love for her brother.

"How was your day?" she asked sweetly.

"Nuh," he grunted.

Jane felt serious, almost prayerful. She knew that her life had irrevocably changed and she thought she should commemorate it in some way. They passed St. Michael's Church and she thought about going in to light a candle, but she would never be able to explain that to Jamey.

Jane was not innocent of how children came into the world. She also knew what happened to the unmarried girls who were with child. Somehow, though, she was not worried. She knew everything would come right.

The next day it was raining sideways and she was soaked and chilled when she arrived at the Union, but she didn't care. There would be a fire in the studio and Rossetti would stand beside her and talk to her while she dried herself off. He would make her tea and toast.

Morris answered the door. She nodded a greeting, walked past him to Rossetti's place, and began removing her wet coat and hat and gloves. It appeared that she and Morris were the first ones there. Rossetti was nowhere to be seen, but she thought that perhaps he'd gone out for supplies. He would need drying out and warming up, too, when he got back. Morris had followed her across the room, she noticed with annoyance. He was standing behind her clearing his throat.

"Miss Burden?" he said.

"Yes?"

"Mr. Rossetti was called back to London on urgent business. He sends you his most heartfelt apologies."

Rossetti's easel was exactly as he had left it. The drawing from the day before was still pinned to it. The charcoal he had dropped was still under his table.

"Is he all right? Is he ill?" Jane did not understand.

"He's quite well," mumbled Morris, looking at his feet.

"What is it then?" she said with growing alarm. "Someone in his family? His father?"

"No," Morris said. "They are all fine."

"When will he be coming back?"

The pause before Morris spoke was practically unendurable.

"He has no plans to return in the immediate future," Morris said. He held a crumpled letter in his fist and now he began to nervously tear it. The white pieces floated to the floor like chips of paint. "In this note he asked me to pack up his supplies and bring them back with me when I'm finished. The last two of his murals will have to remain unpainted. Perhaps we can fill in the space with some sort of stenciled decoration."

Jane scarcely heard Morris talking about the murals. She no longer saw the hall. She had receded to a still point in her mind where her own voice repeated, "Rossetti has gone."

"You're very white," she heard Morris say. He sounded miles away. Jane did not feel his hand on her trembling shoulder when he led her to a chair and sat her down in it, and went to find dry clothes and hot tea. In a few moments a warm robe was placed over her shoulders and a steaming cup was in her hand.

"I didn't know he was leaving either," said Morris miserably. "I found the note when I came down to breakfast."

"Rossetti has gone," said Jane stupidly.

"Shall I send for the doctor?" asked Morris, looking alarmed. With difficulty Jane roused herself.

"That won't be necessary," she said, placing her cup carefully in its saucer. "As I am no longer needed, I will go home. Thank you for your kind attentions."

Jane thanked God her mother was gone for the day, sitting with a neighbor who was in childbirth. She sat in front of the fire with her sewing basket in her lap, but she did no work at all. Rossetti has gone, she said to herself. He has no plans to return.

Why would he leave so suddenly? Even if he didn't care at all for her, why would he leave his work unfinished? Why, if some emergency called him away, could he not attend to it and then come back? Why didn't he say goodbye?

There was something Morris was not telling her. Jane turned over in her mind all that she knew about Rossetti, but she couldn't figure it out. When she couldn't stand it any longer, she stood, spilling her sewing basket on the floor. She did not stop to pick it up. Morris might not be willing to tell her what he knew, but Miss Lipscombe would.

"Lizzie Siddal," Miss Lipscombe said, handing Jane her cup. She had evinced no surprise when Jane appeared at her door, nearly in tears. She had greeted Jane quite cordially and ushered her into a comfortable sitting room.

"She was found in a hat shop," the young lady went on. "Can you imagine that?" Jane cringed, but Miss Lipscombe didn't notice.

"Somewhere called Cranborne Alley, off Leicester Square. She was working there. It wasn't Mr. Rossetti who found her, it was one of his friends. He'd accompanied his mother there. Such a funny story. And then Mr. Rossetti went back to see her and convinced her to model, and not long after they got engaged. That was, I think, six years ago. I can't think why they haven't married, though I'm sure they will now. Of course, Lizzie might die. They say she's always been delicate, but she may have full-blown consumption this time."

Impeccable timing, Jane thought in spite of herself. It was as if Lizzie knew Rossetti was slipping away. "Why didn't you tell me?" she reproached Miss Lipscombe.

The girl looked truly penitent. "I didn't think," she said. "It didn't seem as if you liked him. Is your heart quite broken?"

Jane could only stare into her cup, the tears falling off her cheeks into her tea. "Can he really love her so much, if they've been engaged for six years and never married?" she choked.

"Well, I don't know," evaded Miss Lipscombe. "They say that almost all of his paintings and drawings are of her." Jane realized that she had never seen any of Rossetti's paintings and drawings, other than the ones of herself. Despite her questions and Rossetti's loquacious answers, she really knew nothing of his life in London. Chatham Place and armadillos, that was all she knew. Even if she'd wanted to go to London, she would not know how to find him.

Jane knew it was wicked, but she fervently wished that Lizzie would die. Then Rossetti would be free. But if he loved her . . .

"Let me think, what else do I know about it?" said Miss Lipscombe. "They say Lizzie wants to be an artist herself and is quite good."

"Is she very beautiful?" asked Jane.

"Like an angel," confirmed Miss Lipscombe.

They were not married. That was some comfort. But what she had heard spoke to Jane of a shameful illicit relationship. Though she supposed if Rossetti had asked, she would have done it, just as this delicate, possibly dying Lizzie had done. But he had not asked. He had left, and he had not even written her a note!

Jane dreaded going home, but it was already dark and she was late. Miss Lipscombe had things to attend to, though she pressed Jane's hand sympathetically as she left.

"Don't think of him again," she said. "He's a beast. All London men are. They're great fun for flirting, but when the time comes I'll marry an Oxfordshire man."

When Jane got home her sewing basket had been picked up and was sitting on the kitchen table. Her mother was there, pulling the innards from a chicken. Blood dripped from her hands and the smell made Jane feel faint and nauseated.

From the look on her mother's face, Jane guessed she had been talking to Mrs. Harris again. "So your Italian gentleman has gone," Mrs. Burden said with satisfaction. "Back to his wife?"

"Yes," said Jane. There was no point in explaining. It would only make things worse.

"We'll have to arrange for a meeting with young Tom's family then," said Mrs. Burden. "We can't waste any time. If your reputation's not already ruined from posing for those gentlemen. And if we didn't make the Barnstables too angry, calling it off the last time. It may be that even Tom won't have you now."

Now Jane stayed at home. After her time at the studio, Holywell Street seemed even bleaker and more desolate than before. She prayed desperately that Rossetti would send her a letter. Even if he told her that he loved her but could never be with her, that would be something. She could live on the memory of him, if she had to. But nothing came.

A week later Tom and his parents came to tea. It was a dismal affair. Tom looked as unhappy with the arrangement as she felt. Tom's mother looked at her as if she were a piece of livestock. "She looks strong," Mrs. Barnstable said.

"Oh, she is," agreed Mrs. Burden. "She can lift that heavy copper pot when it's completely full. And she almost never catches cold, even when the rest of us are too feverish to get out of bed."

"Can she read and write?" asked Mr. Barnstable.

"Well enough," said Mr. Burden, who had stayed home from the pub for the event. Jane knew that her father had never bothered to find out if she could read, or how well, or if she enjoyed books. He gave the answer that he thought would most please Tom's parents.

"But not too well," lied Mrs. Burden, anxious to make sure the Barnstables knew that sitting for the artists had not made Jane think too highly of herself. Everyone but Jane laughed.

Jane contemplated drowning herself in the river. It wouldn't take long, compared with a lifetime on Holywell Street. She wondered if Rossetti would ever hear of it, if she were to kill herself. Would he understand why she had done it? Would he feel remorse? But she stared too long at her reflection in the bottle green water and by the time she had made up her mind to do it, she was late to feed the chickens. Well, there's always tomorrow, Jane thought as she ran.

That evening she began to bleed. As she pinned a thick cloth to her underclothes, Jane wept. She was not sure if it was with relief or with sorrow. Her only remaining link to Rossetti had been the child she could have been carrying. Now she had nothing.

The next day there was a knock at the door. Jane's heart leaped with hope.

"Don't imagine it's the Italian," said Mrs. Burden. "It's most likely Tom. Mind you don't stand up too straight when you're walking. I think he's not quite as tall as you."

But it was neither Rossetti nor Tom. It was Morris. He looked very uncomfortable standing on their doorstep, and very much disgusted by the squalor all around him. He lifted one foot and then the other, as if to keep them from spending too much time in the dirt.

"Miss Burden," he said when she answered the door. "You must help me. My Guinevere is all wrong. If you were to pose for me, I'm sure it would come out right."

"And who is this one?" said Mrs. Burden, coming up behind Jane. "Not another foreigner, I hope."

Jane made the introductions, and Morris addressed his request to her mother.

"And why should she, when the other fellow used her so cruelly?" Jane thought she would die of shame.

"Because I'll pay her two shillings an hour," he said.

Jane and her mother both gasped. It was twice what Rossetti had paid her. Morris was not as callow or as foolish as he looked.

"Can you come tomorrow?" Morris asked Jane.

"She can," said Mrs. Burden.

All of the other artists had finished and gone, so when Jane stepped into the Debating Hall the next day, it was empty except for Morris and his easel. The paintings on the walls above her gleamed. She could not believe the transformation.

"You like it?" he asked, watching her.

"It's like seeing the world through stained glass," she said. She felt that she did not explain herself well, but he looked pleased.

"I understand what you mean," he said. "Rossetti and his fellows are for making everything strictly naturalistic, but they are also partial to these jewel-box colors. I suppose it's inconsistent, but it's turned out well."

The mention of Rossetti's name made Jane feel sick. She tried to change the subject.

"Haven't you completed your part of the ceiling, Mr. Morris?" asked Jane. "Why did you stay behind?"

"Rossetti gave me decorative bits to do," he answered. He seemed unable to complete a sentence without mentioning his friend, oblivious to the pain it caused Jane. "Sunflowers in corners, things like that. But I wasn't given any scenes. I wanted to do at least one monumental figure before I left Oxford."

"I was up there once and saw your sunflowers," said Jane wistfully. "They're lovely."

Morris showed her how to stand and then busied himself at the easel. They were both silent; she could hear the clap of Morris's pencil against his paper. He made a humming sound that was not quite a tune under his breath. The windows were open and out on the street students called to one another. It was nearly spring and everyone was restless. The fields were too muddy for walking or playing, the Thames and the Cherwell were swollen with rain, and everyone was waiting for the air to warm and a few sunny days to dry things out a bit so that they could be outdoors again.

A newspaper rustled on a nearby chair, and then one after another the pages blew onto the floor. It was excruciating. Jane wanted to call to Morris to stop so that she could pick up the sheets and clamp them down with a paperweight, but he looked so fiercely focused that she hated to interrupt him. She tried not to think of Rossetti. It had been nine days since he'd left. She wondered if Lizzie Siddal had died. Perhaps she had recovered, and was even now convalescing in Rossetti's Gothic parlor, wearing a carmine cashmere dressing gown while Rossetti spooned custard lovingly into her mouth. Jane shook her head to rid herself of the thought.

"You moved," said Morris. "Are you tired?"

"I'm sorry," said Jane. "Perhaps I would like some tea."

"Certainly," said Morris. He put down his pencil. "I'll find the porter and tell him to bring it." With a sinking heart Jane realized that there would be no more gossipy chats with Miss Lipscombe. She would have to take tea with this awkward, silent boy.

When the tray came, Jane marveled, as she always did, at the abundance of the meal. There were cream biscuits and lemon curd, currant scones and marmalade so finely cut it was smooth as jelly. Morris poured the tea, fearing the pot was too heavy for her. He dropped two lumps of sugar into her cup and a generous helping of milk. It was when he was handing the cup to her that the mishap occurred. Somehow Morris contrived to drop it before she had a firm grip on the handle. Hot tea spilled over the table and into Jane's lap as the cup fell to the floor and broke in two.

"Forgive me," said Morris, blushing furiously and trying to mop the table with his napkin.

"It was an accident," said Jane. "We'll send for another cup."

He cares for me, she realized with a shock. The knowledge eased her sadness ever so slightly. He is sweet, if clumsy, she thought.

When the mess had been swept away and Jane had poured herself a cup of tea, she looked over at Morris. He was carefully buttering a scone and would not look at her. The silence became oppressive.

"Have you heard from your friends?" she inquired when she could stand it no longer. "Have they all returned safely to London?"

There was a long pause before Morris spoke. "I believe Burne-Jones has gone to Birmingham," he said.

Jane waited, but Morris didn't say anything else. "And the others?" she prompted.

"The others are back in London, though I cannot vouch for their safety."

Jane racked her brain for some way to get Morris to reveal something of Rossetti without asking him directly.

"Except Rossetti," he added abruptly. "He's in Bath with . . ." Here Morris blushed and stuttered slightly. ". . . his brother," he finished.

"I've heard Bath is lovely," said Jane.

"It's a wretched place," growled Morris. "Full of sickly old people and the young people who prey on them. But the architecture is interesting. Roman, you know." He began to tell her about the baths and completely forgot what the conversation had originally been about.

When the post came there was a letter for Jane. Morris scowled and tossed it next to her plate before muttering that he had to prepare for the next drawing session.

The return address was Bath. The forceful hand could only be Rossetti's.

Jane tore the letter open with shaking hands, grateful that Morris had left her alone to read it.

Dearest Miss Burden, it read:

> *You were so kind as to write me a letter and now I find it necessary to return the favor. I wish that we weren't separated by all of these miles, that I could see your sweet face, though I shudder with dread at the thought of the grave judgment in your sea green eyes. How to explain to you, how to apologize, how to beg your forgiveness? I am ashamed that I deceived you; in truth I never meant to. I never meant to fall in love with you. I resolved every day to withstand the siren song of your loveliness and your sweet gentleness, but I was weak. And then I told myself that some circumstance would release me from my obligation and then I would be able to openly declare my love for you. But, alas, the opposite occurred. The person who held a prior claim on my affections became deathly ill and I would be the worst kind of cad if I had not rushed to her side. She is recovering now, though her prognosis is still uncertain. Until she either recovers or expires my duty is to remain with her. I cannot ask you to wait for me, but I dare to hope that at least you will not hold me in contempt.*

I have sent this letter to the Debating Hall, hoping that Topsy will find a way to deliver it to you. I dared not send it to your house, knowing what your mother would think of a letter from me. I breathlessly await your reply.
Ever your servant,
Dante Gabriel Rossetti

It took every ounce of self-control Jane possessed to slip the letter into her pocket and return to her pose. He had loved her! He still loved her! Her mind whirled. She wanted to read the letter again, she wanted to burst into tears, she wanted to skip for joy. Instead she remained still as a statue while Morris hummed and cursed under his breath and tore sheet after sheet of paper off the easel and ripped them into pieces.

Jane considered whether or not to answer him. She knew that she should punish Rossetti's behavior by never speaking to him again, but she didn't think she could do that. And he wanted her to wait for him, that was clear. She had no idea what she should do.

"Do you like poetry, Miss Burden?" It took Jane a few moments to emerge from her reverie and realize that Morris was speaking to her.

"Yes I do, Mr. Morris," she said, "although I don't have as much time to read as I would like."

He misunderstood her. "I'm sorry that our work here keeps you from your books, and I promise you I will be eternally grateful for the sacrifice."

There was a long silence as she tried to figure out what she was supposed to say to that. She could admit that she had no books at home, that the only poetry she heard now were the few things she had committed to memory, but she did not want him to feel sorry for her.

"Who are your favorite poets, Mr. Morris?" she finally asked.

"Keats," he replied. She had to admit she had not read any. Tennyson she had read. He asked if she knew "The Lady of Shalott."

"It is one of my favorites," she said. "I have often wanted to be her."

"But she was imprisoned," protested Morris. "And cursed. She died."

"Yes, but where she lived was beautiful, looking out over the fields of barley and rye, and the river, shaded by willows and aspens. And she had her weaving."

"But she had no 'loyal knight and true,' and was condemned to see the world only as shadows."

"Think how she must have felt when she saw Launcelot," mused Jane. "A peculiar mixture of exhilaration and sadness, I imagine. For she had found love, but she knew that she would die. She was free, and yet she had lost everything."

"I sincerely hope that it will not require your death to free you from your prison," said Morris. Jane blushed. She had not meant to draw attention to herself. She had only wanted to talk about poetry.

"I am not imprisoned," she said. "I do not live in a poem, whatever my silly imaginings."

"They are not silly," said Morris. "It is what poetry is for, to transport us out of ourselves."

"Have you thought of painting her?" said Jane, to distract him.

He shook his head. "Rossetti could, I'm sure. But I am beginning to fear that I will never be any good as a painter. This Guinevere will not come right, and I have the most wonderful model in England."

Now Jane really did not know what to say. The compliment sounded so different coming from Morris. The depth of feeling behind it was alarming. It seemed to imply an obligation on her part that made her want to flee.

"Do you like novels, Mr. Morris?"

"I adore them. Scott especially. I am reading Dicken's latest, *Barnaby Rudge.*"

"I have only read *Ivanhoe*," Jane admitted. "But I would like to read Dickens someday."

"If you like, Miss Burden, I will read some of it to you."

"I would quite like that, Mr. Morris," she said, wondering if it was wrong to flirt with him.

That night she sat for a long time, pencil in hand, trying to organize her thoughts.

Dear Mr. Rossetti, she wrote:

> *I have received your letter. I admit I was shocked by your sudden departure and grieved not to have merited a farewell or an explanation.*

She stopped, uncertain what to say next. Should she give him reason to believe she would wait for him? Should she encourage him to continue to write to her?

> *I wish you every happiness but I cannot in good conscience continue this correspondence. Please do not write to me again.*
> *Jane Burden*

As she sealed the letter, Jane felt a searing pain at the thought of sundering herself from Rossetti, but she had no doubt she had done the right thing. How would she feel if she were in Lizzie's place, sick and helpless? If Rossetti abandoned her she would be reduced to something much worse than a hat shop.

The next day when she arrived, there was a package wrapped in blue paper on the table next to Morris's easel. Morris turned red when he saw her looking at it. He picked it up and handed it to her.

"I saw something in a bookshop yesterday I thought you might like. I hope you won't think it too forward. From one reader to another."

She untied the string and unwrapped the present. It was an illustrated Tennyson, bound in soft leather with the title stamped in gold. Inside, each poem was bordered by pen-and-ink drawings, and every few pages there was a two-page spread of watercolor. She could not imagine how much such a thing had cost. And Morris made it sound as if he had bought it on a whim, with no particular thought or care!

"I don't know what to say, Mr. Morris," she said.

"Say you like it," he mumbled.

"I do," she said, "very much." As she flipped through the pages, she noticed that although she had read most of the poems, a few were new to her. Reluctantly she closed the book. "I shall read a little bit of it every day, to make the pleasure last longer," she said. Morris smiled with delight, but his smile faded as Jane pulled the letter to Rossetti out of her apron pocket and handed it to him.

"Would you be so kind as to post this for me?"

Morris frowned as he read the address. "Yes, of course," he said. He looked at it as if it were a particularly noxious type of vermin, then put it in his pocket.

They worked in silence for most of the morning. Morris had moved on to the canvas now and his difficulties seemed to have multiplied. His face was clenched in determination and his fingers were white from holding the brush. She expected it to fly out of his hand at any moment.

"Rossetti would know how to fix this," he grumbled. "Of course, he would never get into such a muddle. Only Millais is more naturally gifted at painting. Of course Millais drives himself like a cart horse."

He looked up and saw that Jane was standing as still as before, but that tears were rolling down her face.

"Tell me what you thought of *Ivanhoe*," Morris said quickly. "I can imagine you modeling for a painting of Rebecca."

Jane wished she had a handkerchief. "Of course I always wished to be Rowena," she choked.

"Why is that, when Rebecca is such a principled and noble woman, and Rowena is a simpering, helpless fool?" Morris asked.

Jane had to laugh at his blunt appraisal of the characters. "I suppose that's true," she admitted. "But Rowena marries Ivanhoe, while Rebecca ends up in the Jewish convent. Though it always did seem to me that Ivanhoe should have married her instead. It would have been a better story."

"I wholeheartedly agree," said Morris. He lowered his brush and stared out of the window. "I first read Scott when I was a young boy in Essex. I used to ride my pony out into the woods and pretend that I was a knight on a quest. There was a hunting lodge there that had been Queen Elizabeth's, but it was derelict and barely cared for at that time. I used to imagine that it was my castle. I even fashioned myself a costume and a bow and arrow." He smiled at the memory. "My poor pony had to wear a tasseled blanket made of discarded drapery. He was very patient with me."

"Was your childhood a magical one, then?" said Jane. She could hardly imagine having the time and freedom he described.

"For a while," said Morris. "Until my father died and I was sent away to school. I have not seen the hunting lodge in many years. I suppose it will be torn down to build workers' housing. All of the old lovely places seem to be disappearing."

"There is a place here, on the Iffley Road," said Jane without thinking. "The violets grow in the fields along the river in great profusion. There's not a castle, but it is the prettiest spot in Oxfordshire, I think. Do you know it?"

"Is it near the walnut grove?" asked Morris. "The one owned by Magdalen College? We used to sneak over there and steal nuts by the pailful when I was in school."

Jane smiled. "I'm surprised we never ran into each other then.

My sister Bessie and I visit the walnut grove regularly. The violet field is not half a mile away."

"I should like to see it," said Morris. "Will you take me there sometime?"

Jane realized now what she had said, but there was no evading him. "Of course," she said reluctantly. "When the weather improves."

When she left, Jane hid the Tennyson in her coat and somehow slipped past without her mother seeing it. She secreted it away under her pallet.

A few days later there was a sheaf of papers waiting for her when she arrived at the studio. She could not imagine what they could be. She picked them up and read from the topmost page, "Sir Galahad, A Christmas Mystery," by William Morris.

"It is my own poor poem," Morris said. "I am a little bit ashamed to show it to you, but I hope you'll be generous and not despise it."

"I'm sure I won't," she said, not sure at all. How would it compare with the lines Rossetti had recited to her? Rossetti's poetry had always seemed to flow effortlessly from him, fully formed and perfect, as if received from the gods. She had never seen any of them written down like this, words crossed out and ink blots marring the page.

"I am putting together a book of poems," Morris said. "It occupies me at night when I am not at the studio."

Jane suddenly saw Morris's evenings, so full of the thoughts in his own head, so starved of human companionship. No wonder he did not know how to talk to her.

She read Morris's poem that night. It was not so ecstatic as Rossetti's poetry, but she liked the story. In it the knight Galahad voiced his jealousy of Palomydes and Launcelot because they had fair ladies, and bemoaned his own loveless state. She thought she recognized the parallels between Galahad's sorrow and Morris's own. Burne-Jones could easily be Palomydes, wallowing in the self-sacrifice of a distant love and a lengthy engagement. Of course Launcelot was Rossetti, so merry and gallant, with everything coming so easily to him. Then Galahad has a vision of Jesus and is told that to love and serve the Lord is much more important and lasting than earthly love. Jane wasn't sure she liked that, although she knew Morris was just following the tale as he had read it.

"It is not finished, you know," Morris said nervously when she arrived the next day. "It is meant to be a long poem and I have only gotten as far as what I gave you."

"I thought your poem was quite good," she said. She saw Morris's face relax in relief. "It's a familiar subject, of course, but I thought your perspective was original. I really feel as though I understand Galahad in a new way."

"Thank you," Morris said. "Of course I hoped to be able to do that, but one never knows if one has succeeded or failed. Most often I fail. But if you gained even a small measure of pleasure from it, then I have been sufficiently rewarded for my effort."

"I only wondered," said Jane, "if you really believe that heavenly love is to be sought and valued over earthly love."

Morris stared at her for a moment, as if not sure how to answer. "Not really," he said at last. "It's something loveless people often say to give meaning to their loneliness. Of course I am not Gala-had, nor Mallory, for that matter."

"You have portrayed him so convincingly, I am not sure where the author ends and the character begins. But then I have never known a poet before," said Jane, not quite truthfully. She was thinking of Rossetti. "You will have to teach me."

"I'm honored that you think me a poet," said Morris. "If it does not trouble you too much, would it be all right if I showed you more of my poems?"

Jane was torn. She did not want to give him the wrong idea, but reading his poem had been a wonderful treat. The thought of a new poem, to read in secret every night after her family was asleep, was almost better than the lavish Oxford teas. But how to explain this to Morris?

He was waiting nervously for her answer.

"Of course," she finally said.

Having overcome her worst nature in relinquishing Rossetti, it was somewhat deflating to receive another letter from him, praising her scruples and declaring his continued affection. She did not reply. She occupied herself with reading Morris's poems and sitting for his painting. She was amazed by Morris's prodigious energy. He seemed to write a new poem each night, and to attack the painting each morning with determined zeal. There was something utterly prosaic about him, but Jane found it comforting after her experience with Rossetti. His obsession with knights and chivalry notwithstanding, there was something very solid about him. Rossetti had been a dream: magical, ephemeral. He had made her believe in fairy tales, if only for a moment, and for that, she thought, she would never forgive him.

Morris was painting. Jane was looking toward the window, lost in her own thoughts. She was thinking about the patch of blue sky that was just visible over the top of the chapel across the courtyard. She was thinking about spring, not about Morris at all. She was imagining that Rossetti had come back. Miss Siddal had broken off their engagement after she got well. At first Rossetti had been brokenhearted, but then he said, "I was secretly relieved, Miss Burden, for it allowed me to return to Oxford to see you again. I can only hope and pray that you are still free." She told him that she was, and he knelt before her and kissed her hand. He pledged his undying love and devotion in words she couldn't quite work out. Of course they were poetic, much more poetic than anything she could concoct. Instead of focusing on the words, she imagined his eyes, so dark and soft, and his hand, so warm and strong in hers.

"Miss Burden," Morris said. He had to say it several times before she emerged from her daydream. Jane felt very cross at being interrupted. When she turned to Morris, she saw an expression in his hazel eyes that frightened her. Then she realized that he had turned his canvas around to face her. For the first time she saw the work he had been laboring over all of these weeks. The figure, only in the vaguest sense her size and shape, was a crosshatched mess. The background was muddied with wide angry brushstrokes the color of silt and loam. The bottom of the canvas was still startlingly white, and on it Morris had written, in midnight blue: "I cannot paint you, but I love you."

Seven

*J*ANE sat in stunned silence. Though she knew she had been encouraging Morris, she had hardly dared believe he would declare himself, and if she had imagined it, she would not have thought it would happen so abruptly.

"I am shocked, Mr. Morris," she finally said. "I do not know what to say."

"Say you love me as well," he said. In contrast to his bold declaration, he could not meet her eye but stared down at the floor. "No, I know you cannot say that. Say that one day you might love me."

"I do not know," she said. Her head was still filled with Rossetti.

Morris looked encouraged that she had not refused him outright. "Then perhaps I may hope. I apologize for my conduct. I have frightened you, you look most pale. Sit down and I will bring you some water."

While she sat and sipped the water, he told her, haltingly, how he had fallen in love with her.

"Of course I was overwhelmed by your beauty when I first saw you, as we all were, but I would never have thought of approaching you. You were, and are, perfect, like Aphrodite, high on Mount Olympus, completely untouchable. You were sent here for men to worship from afar, and I was content to do that."

He paused to give Jane the opportunity to say something, but she couldn't speak. No matter how much water she drank, her mouth still felt dry. He went on.

"But then I saw how horribly Rossetti had treated you, and how much you suffered. And when I found the courage to visit your home, I saw just what he had left you to. Someone like you should not be doomed to live a life of poverty. You should be celebrated by all. I hope you don't take this to mean I intend to rescue you. In fact, you would be rescuing me from my loneliness and solitude. I know you understand, from the way you have talked about my poems. It was our conversations about poetry that made me think you might one day learn to care for me."

"I love poetry, Mr. Morris," she said helplessly.

"That is something we share," he said. "I believe there are many other things we could share, if we took the time to discover them."

"I don't know," said Jane, again. She could not believe what she was saying but with his ardor so nakedly on display, she was ashamed of herself for being so calculating. "We hardly know each other."

"True," said Morris, who was beginning to look rather glum now that the excitement of his confession was waning. "I apologize. I hope that my outburst will not prevent you from returning to the studio. I assure you such a thing will never happen again."

"I am sure it won't," said Jane.

"Then you will continue to model for me?" pleaded Morris.

"Of course," she reassured him.

Yet both knew that the matter was far from resolved.

Jane considered her feelings on her walk home, and realized that more than anything she felt guilty. She felt that she was betraying Rossetti by receiving the attentions of someone else. But that was ridiculous. Whether he loved her or not was immaterial. He was not free. She was betraying no one.

Of course she must marry Morris. He was not handsome, she had to admit. He was shorter than she, and plump. His thick curly hair refused to lie neatly, but was always sticking out all over his head. His eyes were small and deeply set. His whiskers were sparse and he seemed to have no lips at all.

On the other hand, he was not Tom Barnstable. He was not hideous or disfigured. His smile was pleasant and his eyes were kind. And he was rich.

Jane admitted that she did feel something for Morris. She was flattered that he cared about her, and grateful for the way he spoke with her about poetry, as if she were intelligent and could understand. She had come to enjoy their conversations. If Rossetti had not come, Jane might have convinced herself that these mildly warm feelings could easily be transformed into love, but now she was not so sure.

Of course she did not tell her mother what had happened at the studio, but though the full story never reached her, people were talking. Mrs. Harris's son the porter was as useful as ever. In addition, Morris had accounts with many of the stores in town and an uptick in his purchases had been noticed. The lack of discretion among Oxford's merchant class enabled Mrs. Burden to construct a fairly clear picture of Morris's financial prospects.

"Seven hundred pounds a year," she said that evening, apropos of nothing.

"What?" stammered Jane.

"Mr. Morris, he has seven hundred pounds a year," said Mrs. Burden. "From some kind of mine. Copper, or something. Now that's a good business. Not a fly-by-night thing like picture painting."

"Mr. Morris is a painter, Mother," said Jane.

"He'll get over it," said Mrs. Burden. "His prospects are very good. You're not going to do any better. Though I ought to thank that Italian for drawing Mr. Morris's attention to you. I doubt he'd have paid any attention otherwise."

"Mr. Morris isn't paying me any attention," said Jane, lowering her gaze to her needlework.

"But he is going to propose," Mrs. Burden said. "And you are going to accept."

It was not an observation, it was a command. It was strange, Jane reflected, that while she had decided to accept Morris's proposal, as soon as her mother spoke, she felt that she would rather die than marry Morris.

"I'm not," Jane said.

Her mother, surprisingly, did not lose her temper but continued to sew placidly. "Just wait," said Mrs. Burden.

"Do you think it's wrong to marry someone you don't love, if they love you?" she asked Bessie.

"How is it worse than marrying someone you don't love who doesn't love you either?" Bessie snapped. She could not forgive her sister for bewitching not one but two of the most eligible gentlemen either of them was likely to see.

"At least that's honest," said Jane. "At least no one will be hurt."

Bessie thought Jane was being ridiculous. "Say you marry him," she said. "You go to live in a fine house in London, with servants. You never have to do any real work again. You can eat delicious food, and go to the theater whenever you want, and buy books. Your dresses will be nice. Perhaps you'll travel. Of course there will be the unpleasantness, but how often can that happen? Once or twice a month? You can easily feign illness or a backache.

"Then say you don't marry him. You'll marry Tom and move to a cottage down the street. You'll work even harder than you do now, and you'll still have the unpleasantness! And Mrs. Burden will come by for tea every day. Or say you don't marry Tom. You'll go to work for some lady as a housemaid. Perhaps it will be the new Mrs. Morris! Or at least someone very like her. You'll wait on her hand and foot for a pittance, all the time knowing it could have been you sitting in her chair, if not for your scruples."

Still, Jane hesitated. Each day she returned to the studio, determined to keep things neutral until she understood her feelings better. However hard she tried, though, Morris would not be put off. Now a present appeared for her every single day: apricot jellies dusted with powdered sugar, a picture postcard with an engraving of the cathedral at Amiens, a bag of pears, a volume of William Blake. An arrangement from the florist appeared at her house almost daily: iris and apple blossoms, daffodil and sweet pea, bunches of lilac. It was enough to turn the head of a girl much less deprived than Jane.

"You spoil me, Mr. Morris," she said.

"I intend to be like the lover in 'The Eve of St. Agnes,'" he said, and recited the lines from the Keats poem to her:

And still she slept an azure-lidded sleep,
In blanchèd linen, smooth, and lavendered,
While he from forth the closet brought a heap
Of candied apple, quince, and plum, and gourd;
With jellies soother than the creamy curd,
And lucent syrups, tinct with cinnamon;
Manna and dates, in argosy transferred
From Fez; and spicèd dainties every one,
From silken Samarcand to cedared Lebanon.

These delicates he heaped with glowing hand
On golden dishes and in baskets bright
Of wreathèd silver: sumptuous they stand
In the retirèd quiet of the night,
Filling the chilly room with perfume light.
"And now, my love, my seraph fair, awake!
Thou art my heaven, and I thine eremite:
Open thine eyes, for meek St. Agnes' sake,
Or I shall drowse beside thee, so my soul doth ache."

"Do you like dates?" he asked. "If you do I will bring some tomorrow."

It was worrisome, Jane thought, how consumed he was by her. He said he was writing a poem about her, but that she could not see it until it was perfect. By day, he painted her, and by night, he wrote about her.

He showed her his painting for the first time since the day he'd declared his love, and Jane saw with relief that it was much improved. Though her figure was still little more than a sketch, the background was now complete. The carpet, the curtains, the wall hangings, the bedclothes, all were richly colored and textured. There were oranges and a medieval prayer book on the painted chest next to the bed. In the bed slept a tiny dog. There was a copper jug at her feet and an angel with a harp behind her.

"I think I would like to have such a room someday," Jane said. "Such rich colors and textures—I think I could be happy there, though Queen Guinevere is not, is she? But I suppose she's used to it and takes it for granted."

"I should like to have a room like it myself," said Morris, looking at her meaningfully. "I intend to, someday, when I have my castle and my heart's desire."

Jane dropped her gaze to the floor. Morris saw that she was uncomfortable and quickly turned the conversation.

"Burne-Jones and I have designed some furniture for our flat in London," he said. "A chest just like the one in my painting, in fact. We found that there was nothing to our liking in any of the shops, so we found someone to make us some heavy medieval things."

"It's unlike anything I've seen," Jane said. She thought of the furniture at home, crude, unsanded and unstained pieces her father had made. "But I like it very much."

Morris flushed with pleasure, but could not seem to accept the compliment. "I'm much better at painting objects than painting the figure," he lamented. "I don't know why that is. I try and try, as you know. How many times have I drawn you? A hundred? A thousand? And still your figure is all wrong. As for your face . . . I know I will not be able to do it justice."

"I think the shadows in the folds of the drapery look very well." She did not mean to be too kind, but she could not help trying to be sympathetic, he looked so discouraged and so disgusted with himself.

He shrugged. "Of course. That's the easy part. A child could draw a drapery."

"I know I could not," Jane said.

"You're too modest," said Morris, still scowling at his work. "I knew that painting would be the most difficult thing I could endeavor to do, but I am determined. I will be a painter."

"I believe you, Mr. Morris," she said. "Anyone who works as hard as you do must succeed."

With alarm she saw that she had at last said too much. With a sick feeling in her stomach, Jane knew that the moment had come. Morris came toward her and fell to his knees.

"Miss Burden, I cannot wait any longer. I must know if you will marry me."

She found that when it came to it, she did not know what to do. "I am very honored, Mr. Morris," she said. "May I ask for the favor of a few days' consideration?"

"As long as you accept me at the end of that time," he joked, trying to make light of the situation, but afterward they reverted to their earlier awkward silence. Jane was glad when the day's work was over.

She wondered if Rossetti knew. Had Morris written to Rossetti of his intentions? It became her new daydream: Rossetti rushing to Oxford to put a stop to Morris's attentions. He had not known, he told her, how strongly he felt about her until he heard that she might become another's. Then he swept her into his arms as Morris looked on helplessly. Once she imagined a duel but discarded that fantasy as far too extreme. If Rossetti appeared Morris would abandon the field, she was sure of it. She thought of writing him a letter herself, asking him what she should do, but she could not bring herself to stoop so low.

The next day Morris showed her a letter he had received from Rossetti. It contained a drawing of Morris presenting a ring to Jane. In the drawing Morris's nose was very long and his chin stuck out very far. He was as squat as a duck. Next to him, Jane gazed down at her hand, a hint of a smile on her lips. She looked pleased and pretty.

The drawing was quite kind to Jane and equally unkind to Morris, but she could not find comfort in it. Rossetti knew. And Morris, by showing her the drawing, was discreetly informing her that Rossetti knew, and that he would not come. He might disapprove, he might be jealous, but he would not stop it, he would not take her away.

That night, as if she sensed that the crisis had come, Jane's mother sat her down.

"I've been patient with you," she said, "but this has gone too far. You're to marry Mr. Morris, and if you don't there's no place for you in this house."

There had been girls thrown out of their homes on Holywell Street before. Usually the implication of bad character had prevented them from getting jobs in the big houses of Oxford, and they ended up as prostitutes in the brothels near the university.

"All right," said Jane, feeling almost relieved that her mother had left her with no choice. "I'll marry Mr. Morris."

Morris's smile was almost handsome when she told him. For a moment it seemed he might kiss her, but instead he took her hand and gave it a little shake.

"I will write to my mother immediately," he said.

I will grow to love him, Jane thought to herself. She tried to stifle the voice inside reminding her that marrying Morris was the best way to keep Rossetti from disappearing from her life completely. It was wrong to think such things, but she couldn't help it.

Eight

I T was March 1858, and Jane was eighteen years old and engaged to an Oxford man of independent means. No one on Holywell Street could believe it. A few said Jane must have bewitched Morris. Others shook their heads and thought that he must be a very odd fellow. Mrs. Burden received so many unexpected callers she had to order extra tea and sugar to have on hand for them, but for once she didn't grouse or grumble. She smiled sweetly at everyone who came and said yes, it was true, and yes, it was a miracle.

Jane and Morris went out walking together, and once went to the theater with Bessie, but he did not come to Holywell Street. He had come for supper once and been so embarrassed by her mother's attentions that he refused to come again. Jane could hardly blame him. Most often they spent their time together at the Debating Hall, since Morris had not yet finished his painting.

A week after the engagement was announced, Morris and Jane took a picnic to the field of violets. It was a pretty walk out of town on the Iffley Road, past ancient, ivy-covered stone houses with front gardens carpeted in purple and white crocus. They crossed the Magdalen Bridge and stopped to admire the view. The river below changed with the season and the weather; today it was placid and reflected the pale blue sky. A tentative sun shone and gently warmed Jane's face. On one bank a man in a red jacket was training two young liver-spotted spaniels to flush game. On the other several students were fishing and amusing themselves by distracting the dogs with tossed sticks.

"I have received a letter from my mother," said Morris as they watched the man shouting at the students while the dogs leaped and barked.

"What does it say?" Jane was immediately nervous. From all she had heard, Mrs. Morris sounded like a frightening person, and she doubted the lady was very pleased with her son's choice of a bride.

"Oh, she is well, and happy about the engagement," Morris said with uncharacteristic vagueness. "Shall we walk on? The violets are not going to pick themselves."

Jane thought he was being evasive. "I imagine she is horrified," she said bluntly. "I'm sure she had someone less common in mind for you."

Morris blushed. "What she may have had in mind for me is completely irrelevant," he said.

He paused, and for a terrible moment Jane thought that his mother might have convinced him to break off the engagement after all. How could she return to Holywell Street now that she had allowed herself to hope?

"However, she has asked a favor of you and I hope you will consider it, if not to please your future mother-in-law, then at least to please me?"

Morris was suddenly very interested in the handle of the basket he was carrying.

"Yes?" Jane asked fearfully. "What is it?" She did not want to promise until she heard what it was. It must be awful if Morris was so afraid to tell her.

"My mother wishes for you to be trained as a proper lady. A gentlewoman of her acquaintance, Mrs. Wallingford, has agreed to be your tutor," Morris said, speaking quickly now, as if to get it over with. "Her husband has died and her circumstances are much reduced. Not that you should mention that."

"I don't understand," said Jane. "Are there so many things I need to learn?"

"My mother thinks it would be helpful to see how a great house is run, and learn about clothes, and other things," said Morris. "I know it may seem insulting, but it really might be very helpful to you."

"How long will this training take?" asked Jane. "I suppose I must go and live with this strange woman?"

"Mrs. Wallingford has a house in Gloucestershire," said Morris. "I hear it is lovely, with green hills all around. You'll stay there for a few months. I have to return to London soon anyway." Morris had taken a job with an architect. "By the time I find a house for us and get it set up, your time with Mrs. Wallingford will be over and we can be married."

"How many months is a few?" asked Jane.

"I suppose as long as it takes before Mrs. Wallingford is satisfied with you," said Morris. "I can't imagine it would be more than six or seven."

"What if she's never satisfied with me?" asked Jane. "Will I be her prisoner forever?"

Morris smiled indulgently. "She would have to have a heart of stone not to be immediately pleased with you. I'm sure it will take no time at all."

They had arrived at their destination and gazed admiringly at the profusion of purple. Their delicate scent was delicious. While Jane laid out the cheese sandwiches and chocolate biscuits, Morris filled the basket with hundreds of fragile violets.

As they ate, Morris earnestly described his most cherished dreams.

"I hope to be a great painter, of course," he said. "Also a good architect, and a good poet. And I'd like to increase the measure of beauty in the world, and make things better for others, if I can." He blushed a little. "That is my motto, you know. *Si je puis.*"

"If I can," repeated Jane.

"Yes," said Morris. "It may seem silly to you, but I want to do as much as I can, try as many things as I can, not be daunted by my own ignorance or discouraged by my lack of ability. I don't want to be lazy or complacent. I don't want to be some silly fop drinking champagne and gossiping about dancers."

Jane thought he looked very noble as he said this, and she had to admit that such sentiments would never pass Rossetti's lips. He was a thoughtless, careless, pleasure-seeking hedonist. She resolved to stop loving him immediately.

When the portrait was finished, Jane had to agree with Morris that he had little talent for figure painting. She thought her face looked splotchy, as if she had a pox. There was no animating life in her eyes; she could have been made of wax. She told Morris that she was pleased, that she felt honored to have been made a queen, but a small inner voice she tried to stifle told her that Rossetti would have done it much better.

The painting complete, Morris left Oxford to return to London, leaving Jane behind. Soon after, Jane left Oxford herself for the first time in her life. On the day of her departure, her father left for the stables before it was light, not bothering to say goodbye. Jamey nodded to her as she left the house, but her mother barely looked up from the washing as Jane picked up her small bag and opened the door. Bessie walked her to the train station. She presented Jane with a packet of mint candies that had been a present from her beau and which she didn't like. Still, her sister's tearful exhortations to write made Jane feel weepy and sentimental. But when Jane opened the window of her compartment so she could wave to Bessie as the train pulled away, she saw that her sister was already walking toward the exit.

Jane wiped her eyes and vowed not to waste any more tears on her family or her town. Soon she became engrossed in the view of the countryside from her window. The verdure of flat pastures went on for miles and miles. Every so often they would pass a wide marsh thick with geese and ducks. They stopped at several towns along the way. After a time the countryside became hillier, the trees thicker. The sky darkened. They were entering the Cotswolds. Halfway into the trip it began to rain. Jane had brought two hard-boiled eggs and an apple for her lunch, which she ate while she watched through a scrim of rain as goats grazed the rocky fields.

A carriage met her at the station in Cheltenham and a driver took her small bag as if it were a dead animal and placed it above. She had not wanted to give it to him; she did not like to be parted from her few possessions. The driver's withering look, however, cowed her and she meekly gave the bag to him.

Cheltenham had been built in the eighteenth century as a spa town. As they drove past rows of white and yellow Regency hotels, she wondered what Morris would think of the place. She decided that with his fondness for the ancient and medieval he would probably dislike it, since the stone cottages that had once been there had been torn down to make way for the stucco buildings lining the streets. Jane thought them very pretty, though it made her feel disloyal to admit it. She was sure that if Morris were there to explain to her why the old buildings were wonderful and why the new ones were shoddy, she would come to agree with him.

The carriage continued west, out of the town, and the landscape was much the same. Jane began to feel sleepy and dozed off until a lurch of the wheels woke her. It took her several minutes to realize that they were no longer on the main road, but on Hartford Hall's private drive. They trotted between towering yew hedges for what seemed like hours, until the view opened onto the largest park she had ever seen. Groups of elms and oaks were interspersed with rolling lawns of immaculately kept grass. Then she caught sight of the house itself. It was a palace. The central section was made of the same sandstone as the village cottages, but smoothed into large ochre blocks. The wings had been added later, and were of white marble. She had never seen so many windows, so much glass. The driver helped her from the carriage and disappeared with her bag. She had never felt so small as she stood in front of the enormous oak door. Not sure what to do, she waited to see if anyone would come out. When no one did, she rang the bell.

An old woman in a starched uniform opened it. She stood and waited with a blank expression while Jane stuttered out who she was and why she was there. Then she said, "Your coat, miss," and without another word led her to a room on the main floor in the back of the house. It was papered in sky blue silk and decorated in the French style, with elaborately carved and delicately proportioned gilt furniture, an ormolu clock, and many Chinese vases. The woman gestured toward a Louis XVI chair covered in peach velvet and Jane sat in it to wait for Mrs. Wallingford.

She was surprised to discover that Mrs. Wallingford was only forty. She had not a gray strand in her loosely tied auburn hair. She was quite pretty, with a prim, narrow mouth and porcelain skin. Her dress was sumptuous and well cut, in an hourglass shape.

"So you're Jane," she said. "The pauper who is to become a princess."

Jane said nothing, as it was clear she was not expected to speak.

"Stand up, please, so I can look at you," Mrs. Wallingford said. Jane stood, feeling like a cow at an auction.

"You're very vulgar, I can see," Mrs. Wallingford said. "Your clothes, though abhorrent, are of little interest, as they can easily be changed. It is what is underneath that is important, as it is all we have to work with. That, and a great deal of Mrs. Morris's money. Money can camouflage a world of imperfection, but not all, of course. Not nearly all." She circled Jane and examined her carefully.

"Your forehead is very low, but that is to be expected with your class. Your hands are ridiculously large. Perhaps a skillful glove-maker could help, but it would be better for you to keep them hidden in the folds of your dress at all times. Your hair, of course, is a fright, but we can do wonders with that. Your posture is bad, your facial expression worse, and I do not even want to consider what your voice will sound like when you open your mouth. I imagine you're very stupid and will be unable to remember half of what I tell you. However, we will try."

Jane said nothing.

"Well?" said Mrs. Wallingford. "Will you not thank me for all of the efforts I am willing to make on your behalf?"

"Thank you," said Jane. It came out in a croak.

"If you must clear your throat, do it quietly and discreetly before you are called upon to speak. And say 'Thank you, Mrs. Wallingford.'"

"Thank you, Mrs. Wallingford," said Jane.

"We must raise your voice at least an octave," said Mrs. Wallingford. "I've no objection to a rich contralto, it can be lovely on the right woman, but you sound like my uncle Hugo."

Mrs. Wallingford's first letter to Mrs. Morris, which she read out loud to Jane before she posted it, was not encouraging. She enumerated Jane's many faults and expressed doubt as to whether the course could be completed in six months. In fact, she expressed doubt as to whether Jane could ever be made suitable.

"But as your son is determined," wrote Mrs. Wallingford, "so shall we be."

The mornings were devoted to housekeeping, the afternoons to dress, manners, decorum, and social training. Jane followed Mrs. Wallingford as she went about her duties in her grand house. Jane found that the housekeeping abilities she had were not required. She was never to boil water for laundry, or prepare the lye for soap making, or chop vegetables, or scour pans. Instead she had to learn how to instruct the servants in their duties, how to keep the account books for the many tradesmen who supplied the house, how to make a household inventory down to the last dish towel, teaspoon, and candlestick. Sewing was acceptable, but only the most delicate embroidery and tatting were appropriate. She was not to darn stockings or repair torn hems, but to give them to someone else to do. There were ways of keeping a large house and its staff running smoothly, methods of organization and planning, and Mrs. Wallingford taught her all of them, though she was quick to sigh that when her husband was alive she had twice as many servants.

"We had forty guests, for hunting during the day and dancing at night," she said wistfully. Jane did not think that Morris would enjoy either activity very much. But then she reflected that she did not know him at all well.

Once Jane had timidly asked if learning to manage such a large staff was really necessary. She could not imagine Morris in a house like Mrs. Wallingford's, even short staffed, even when dozens of rooms were shut up to save on heat.

"These rules apply whether one has two servants or two hundred," Mrs. Wallingford replied majestically.

The staff knew her story and as a result did not respect her. They glared at her when they served her dinner, until she was so discomfited she dropped her fork and was reprimanded by Mrs. Wallingford. They lost the lists she gave them, and told Mrs. Wallingford they had never received any. They ignored her instructions and laughed at her mistakes.

Jane wrote to Morris and confessed how miserable she was, but no one would post her letters. Finally she resolved to walk to Cheltenham and post them herself. She was halfway there, already wet and bedraggled, pulling her heavy skirts through the mud, when doubt crept in. He might not believe her. He might tell her not to worry, and to keep her chin up, and maintain a cheerful countenance. Or he might tell his mother what she said and it could get back to Mrs. Wallingford. She faltered, and turned back. After a week she thought she would call off the engagement and return to Oxford. But return where, exactly? She doubted that her mother would take her back. No, she was virtually a prisoner, and she would have to figure out a way to survive. She had never known that a big house with fine things could be so odious, so unpleasant to live in.

Jane finally had all of the books she desired, though Mrs. Wallingford disapproved of reading.

"Books are lovely," she said. "They add such finish and refinement to a room. But they sit better on the shelves if their pages have not been cut."

Mrs. Wallingford endeavored to teach Jane French, but found it slow going. Likewise she was taught to play piano and sing.

"It will not matter that you are very bad," Mrs. Wallingford consoled her. "All that matters is that you have been taught." Jane learned to play "The Ash Grove" adequately, but she did not enjoy it. Next Mrs. Wallingford tried a soprano/alto duet from Handel, but soon gave it up, as Jane could not keep to her part.

Jane's favorite activity was the daily walk she took about the grounds. Slowly over the weeks she lengthened it until she was gone two, sometimes three hours a day. She took her favorite books and the letters she received from Bessie, full of Holywell Street gossip, and from Morris, who was traveling in France with fellow architect Philip Webb. He wrote that he had conceived an idea for the house he was going to build for her.

"We've been traveling down the Seine from Paris," he wrote, "sketching ancient castles. I've enclosed a drawing of our house. You can see it is in the style of the thirteenth century. When Webb and I return to London we will look for a site. I'm thinking of Kent."

Jane unfolded the drawing and saw a medieval house with oriel windows and Gothic arches. It looked like something from a fairy story and the sight of it cheered her. She would not be stuck here in the gloomy Cotswolds forever. She did not know Kent but she hoped it was a sunnier place, with lots of orchards.

"She's much improved," Mrs. Wallingford said to the vicar as the three of them sat at tea. "I've given up trying to get her to smile, though her teeth aren't good enough for that anyway. But she seldom trips on the carpet now and she can pour tea quite adequately."

"I very much wonder at Mrs. Morris, undertaking such a project," said the vicar, looking at Jane severely over his spectacles. "Dr. Howell has proved beyond a doubt that the brains of the lower classes are smaller and feebler. But you are very brave, Mrs. Wallingford."

"I never shrink from my duty," admitted Mrs. Wallingford. "There have been many times in the last few weeks when I doubted I would succeed. You should see this girl eat an artichoke! But I have always been known for my tenacity. Mr. Wallingford always said he could not talk me out of anything once I had made up my mind. Mrs. Morris is such a dear friend that I could not say no to her in her hour of need."

"An act of pure Christian charity, indeed," said the vicar, and Jane clenched her offending teeth and thought to herself that it was fortunate Mrs. Burden had trained her before she arrived at Mrs. Wallingford's. Years of insults had taught her how to bear them.

"Webb and I look at properties every weekend," Morris wrote in September. "He makes me do without lunch, which is extremely trying. I haven't found anything yet but I've narrowed it down to the Cray Valley, in Kent. The area reminds me of Essex. It's a gentle landscape, mostly open fields, apple orchards, and oast-houses, which perhaps you have never seen. They are large kilns for drying hops, which are used to make beer. They have funny conical roofs and add quite charmingly to the scene. I have been thinking about incorporating their shape somehow into the design of the house."

And then, a jubilant letter in October:

"I've found a spot for our castle, very near a Franciscan priory where pilgrims would have stayed on their way to Canterbury. What could be more perfect than that? When the house is finished, we can have great banquets and imagine that we are pilgrims ourselves.

"Webb is hard at work finishing the drawings and working out the materials. His latest idea is red brick with a red tile roof. What is your opinion?"

A castle made of red brick. A gentle landscape of barley fields. As she trudged across the frozen Cotswold hills, it seemed that winter would never pass.

In January Mrs. Morris wrote to say that her son was getting impatient and was his bride nearly ready? Mrs. Wallingford wrote back that although Jane would never be really suitable, she was now at least properly trained. With this imprimatur, the wedding was planned for April. The violets will be blooming, thought Jane when she heard.

Mrs. Wallingford oversaw the making of Jane's wedding dress to Mrs. Morris's specifications. Morris's mother had chosen an opal-colored taffeta in a severe style that Jane did not like, but no one asked her opinion. Mrs. Morris also sent her a plain gold brooch that had been in the Morris family for generations, with the understanding that she was to wear it to the wedding. A taffeta bonnet adorned with peach-colored roses, and a paisley shawl, completed her wedding ensemble.

The wedding was to be held at St. Michael's Church. Jane's family attended the resolutely low-church St. Luke's, but Morris had written to her that St. Michael's was the only church in Oxford that was at all atmospheric. Its tower was built in 1040 and was the oldest building in the town. It had been part of the town prison, and Latimer, Ridley, and Cranmer were held there before they were burned at the stake by Queen Mary for refusing to convert to Catholicism. Though St. Michael's was old, he continued, it had just been restored by his employer, the architect George Edmund Street. It will mean so much to me, he wrote, to be married in such a beautiful and historic place returned to its former glory. Jane had never been in St. Michael's Church, but the way that Morris described it fired her imagination. It would be so much more romantic than the usual wedding.

She arrived back in Oxford just over a year after she had left. She had written to her family of her return, but no one was there to meet her at the station, so she walked home. Her heart began to pound as she approached Holywell Street. Would her family be glad to see her? Would they be changed at all? The street seemed even more squalid than before. I've become soft, she thought to herself. Then she reflected that it hardly mattered, since she would not be expected to live there after the wedding, which was in two days' time.

Her mother was in the kitchen when she arrived and eyed her appraisingly.

"So you're back," she said.

"Yes," said Jane.

"With that dress on I can't ask you to feed the chickens, I suppose, but if you take those fine gloves off you can peel potatoes."

"Where's Bessie?" Jane asked.

"Out walking with a new beau of hers," said Mrs. Burden. "He makes eyeglasses. I hear it is a very difficult art. He is certainly well paid for it."

"I'm glad," said Jane, feeling a little blue Bessie was not there to greet her.

"Your father and your brother will want to see you, but I don't expect them tonight," said Mrs. Burden. "They'll be down at the pub." She dumped the basket of potatoes on the table in front of Jane.

When Bessie finally came home, she squealed over Jane's new clothes and her new traveling case, which Mrs. Wallingford had bought her when she saw the bedraggled bag Jane had arrived with. The new one was calf's leather with brass studs.

"Very smart," proclaimed Bessie. "I will have to ask Charlie—that's my latest beau, you know—to buy me one like it." Inside the case were Jane's new undergarments, trimmed with machine-made lace; silk stockings; kid gloves; a Spanish fan; and her wedding ensemble. Bessie sighed enviously over all of it.

"Why couldn't Morris have taken a fancy to me?" Bessie pouted. "It's all because of that Rossetti. Who knew when he approached us like a lunatic that your life would completely change and mine would stay exactly the same? It's unfair."

"It's not all so wonderful," said Jane. "Didn't you read my letters?"

Bessie was trying on the new gloves and waved her hand majestically. "It didn't sound so terrible to me, living in a grand house like that. Meanwhile I was slaving away here and getting all of the blows that were meant for you."

"I'm sorry," said Jane.

"Don't pity me," said Bessie, with a toss of her head. "James is going to propose and we are going to live in Gloucester. Mrs. Burden will have to abuse someone else, the neighborhood children, I suppose."

The morning of the wedding a large bouquet of white lilies and stock arrived on top of a large white box. Inside the box was the most beautiful dress Jane had ever seen. In its shape it was not so different from the Elizabethan dress she had worn to model for Rossetti. White silk organza dropped straight and soft into a puddle at her feet. There was embroidery on the bodice, a square neckline, and lace sleeves.

"Something you might like better than Mrs. Wallingford's taffeta," the card read. "All my love, William."

"How very thoughtful of him," said Bessie. "I just hope his mother isn't angry that you're not wearing the dress she wanted."

"She's not coming," said Jane.

"All that expense and she doesn't want to take a look at you?" Bessie was shocked.

"Evidently not," said Jane. "She blames it on sciatica."

"More likely she doesn't want to have to shake hands with Mrs. Burden," Bessie said, nodding sagely. "You're lucky, though; the less you meet Mrs. Morris the better, I think."

Jane had to agree. Later that afternoon, though, a letter arrived from Mrs. Morris. Mrs. Morris might not want to meet her daughter-in-law but she still had a lot of advice to give her about her son.

"Do not ever prepare liver, veal, or cheese soup," she wrote. "He dislikes mussels, oysters, and other shellfish. He is partial to strawberries and cream, and to potatoes of almost any kind. Do not allow him to take walks on rainy days, as he is prone to influenza. He must never lift anything above fifty pounds; he has a weak place in his back. Blooming chestnut trees make him sneeze and lilacs make his eyes water. When he is in a temper, he is often soothed by my piano playing, although Mrs. Wallingford tells me you are sadly deficient. If you could learn to play Chopin, it would be a great help to him.

"My son is a genius, you know," she wrote in conclusion. "He must be allowed to prosper. Now that is up to you. Do not fail."

Jane folded up the letter feeling daunted, as Mrs. Morris no doubt expected her to. Morris had made it seem as if their life together would be simple and easy, that anything she did would be all right with him, but now she realized that it wasn't true at all. Morris had a lifetime's accumulation of preferences and quirks she would be required to learn and cater to. It was a shame, really; she had tasted mussels once and thought them delicious.

When Jane arrived at the church for the ceremony, she saw the interior of St. Michael's for the first time. It was simple and weighty, with heavy piers and Gothic stone arches.

"Rather gloomy and dark for a wedding," observed Bessie. "But at least he's bought plenty of candles and flowers."

Jane felt a rising panic. It was all happening too fast. Why had she said she would marry Morris?

They carried Jane's dress into the bride's room.

"Lord Almighty," groaned Bessie when they had laid it down and begun to remove the tissue that covered it. "This thing must weigh forty pounds. What's it made of, iron?" She was sullen that the silk on her burgundy dress was not nearly as fine as Jane's.

"It's the embroidery, I suppose," said Jane.

"Well, I hope you don't faint," said Bessie. She lifted up the dress and held it open for Jane to step into. "Hurry," she gasped.

Jane slid her hands through the gossamer sleeves but her fingers caught in the fine French lace and nearly tore it.

"Be careful," snapped Bessie, but she grabbed Jane's hand and pulled hard. "Ridiculous sleeves," she complained. "Who wears lace this fine? It's more cobweb than clothing. Maybe if your elbows and wrists weren't so bony it wouldn't be so difficult."

"You admired the sleeves earlier," said Jane.

"That's before I tried to put you into them," said Bessie. "I suppose the richer you are the more impractical your clothes become. Well, at least this sack I have on is comfortable."

Jane was hurt. "That silk was the nicest they had in Cheltenham," she said.

"Cheltenham," snorted Bessie. "That explains a lot. There, you're buttoned, top to bottom. I've got to find my seat." And before Jane could ask her to stay, she was gone. Jane was alone.

Her father arrived, sobered up, shaved, and dressed in a suit Morris had bought for him.

"I hope you'll be happy, Janey," he said doubtfully. He put his hands in the pockets, then pulled them out and began to clean his nails.

"If I'm not, I won't be the first," she whispered. The dress made it difficult to breathe and she thought that she might faint.

"No," he agreed, "nor the last. But if you do as Morris tells you, and are a good girl, you'll be all right." He stopped, and Jane watched him struggle to find something else to say. Then the acolyte came to lead them to the narthex.

Jane heard the music start to play and the guests rise and turn to catch the first glimpse of her. A quick scan of the sanctuary revealed no sign of Rossetti. She could not decide if she was relieved or disappointed. Perhaps he is late, she thought to herself. Perhaps he is hidden behind a column.

Jane had never seen Morris in fine clothes and she halted in the middle of the church in panic when she saw his blue frock coat and quilted waistcoat.

I can't do it, she thought wildly. I have to leave.

"Come on," her father hissed, dragging her forward. A few steps more and she recognized Morris, though he was freshly shaved and his hair was successfully plastered down with a copious amount of hair oil. His face glowed with happiness and delight.

Jane's father pushed her toward her groom and left to take his seat.

Morris's friend Dixon, looking very young and slightly ridiculous in his ebony vestments, gave Jane an encouraging smile as he began the service.

"'Dearly beloved,'" he began. "'We are gathered together here in the sight of God, and in the face of this congregation, to join together this Man and this Woman in holy Matrimony . . . '"

Jane recovered her nerves as he spoke and looked out into the sanctuary. Her mother was in the front row, smirking. When her eyes met Jane's, she gave a little wave of her handkerchief and pretended to cry. Bessie appeared to actually be crying; she was bowed over the church rail, her head buried in her arms. Her father was deep in conversation with her brother about something. She caught sight of Burne-Jones, and Brown, but after scanning every face she had to acknowledge that Rossetti had not come.

"'I require and charge you both, as ye will answer at the dreadful day of judgement when the secrets of all hearts shall be disclosed, that if either of you know any impediment, why ye may not be lawfully joined together in Matrimony, ye do now confess it. For be ye well assured, that so many as are coupled together otherwise than God's Word doth allow are not joined together by God; neither is their Matrimony lawful.'"

Jane's hands began to shake and she nearly dropped her *Book of Common Prayer*. For she did know a reason they should not be married. Her heart belonged to another. Would she be struck down at the Day of Judgement for marrying Morris anyway?

She heard Morris say, "I will."

"Mary," Dixon intoned, turning to her, "'wilt thou have this man to thy wedded husband, to live together after God's ordinance in the holy estate of Matrimony? Wilt thou obey him, and serve him, love, honour, and keep him in sickness and in health; and, forsaking all others, keep thee only unto him, so long as ye both shall live?'"

Jane wasn't sure what to do. Had anyone else heard the mistake? Should she say something to correct him? If she was married under the wrong name, was she really married?

Everyone was waiting. Morris began to look pained.

"I will," she finally said.

The congregation exhaled as one and there were scattered claps. The triumphant music began and Morris led Jane proudly down the aisle and out of the church.

As they stood on the steps shaking hands with their well-wishers, Morris whispered that they must go back inside.

"I have to show you all of the stained-glass windows. I imagine you weren't able to get a good look at them before."

"No," said Jane. "But won't everyone be waiting for us?"

"They can wait a few minutes," said Morris. "Come with me."

They stood before the altar as they had done a few minutes before, but now Morris pointed to the stained-glass medallions above it. "Here is the oldest stained glass in Oxford," he said. "It dates to 1290." He waited for Jane to say something.

"It's very pretty," she said.

"The techniques of the time were far superior to those we have now," said Morris. "It's the fault of Protestantism, really. Stained glass was purged, and clear glass came into fashion. You see how the colors are so clear and true? They used natural compounds in ways that are now lost to us." Next he took her into the lady chapel to show her a fifteenth-century window of Christ crucified against a lily. He showed her how the design of the window was different from the one done two hundred years before.

"You see how the shading on the figure of Christ is so much more elaborate?" he said. "They had developed new ways of painting by this time, stippling and matte shading. You should read Charles Winston's *Hints on Glass Painting*. He has a whole section on painting techniques. But I don't like this window nearly as well as the other, do you? The pieces of glass are larger, true, but the colors look washed out."

It was endearing, really, Jane thought. He was like a small boy at a fair.

"Dixon called me Mary during the service," she said to him.

"Did he?" Morris laughed. "So that's why you took so long to answer. I was beginning to be afraid you were going to say 'I won't.'"

"Oh no," said Jane. "I just didn't feel right, saying 'I will' as Mary."

"You can't get away that easily," said Morris. "You are Mrs. Morris whether your first name is Jane or Mary or Guinevere."

When they had examined every piece of glass in the church,

they took a short carriage ride to Jane's house for the wedding breakfast. The feast of lamb, cold duck, chicken pie, tongue, jellies, and fruit was paid for by Morris. A few people from Holywell Street had been invited so that they could spread the word about the fine food at the Burdens's. For what was the point of making an auspicious marriage if not to make one's friends and neighbors jealous? The artists ate prodigiously, seemingly oblivious to the squalor of Holywell Street.

Jane's mother sat beside her during the meal.

"You'll send money home every month," she said.

"Of course," said Jane.

"You'll visit every year."

"If I can," said Jane.

"Robert's a good name for a boy," her mother said. "For a girl I'm partial to Elizabeth, after Bessie. You could call her Beth, or Eliza, as you choose."

Jane blushed and looked over at Morris to make sure he hadn't heard.

"No need to be shy, girl," blared her mother. "That's what marriage is about, isn't it? If you don't like Elizabeth, I think Sarah is pretty, too."

Jane tried not to think about Rossetti's absence. Perhaps it had been too painful for him to come, she thought, but in her heart she knew it wasn't true. Brown informed her that he was on holiday in Cornwall with Lizzie. In late afternoon a carriage came to take Mr. and Mrs. Morris to the train station. The train would take them on to London.

Nine

ORRIS was rereading *Kenilworth*, and he turned to Jane every few minutes to read her a passage he thought particularly good, until she begged him to stop so as not to spoil the story. With her new husband quiet and absorbed, she occupied herself with looking out of the train window. The day, which had been bright when they left Oxford, became progressively grayer as they traveled east. When the first rows of brick houses appeared, Jane could barely make them out through the gloom. She thought they must be in London then, but Morris said no, they were in Willesden. London was still four miles away. It was astonishing to her that the terraced houses continued uninterrupted for the entire four miles. They passed shop after shop, the names flying past: Timmins' Watchworks, Underhill Sundries, Hoyle and Marchmain Booksellers. They passed auction houses and jewelers and grocers and haberdashers. They passed tea houses and restaurants, solicitors' offices and flower stalls. Everything was black with soot: the sidewalks, the windows of the shops, the iron gates of the many courtyards around which the grimy stone town houses were grouped. The lamps were lit and glowed dimly. Jane had never seen such crowded streets. Everyone seemed to be walking very quickly. Their clothes, she realized, were powdered with ash.

"Will it be so dirty where we are?" asked Jane.

Morris sighed. "Terrible, isn't it? But it's only for a few months, until the Kent house is finished."

Jane did not like the idea of exchanging one kind of filth for another, but she supposed ash and coal dust were preferable to what she had left behind.

Paddington Station was terrifying. Suddenly Jane was in the crush of people that she had seen from the train. People were pushing every which way, and it seemed dangerous to stand still, so she blindly followed Morris, who held her elbow firmly. Everyone was very noisy, calling for cabs, cursing each other for being in the way, hawking newspapers and roasted peanuts. The conductor shouted that the train to Dover was leaving in two minutes, and there was a mad dash of people toward it. Porters banged her legs with heavy luggage as she passed them, and did not stop to apologize. Somehow Morris did not lose her in the crowd but pushed her into a cab.

"A bit overwhelming at first, but you'll get used to it," Morris said. He directed the driver to Claridge's hotel. "Go by way of Bayswater Road," he instructed. "I'd like my wife to see the park."

"Exactly how many people live in London?" Jane asked. It was hard to imagine that she hadn't seen most of them already.

"Around two and a half million, I believe," he said, smiling at her astonishment.

"How will I manage with so many people?" she wondered aloud, thinking of tiny Oxford, where she knew every face and could walk anywhere she needed to go.

"For one thing, they won't all be living with you," Morris laughed.

Then Jane saw the open green expanse on her right.

"Kensington Gardens," Morris said. "A little farther on is Hyde Park. When we come back we will go walking there on Sundays. It's almost like being in the country."

On a nearby rise she glimpsed a pond with a flock of geese

afloat on it, and a little gazebo next to it. It was comforting, amid all of the oppressive stone and glass and smoke, to see the birds and the water.

The London house Morris had rented would not be ready until they returned from their honeymoon, so for their first night of marriage they stayed at Claridge's. It was a very grand hotel. Morris told her that King William III of the Netherlands had recently stayed there. Despite having spent many months at Mrs. Wallingford's estate, Jane was intimidated. She saw that the ladies taking tea in the lounge eyed her critically as she passed. She did not know if they thought her gown shabby or her cloak out of fashion, or if they were only wondering idly who she was, but it made her nervous. She wished she did not have to go down for dinner.

Their room was hung with coral pink silk and Jane pretended to inspect a portrait of a Lady Ogilvie so that she could surreptitiously stroke the wall. It was as slippery as soaped glass.

"It's by Lord Leighton," said Morris, and Jane quickly dropped her hand. "Academic, but not garbage. Someone has to paint their portraits after all."

Lady Ogilvie had white hair that stood out from her head in a frizz, a severe mouth, and round black eyes. She reminded Jane of a sparrow. She wondered if Lady Ogilvie had looked like that, if the portrait had pleased her. Had she fallen on hard times? Was that why her portrait was now in a hotel?

"I think she disapproves of me," said Jane.

"Impossible," said Morris, tentatively touching her shoulder.

Jane ducked out of his embrace and went to the window. Their view was of a street of limestone town houses and a row of sickly plane trees.

"I hope it won't be too loud," said Morris apologetically. "They assured me that it wouldn't be. If it is, we can change."

"I think these curtains will block the sound," said Jane, looking at the heavy brocade, the same color as the walls.

As she hung her dresses in the hulking armoire, with Morris across the room unfolding things from his trunk and putting them in drawers, Jane cast a nervous eye toward the tester bed. At last it seemed real to her: they were husband and wife. She would have to share this room with him, and this bed.

Did he already suspect that she wasn't a virgin? Jane couldn't believe that Rossetti would have been such a cad as to tell him. If Morris was as inexperienced and naive as she believed him to be, he might think she and Rossetti had exchanged letters, or touched hands, at most shared a kiss. If he realized that she was not a virgin, would he throw her into the street on the spot, or return her to her parents in disgrace? It made her sick to think of it.

"Would you like to rest before dinner?" Morris asked after a while. Jane started, not sure how to reply. "I could go downstairs to the lounge for an hour or two," Morris added quickly, seeing that she was nervous.

"That would be very nice," said Jane. "I am quite tired."

"I'll be back at seven," said Morris, nodding at the brass pendulum clock next to the door.

After Morris had gone Jane found that she wasn't tired after all. She spent the time looking through her clothes, trying to decide what would be suitable to wear to dinner. Judging from the jewels she had seen at the throats of the ladies taking tea, she had nothing grand enough. And what was a suitable color for a new bride? Something soft and delicate, no doubt, just what she hated. At last she settled on dove gray satin. She had no diamonds, but Morris had given her a necklace of amethysts set in white gold. As she tied up her hair, Jane thought that she caught Lady Ogilvie's eye, which seemed to have softened. She would not be ashamed to go downstairs after all.

To Jane's astonishment Morris ordered a dozen oysters as a first course. Perhaps his mother didn't know everything about him after all. He told Jane she could have anything she liked. She could have mussels, and tenderloin of beef, and fish soup, and melon and raspberries. Morris watched her eat with delight.

"You are enjoying your meal?" he asked.

"It is the most delicious food I have ever tasted," Jane said.

"It is good," agreed Morris, "but there are half a dozen other places that are just as fine. I will take you to all of them: Sherry's, the Dorchester. And then of course the food in France will put all of them to shame. I can't wait for you to try the cheeses, and the game. When we get back we'll engage a cook who can make all of your favorite dishes.

"It's a shame you can't see more of London before we leave," Morris went on. "But when we come back, I'll take you to the National Gallery to look at all of the paintings, and to the British Museum to see the artifacts brought back from Egypt. Of course we'll have less time then, as I'll be back at work and you'll be busy setting up the house. But we can take outings on Sundays."

"Yes," said Jane. She hated how cold and laconic she sounded but she didn't know what else to say.

"There is quite a stir about you here, you know," Morris continued. "Everyone is dying to see you and to meet you. When we return from France, we will probably have a dinner invitation every night for a month."

"Really?" asked Jane in surprise. She did not know what he meant by "a stir," but it sounded slightly ominous. She was already petrified at the thought that London society might laugh at her behind her back, mocking her manners and her looks as Mrs. Wallingford had done.

"Everyone in my circle has read 'Praise of My Lady,'" Morris said. He had published a book of poetry, *The Defense of Guenevere*, that year, and it was filled with encomiums to Jane. "Between that volume, my letters, and of course Rossetti's ravings, you've become the talk of London." Morris beamed at her proudly.

"Who are these people who are talking?" she asked, trying not to wonder what exactly Rossetti's "ravings" had been. "I thought I'd met most of your friends already."

"Well, there's Webb, of course, and Street. Georgiana. Millais and Effie, Swinburne, William Rossetti, Hunt, Boyce, Marshall . . ." Morris rattled off a daunting list of names.

"You have so many friends!" said Jane. She had become aware that she had finished her tarte Tatin and that soon they would have to return to their room.

"All eager to meet you," said Morris.

Neither of them could think of what to say next.

"Is everything all right?" asked Morris finally.

"Of course," said Jane. But she began to feel queasy and to wish she had not eaten quite so much.

At last they had no choice but to leave the table. By the time they had climbed the stairs and walked down the hall to their room, Morris was as silent as Jane and neither of them was able to look at the other. In her great anxiety about the marital act, Jane had forgotten that she would have to undress in front of Morris. She was not at all sure she could do it. The door shut behind them and they stood on either side of the bed, eyes averted.

"If we move the screen, perhaps you could . . . inhabit one side and I the other," said Morris, reading her thoughts. They moved the gilt Chinese screen and Jane moved her valise to the sofa behind it. Slowly, acutely aware that there was someone else there, she began removing articles of clothing. There was a terrible moment when all she had on was her chemise, her stockings, and her shoes. Quickly she threw her nightdress over her head and covered that with a printed robe. She removed her shoes and stockings and replaced them with slippers. On the other side she could hear rustling and, once, a shoe dropping heavily to the floor.

"May I come out?" she asked.

"Of course," said Morris, in a thick voice.

When she emerged he was already under the bedclothes, wearing a dark blue robe and reading a book. She slipped in beside him, but he did not look up. Jane took a volume out and pretended to read, but it was impossible. The words floated in front of her, meaningless. At last Morris shut his book.

"It's been such a long day," he said. "Perhaps we should retire early."

"Yes, it has," agreed Jane. Morris blew out the lamp. Jane lay back stiffly and waited for Morris to approach her. It took more than five minutes for him to work up the courage to touch her hand. When he did, it felt like a spider crawling on her skin and she almost jumped out of the bed. His hand retreated.

"Are you all right?" Morris asked. "Should I stop?"

Jane wanted to say yes, but she knew that if it didn't happen tonight, it would happen tomorrow. It seemed better to get it over with.

"No, I'm fine," she said. After a few moments his hand had returned. Now it was on her side, and began to awkwardly stroke her. It tickled and her muscles tightened. She wanted to guide his hands, but she could not. She tried not to writhe or giggle hysterically.

He was trying to push her nightdress up over her legs. Eventually he rolled onto his stomach and leaned on his elbows. He brought his face close to hers and kissed her on the mouth. His lips were slightly dry. His breath was coming fast now. The weight of his body on hers was oppressive. In the dark she could not see the expression on his face, and for his sake she was glad he could not see hers. He sat up and took off his robe. He hiked up his nightshirt. He tossed the bedclothes aside and finally managed to push up her nightdress.

He groped around between her legs for quite a while. He did not seem to know what he was looking for. More than once she felt a fleshy spike poke her belly and then again, much farther down. She was not supposed to know what to do, so she could not help him. He seemed to think it was her virginity that was making it difficult and he tried pushing very hard in various places. Her cries of pain drew whispered apologies from him. The procedure seemed to go on forever. Just as it seemed that he would never find it, that he would have to return her to her parents as defective rather than admit his own inadequacy, it slid in.

Now that he was there, Morris was both so astonished and so aroused that he gasped and shuddered and it was over. He stayed inside her for several minutes more, wriggling and tentatively thrusting as if he thought it would give her pleasure, and then he disengaged. He kissed her on the face and she tasted his sweat. He said nothing, and neither did she.

Jane wanted to cry, but could not. With Rossetti it had been terrifying, but it had not been ridiculous. She felt invaded, and mishandled. She felt empty, and very lonely.

When she was sure Morris was asleep, Jane crept across the room in the dark and found her hatbox. She stabbed her middle finger with a hat pin, wincing. When she knew she had drawn blood, she stepped carefully toward the bed and slipped under the covers. She wiped the blood onto the sheet. Then Jane tried to make herself very small in the bed so as not to touch her husband. It was hours before she finally fell asleep.

Ten

N the morning they went to breakfast and pretended nothing had happened. Jane hoped that the night's excitement would be enough to satisfy him for a few days at least. The seas were rough crossing the channel and it was easy to feign seasickness. Jane had never been on a ship before and would have liked to walk the deck and admire the view, but then Morris would have realized that she was not sick after all. He might have expected something. From the porthole in her cabin, she could glimpse a bit of railing and then the gray sea behind it, the same hue as the slate-colored sky.

Their first day in Paris they spent at Chartres.

"The first of the High-Gothic cathedrals in the Île-de-France," said Morris. "It is fitting that we begin here, although we will have to skip back in time when we go to Notre Dame, which is Early Gothic."

"What is the difference?" asked Jane. In the daylight she found she liked her husband, who gamboled through the sacred space like a St. Bernard puppy.

"The High Gothic is taller, and lighter, not as massive. The builders had learned how to support the building with less heavy masonry, using flying buttresses. If we walk around the perimeter of the cathedral, I can point them out to you."

Morris was encyclopedic in his knowledge and the lesson went on all day. He showed her which were the oldest parts of the church and explained how the various pieces had survived a series of fires. He expounded on the architect's influences, the cathedrals of Laon and Saint-Denis. He elucidated the chronology of the sculptures on each facade, from the earliest, Romanesque-looking jamb statues of the west facade to the High Gothic figures of the north transept. They climbed the bell towers to see the vaulting up close and he even coaxed her onto the roof to examine the gargoyles.

"What is it with you artists and high places?" she complained good-naturedly.

"Perspective," he said. "To see things in surprising ways, you have to extend yourself a bit."

Jane had to admit that the view of the town and the surrounding countryside was lovely.

Their second day they spent at Notre-Dame de Paris. On the way there she looked longingly at the lace and linen shops they passed, but Morris didn't notice. He was consulting one of his books to verify the dates of some of the statuary on the tympanum.

"Do you think we could have tea at that little place we passed, the one with the striped awning?" she finally ventured in late afternoon, when they had been walking for six hours.

Morris looked surprised. "We haven't been to the crypt yet. If we leave now we won't get the chance to see the tunic of the Virgin. It has been here since 1020."

"I didn't realize," said Jane, trying not to sound tired.

"If you'd rather go back to the hotel, I can take you," said Morris, looking longingly toward the massive gate in front of the stairs.

"Of course not," said Jane. "I wouldn't dream of missing the crypt."

On the third night in Paris, he approached her again. This time it was not so awkward, but it was no more pleasant. Afterward, as they lay in the dark, he ventured to ask her, "And how was the experience for you?"

"It was fine," she said, not sounding the least bit convincing.

"I'm glad," he said, obviously relieved. They did not discuss it again.

As their return to London approached, Jane began to feel apprehensive. She had tried to forget what Morris had said that first night, that London society was talking about her, but now she lay awake at night and worried about what would be expected of her. She was sure she would make terrible, unforgivable mistakes and everyone would ridicule her. When she broached the subject with Morris, he just laughed and assured her that everyone would love her. But Jane was not convinced.

At the end of a month they sailed back to London, and at last Jane saw where she would live while the house in Kent was being built. It was a very fine brick town house in a fashionable district, so similar to what she had once fantasized about that she immediately sat down and wrote a letter to Bessie. She even had a key to the garden across the street. But the garden was closed in and shaded by the thick ivy that grew on the tall iron fences, and she didn't like it much. She much preferred the open promenades.

The house was larger than anything Jane had known before she met Mrs. Wallingford, though by that lady's standards it was oppressively small, having only four bedrooms. Jane now had a kitchen and a scullery and a larder, and a cook and a housemaid to go with them. She had a dining room and a parlor on the first floor, and a sitting room upstairs.

The furniture that Morris had made was arranged throughout the house, and Jane saw that her rooms looked very much like the one in the painting Morris had made of her. In the dining room stood a massive round table of unvarnished oak. Two large, throne-like chairs painted with red and blue stars and moons sat opposite each other. A heavy wooden sideboard had a scene from *The Song of Roland* sketched on it, though it remained unpainted. The walls of the parlor were hung with paintings done by Morris's friends, and the furniture was draped with antique embroidered velvet.

"When all of the things we bought in France arrive, it will be perfect, don't you think?" asked Morris, with pride, and Jane had to agree.

In the bedroom, most marvelous of all, was a brightly painted wardrobe, depicting the Virgin giving the Host to a small haloed boy.

"A wedding present from Ned," said Morris. "You see the story is from Chaucer. It's Sir Hugh of Lincoln."

"Poor little fellow," said Jane, reaching out to touch his glowing face. The surface of the wardrobe was glassy with varnish. She examined the painting carefully, marveling at the intricate detail of the work.

"If he disturbs your sleep, we can move him into the hall," said Morris.

But Jane wouldn't hear of it. "It is the most wonderful gift," she said, near tears. "I want it to be the first thing I see when I wake up in the morning."

"I hope it's not," said Morris.

The next day he went to the South Kensington Museum to sketch, and from then on he was gone most of the day. Jane was sometimes lonely, but she wrote letters to her mother and her sister, she read assiduously from the many volumes Morris had collected, and she ventured out to the market and took walks in their neighborhood. She found that it was something of a relief to have Morris gone. When he was there she was nervous and tense, trying to please him, trying to do and say the right things. When he was gone she could relax.

When he came home in the evening, they had dinner and then

sat together in the parlor until bedtime. Usually Morris read aloud while Jane sewed.

One night he did not seem to be able to keep his mind on his book. He kept losing his place. Finally he dropped the book in his lap and stared at her instead.

"What is it?" said Jane, feeling self-conscious.

"You sew very well," he observed.

"I learned from my mother," she said, "and then at school."

"Not from Mrs. Wallingford?"

"Girls who are to go into domestic service are much more skillful with the needle than ladies who make samplers for their own amusement." She thought it strange that he was so interested in her sewing. But then she remembered the dress he had designed for her.

"Do you use patterns?" he asked. She turned over her work to show him the paper grid that marked out the orchid design and the different colors to use.

"Do you like the patterns that are available?" he asked.

"Not always. I switched the colors on this one," she said. "It was meant to be pink flowers on a grayish-green ground but I thought crimson and yellow would be better."

"Quite right," said Morris admiringly. "What will you do with it when you're finished?"

"It's meant for a wall hanging, for my sitting room," she said.

"Could you make wall hangings for all of the rooms?" Morris asked. He fidgeted in his chair with excitement.

"Of course," she said. "It will take time, though, especially if the hangings are large." She did not see what the fuss was about.

"If I were to draw up a pattern for you, could you make it?" he asked.

"Certainly," she said.

"I imagine a dark blue ground embroidered with yellow daisies.

Maybe four feet by six feet. I could make it myself, if you would teach me. You'll have to show me how it's done and what will work."

"I must warn you, I'm very strict," teased Jane. "I make Mrs. Wallingford look like a cherub."

"Be gentle," pleaded Morris. He took her hand and kissed it.

"I'll look for the cloth when I'm out shopping," Jane said. "Then you can direct me on the embroidery. I'll need embroidery silk, too."

"Make it wool," he said. "Silk is too fine. A skein of golden yellow, one of fiery orange, and one of spring green."

"Rough wool embroidery thread is not very common," she told him, knowing that the shopkeepers would think her crazy if she asked for such a thing.

"Nevertheless, that's what we must have. Perhaps in a not so nice part of London it would be more readily available," he said. "You should go to Cheapside tomorrow. If it can't be found, we may have to spin and dye our own."

The next day Jane came back from shopping with a very large piece of blue serge she had found, feeling pleased with herself for how little she had paid. Morris would like it, she felt sure. He would sketch out the embroidery for her and she could start work on it that night. It was very enjoyable, she reflected, to have a project that she and her husband could work on together. She couldn't imagine her mother and father sitting close together night after night, engrossed in a piece of sewing. Perhaps her marriage would be a success after all.

Morris and Jane attended a party at Ruskin's exactly one week after their arrival in London. Jane wore a violet wool dress printed with scarlet poppies. Now that her budget for gowns was virtually unlimited, she could indulge herself with the richest fabrics and embellishments. She discovered that Mrs. Wallingford had been wrong: Morris encouraged her to sew her own clothes and was proud of her talent for it. Discarding any pattern, she had sewn it loose and wore it without a corset. She hadn't chosen the style to influence anyone or to set a fashion, but because she found that tight corsets hurt her back and made her faint. Her willowy figure meant she did not have to worry that the gently gathered material would make her look dumpy. The long, flowing lines suited her. And, since her features and coloring were already exotic, it made no sense to try to conform her looks to ordinary styles. The dramatic and the unusual suited her. It made her look mysterious. Not that Jane had thought about it so carefully. The changes she had made in her wardrobe had been gradual and instinctive.

When she arrived at the party, Jane at last understood what her husband had meant by "a stir." She had hardly taken off her coat and greeted Ruskin when he began to recite, loudly enough for anyone nearby to hear:

> My lady seems of ivory
> Forehead, straight nose, and cheeks that be
> Hollowed a little mournfully.
> > *Beata mea Domina!*

he declaimed. He circled her as though she were a prize marble dredged from the bottom of the Adriatic.

> Her forehead, overshadowed much
> By bows of hair, has a wave such
> As God was good to make for me.
> > *Beata mea Domina!*

> Not greatly long my lady's hair,
> Nor yet with yellow color fair,
> But thick and crisped wonderfully:
> > *Beata mea Domina!*

Heavy to make the pale face sad,
And dark, but dead as though it had
Been forged by God most wonderfully
    Beata mea Domina!

"So far he has captured you very well in verse," Ruskin said, continuing to scrutinize her. Jane was not sure if he remembered that he had met her before. "You do appear made of ivory, and sad, your hair is quite dark and dead. Let me see, how does it go on?" He turned to another guest, a fair-haired, handsome young man, and pulled him toward where Jane stood, frozen with embarrassment.

"You know the poem, Webb. What's the next line?"

Webb carried on the recitation:

Of some strange metal, thread by thread,
To stand out from my lady's head,
Not moving much to tangle me.
    Beata mea Domina!

Beneath her brows the lids fall slow,
The lashes a clear shadow throw
Where I would wish my lips to be.
    Beata mea Domina!

Another young man, dark and stocky, hearing them, joined their group, and soon there was a chorus of them, chanting Morris's poem about her. Everyone at the party stared at her. She only wished they would stop, but they were having a wonderful time. It was clear that they intended to recite the entire poem, and there were sixteen verses to go. At last Morris, who had been across the room with Burne-Jones, heard them and came to her rescue.

"Stop it!" he cried. "My wife is shy and not used to your London antics. You must give her time before you spring such things on her."

"We did not mean any harm, Mrs. Morris," said Webb apologetically. "We only wished to make clear in what high esteem we all held you, even before we were so lucky as to meet you."

She could not be angry at that. Jane Burden, who was homely and awkward and born into an excruciatingly poor and coarse family, was held in high esteem by London gentlemen.

Seeing that she was trembling, Morris excused them both and led her away to a corner chair to restore herself.

"Well, you did warn me," she said shakily.

"Those degenerates," fumed Morris. "I intend to pummel them at the first opportunity."

"They meant no harm," said Jane. "It's silly of me to make such a fuss about it."

"It's understandable," said Morris. "Anyone would be overwhelmed. Can I bring you anything? Water? Smelling salts? Something to eat?"

"I might like some wine," ventured Jane.

While Morris was gone a doll-like young woman in a simple gray dress approached her. She had a pointed chin and eyes of such a light blue they seemed almost white.

"Forgive me if it's rude," she said. "Mr. Morris sent me to sit with you. I'm Georgie Macdonald. I'm Edward Burne-Jones's fiancée." She blushed when she said it and Jane remembered that her father was a Methodist minister. Jane hoped she would not accidentally do anything that would make the girl disapprove of her.

"I've been very nervous about meeting you," the girl confessed. "Ned has raved about you for so long, I feel as if I'm in the presence of a pagan queen. Not that you're un-Christian, I didn't mean that . . ." She blushed again.

"You must be quite disappointed," said Jane, trying to ease her discomfort. "I'm sure I do not live up to it."

"Oh not at all," said Georgie eagerly. "Though I must confess it's strange to hear you talk! I had not imagined your voice would be so nice and rich, not like my little squeak. I do like my singing voice. Singing and speaking are quite different for me. One comes easily and the other doesn't."

"Do you play?" asked Jane.

"Yes, I play very well," said Georgie matter-of-factly. "I love to play the old hymns, even though they're quite unfashionable. It comes from having so many ministers in my family. My father, of course, two of my brothers, an uncle. They were all distraught when Ned gave it up to be an artist. They thought they had settled on someone safe for me and then he goes and changes on them. I quite like it, though. I think it's wonderful. A girl can get tired of ministers. And being a minister's wife is very hard work, you know."

Jane smiled. It was difficult to maintain a cold reserve in the face of Georgie's open friendliness, and the prospect of a friend was not unwelcome. Georgie admitted that she, too, knew few people in London and was a little bit lonely.

"At home in Birmingham there were eight of us," said Georgie. "Now I'm staying with my aunt and uncle, and I hardly know what to do with myself. Though there's my friend Lizzie. I spend quite a lot of time with her."

"Lizzie Siddal?" Jane had trouble saying the name.

"Do you know her?" asked Georgie in surprise.

Jane shook her head. "Will she be here tonight?" she asked, feeling a little guilty for extracting information from the guileless girl but glad of an opportunity to learn Rossetti's whereabouts. "I would like to meet her."

"They're in the country," reported Georgie. "Lizzie's had trouble with her lungs, you know. The city air isn't good for them." She chattered on innocently about Lizzie's health and Rossetti's tender care of her until Jane thought she would scream.

"Well, you must come and see me," said Jane when she could take no more.

"I would love that," replied Georgie. "I'd like to see how you keep house. I'm terribly afraid I'm not going to make Ned a very good wife. Of course I know how to do all of the required things, but sometimes when I'm playing music or reading a book, I find that the afternoon has passed without my knowing it. I'm sure that when I'm married, I'll let the fire go out and forget to buy anything to make for dinner."

"I'm sure you won't," said Jane. "Anyone with seven brothers and sisters can take care of one husband."

"I hope you're right," said Georgie anxiously as Morris and Burne-Jones appeared, each carrying two glasses of claret.

The next day there was an account of the event in the papers. It was noted that Mrs. William Morris wore a very unusual dress. It was quite loose, the papers reported, delicately refraining from mentioning her lack of a corset, and was of an artistic shade of purple. Only the wife of an artist could get away with it, they said, disapprovingly.

Eleven

THE house in Kent was nearly finished and one Sunday in March Morris took Jane to see it. They took the train to Abbey Wood station and hired a carriage to drive them the three miles to the house. They passed the immaculate stone cottages of Upton, then turned onto a lane with orchards on either side. They drove past row after orderly row of apple trees, knobby and bare and glistening in the rain.

"Wait until next month," said Morris. "They will be as white and diaphanous as fields of clouds. There is an apple grown here, called Gascoigne Scarlet. I imagine you have seen one. It is as large and red and sweet as the original, biblical fruit. I can't wait for you to taste it."

They were driving alongside a crumbling, mossy stone wall, and Jane could tell from the way Morris was craning his neck and then looking at her expectantly that they were getting close. Her first glimpse of her new home was of a red tile roof and two hulking oak trees, misty and indistinct.

"How lovely," she gasped.

"I've called it Red House," said Morris. "Not a poetic name, I know, but what else would suit it so well?" They turned onto the drive and the carriage stopped in front of an odd-looking, redbrick house, built in the style of an ancient forest lodge.

"It's so bright!" said Jane. Morris helped her from the carriage, opened an umbrella, and held it over her.

"Don't worry," he said quickly. "Soon the ivy and jasmine and climbing roses will mute the color and make the house seem as if it has been here forever."

"It's like a fairy story," said Jane. "I expect a princess to be unfurling her hair from that window." She pointed to the many-paned oriel window projecting from the right-hand side of the house.

"I imagine you sitting there in the window seat, gazing out upon your domain," said Morris.

But Jane was already on the front porch looking at the massive wooden front door. "A truncheon couldn't break this down," she laughed.

"I don't expect anyone will lay siege, but I wanted to be prepared," Morris said, smiling.

Jane read aloud the inscription on the heavy arch above the door: 'God preserve your going out and your coming in.'"

"You like it?" asked Morris nervously. He came and stood beside her on the porch.

"I like it," she affirmed. She was so giddy she kissed her husband on the cheek, in front of the carriage driver who was still sitting there in front of the house.

Morris looked embarrassed but pleased. He took her hand and led her back out into the rain. "Come out and see the grounds," he said.

"The grounds," said Jane, relishing the sound of the word in her mouth. "We have grounds!"

"We do," said Morris. "And we'll have gardens, and a lawn. Let me show you how I want to lay them out."

The land around the house was mostly bare and muddy from the construction, but Morris had saved several rows of pippins and pearmains from the orchard that had been there before. They would lend a mature look to the landscape very quickly, he said. He led her down a rough path and showed her the series of trellises in place on either side.

"Here will be the hollyhocks and morning glories," he said, pointing at two of the trellises. "Over there I've planted a row of sunflowers, and in that sunny spot a bunch of lilies. I want to plant antique flowers in beds here, separated by sweetbriar hedges, but I wanted to wait and ask you what you particularly like."

"Perhaps sweet peas," said Jane. She had always thought that growing flowers for pleasure was somewhat impractical and unnecessary, but Morris's excitement was infectious. She began to see a fairy garden next to her fairy house. "And lilac."

"I like woody plants, too," he said. "I'll see if any of our neighbors has a plant I can take a cutting from."

Jane thought that the woodsy, uncleared corners of the property, hemmed by the mossy stone wall, would be cool and inviting in the summer. At the back of the house, Morris showed her the well, which he had designed to look like a small oast-house, and the open courtyard.

"We thought an L-shaped plan would be the easiest to add on to," said Morris. "We can build another L and enclose the courtyard completely, if our family gets too large."

Jane could not imagine how many children she would have to have to make the house seem cramped. The wind drove the rain into her face.

"I'm dying to see my kitchen," she said hopefully.

"By all means, let's go inside!" exclaimed Morris.

He led her by the hand through the back entrance. "I call this hall Pilgrim's Rest," he said. "It's the portion of the house closest to Canterbury. I hope we can succor many pilgrims here."

"If by pilgrims you mean poor hungry artists, I'm sure we will," said Jane, stopping to examine the two small rooms that opened off the porch.

"I thought this one could be sleeping quarters for guests," Morris said, "and that this one could be a sitting room for you, if you like."

The entryway had a red travertine floor, simple and roughly hewn. On its way upstairs, an oak staircase turned past two large leaded glass windows with diamond-shaped panes.

"I want to etch some glass with the Morris coat of arms," Morris said. "I know it's feudal, but it will fit with the theme of chivalry. And I want some glass and some tiles to have my motto painted on them."

"You are living up to it very well so far," Jane teased. "Is there anything you can't do?"

"Well, I tried to make the weather better for your first visit to Red House, but you can see I've failed," he answered, flushing with pride at her compliment.

The upstairs comprised a library, an office for Morris, a master bedroom, and several rooms for servants' quarters. The ceilings were not especially tall, and they weren't finished with the moldings and cornices and capitals that a regular Victorian home should have.

"Well, it's far from complete," said Morris. "This is more of a shell than a house. But between ourselves and all of our friends, I am sure we can decorate it sublimely."

Morris opened every closet for her, explained every nook and every window. As the final flourish he took her to the kitchen and the downstairs storage areas. He showed her all of the storage space he had built there.

"The coal cellar seems a bit small," she said, and wished she could take it back immediately. Morris looked hurt.

"The winters are milder here than in London," he said. "And we won't have many servants. But if you like I can have the workmen knock out the wall and combine it with the second pantry."

"I'm sure it won't be necessary," said Jane. "I'm sure it will be fine."

Gratitude washed over Jane as it dawned on her just how much Morris had done, and for her. He had built the house for her. She promised herself that she would fall in love with him, to repay him. In his excitement Morris had allowed his shirtfront to come untucked and it flapped in a ridiculous way when he walked. His hair stuck out all over his head and his trousers were covered with mud from the garden, but somehow it suited him. Jane thought for a moment of flinging her arms around him, but she was too shy, and the moment passed.

Back in London Jane concentrated on readying things for the move. The contents of the house had to be carefully inventoried and Jane went shopping for a calf-bound ledger for the purpose. She was very proud of the price she had gotten, and the length of antique Spanish lace she had found. Preoccupied with her purchases, Jane almost didn't notice Rossetti's card in the hall. When she saw it she nearly fainted. Morris had not told her that Rossetti was back in London.

Jane left the card on the table but kept returning to look at it. The stock was cream colored and heavy, but the typeface was very plain: DANTE GABRIEL ROSSETTI. She ran her finger over the letters as if they were Rossetti's lips. He had been in her hall, had laid the card on her table with his own hand. The thought made her heart pound wildly, and after unsuccessfully trying to go on with her chores for the day, she went to lie down.

That night Morris laid the lace out on the floor and began to unpick one side of it, trying to see how it was made.

"This was done with a needle," he said. "You see it's entirely looped stitches." Jane tried to pay attention, but she was no longer interested in it.

"You saw Rossetti's card?" she asked.

"Yes," he said. "We must return the visit. Perhaps on Sunday."

"Is it all right to go?" asked Jane, not sure how to phrase her question. As much as she desperately wanted to see Rossetti, she wasn't sure she wanted to meet his lover. But Morris understood her.

"You must not snub Lizzie," he said. "It would look very bad, and Rossetti would never forgive me. By going, you indicate that you don't consider her beneath you."

Jane found the idea that Lizzie might be beneath her amusing. Jane knew that in the eyes of many London ladies she was beneath notice because of her background. Many of them would not call on her, or receive her into their homes, no matter how many courses she took with Mrs. Wallingford. It would certainly be hypocritical of her to turn up her nose at Lizzie.

"All right," Jane agreed. "We should dine with them on Sunday."

"I'll write him a note," said Morris.

Twelve

ANE now had many worries, foremost among them what she would wear to meet Rossetti. It had been two years since she had last seen him. Of course she wanted him to think that she was even more beautiful than before, but she didn't want him to think she was still in love with him and trying to impress him. Which of her new dresses would strike just that note? She tried and discarded the poppy red taffeta, the aubergine wool, and the lavender bombazine. Finally, she decided upon the Aegean blue brocade. It had a brilliant sheen to it but was simply made and trimmed with only some dark blue braid. It suited her. Morris would say it was too bright, but she would ignore him.

As she looked in the mirror, she wondered if Rossetti would find her changed. But no, she looked exactly the same: same pale skin and unmanageable hair, same lugubrious expression, same luminous eyes. She was still tall and regal. The only difference was that she was better dressed. She was also his friend's wife.

The carriage ride seemed interminable. A cart had overturned on the street, ahead of them, and vegetables were strewn everywhere. The driver was arguing with a policeman.

"Are you all right, my dear?" asked Morris as they waited for the road to be cleared.

"I'm afraid Lizzie won't like me," Jane confessed. She did not want her husband to guess the real reason she was anxious.

"You must be very kind to Lizzie," said Morris. "She is still far from well."

"Will she be kind to me?" asked Jane.

"Of course," said Morris doubtfully. "Once she knows you. I'm sure Georgie has painted a glowing picture." Jane wondered what, if anything, Rossetti had said to Lizzie about her.

When the door opened it seemed for a moment that everything but Rossetti was blocked from her vision. She had wondered if he would be the same, and he was: his eyes were as black and penetrating as before. He seemed to be looking straight into her heart. He paid no attention to Morris, but came straight toward her. He stood a little too close, and brushed her cheeks with his lips three times.

"Guinevere," he whispered. Jane did not trust herself to say anything, but she tried to smile. Only when Rossetti stepped away from her was she able to discern the person standing behind him. Lizzie was not at all what Jane had expected a libertine to look like. She was not as tall as Jane and seemed dwarfed by Rossetti. Her skin had the dull pallor of someone who sleeps and eats very little, and her heavy eyelids made her look tired. She had eyes the color of amber. Next to her skin her hair glowed a golden red. Jane thought her very plain. This was the great beauty she had been so terrified to meet?

Lizzie's grip was surprisingly strong. "How do you do?" she said in a darkly colored alto. Their eyes met and Jane quailed at Lizzie's expression. She knows everything, thought Jane.

Somehow they passed through the hall and into the parlor. Rossetti's house was as he had described it to her so long ago: dark and richly decorated, masculine and strange. Jane sat on an ornately carved wooden settee, across from a row of Rossetti's drawings of Lizzie: Lizzie brushing her hair, Lizzie asleep, Lizzie petting the cat.

"There were some of you on the wall," said Lizzie, following Jane's gaze, "but I pitched them out of the window."

No one knew what to say to that.

"That settee used to be a church pew," said Rossetti, breaking the awkward silence. "A place in Hackney that burned. It's quite medieval, don't you think?"

"It would be perfect if you hadn't put that awful red cushion on it," admonished Morris. "So common. And a green tablecloth. Really, Gabriel!"

"Yes, it's far too fashionable," agreed Rossetti, "but without the cushion it would not be fit for your lady to sit on. But you must know," he said to Jane. "You must have sat upon many like it during your tour of the cathedrals."

"Yes, I did," admitted Jane.

"It must have been very tiresome," said Rossetti. "Did you make poor Jane crawl out onto the flying buttresses and examine the gargoyles' teeth?"

"She enjoyed it," retorted Morris. "Especially Chartres."

Rossetti winked at Jane. "I'm sure. What was your favorite part?"

"But I don't think any of your sketches did justice to her eyes," Lizzie went on as though no one had spoken. "They are such a lovely ocean gray color. And you never quite captured the expression in them. Your Jane often looked somber, but not quite so observant and keen as the real Jane does."

Now it was Rossetti whose gaze was upon Jane. "I see what you mean," he said. "It has something to do with the outer corners, the shadows there, and also the brow."

"You should make some more sketches," said Lizzie. "I'm sure Jane wouldn't mind coming to sit for you, would you, Jane?"

Jane glanced helplessly at her husband.

"Come see what I've been working on," said Rossetti, springing from his seat. So the party got up and went to Rossetti's studio on the other end of the house.

"I read about your style in the *Times*," said Lizzie as they walked down the hall together. "They made it sound so shocking! But the way you wear it is completely natural."

Jane could not detect a barb in this. "It's just what suits me," she said warily. "I had no idea I would be caricatured."

"And copied!" said Lizzie. "I saw three ladies last night with Indian shawls on their shoulders and bits of ribbon tied 'round their waists. Everyone wants to be Jane Morris."

"Not the girls with sense," said Jane.

Lizzie laughed in surprise. "You're unhappy with your marriage already?" she asked. "Some might consider you ridiculously fortunate."

"Oh no," said Jane. Lizzie seemed determined to misconstrue everything she said. "I just meant that it would be silly for a really pretty girl to use the techniques I employ to conceal my flaws."

"Quite right," said Lizzie, with a startled look. "Well, you're not vain, I'll concede that."

In the studio Rossetti pulled the sheet off his canvas with a flourish and Jane saw with amazement that the figure of Beatrice was herself. Her face was unmistakable: her nose in profile, her eyes and hair. In the left-hand panel, she and Dante gazed at each other as they passed, and in the right-hand panel, Beatrice removed her veil to reveal herself directly to the poet.

"I had been modeling for it, but then Gabriel decided that Beatrice must be dark," said Lizzie matter-of-factly. "I'm right for the good old British angels, but I certainly don't look the least bit Italian."

"I had so many sketches of you done already," said Rossetti to Jane, "it was easy to work from them."

"Until they flew away, like little birds," laughed Lizzie.

"The first panel is more like her," observed Morris. "You've got the light in her eye just right, and the curve of her upper lip. The second is more of a faded copy."

"How is your painting going, Topsy?" asked Rossetti bitingly.

"Not well," admitted Morris. "The painting I did of Jane is the only good thing I've ever done and it's better than it has any right to be."

"Jane is going to become vain with too much praise," said Lizzie.

"I doubt that any amount of praise could spoil Jane," said Rossetti admiringly.

Lizzie leaned against the wall and coughed into a handkerchief. Immediately Rossetti was at her side. She slumped into his jacket, and though her whole body shook, the sounds were muffled.

Jane was alarmed.

"Shall I call a doctor?" asked Morris.

"I'm fine," choked Lizzie.

"It's the London air," said Rossetti. "The doctors tell us to go back to Bath, but we were so bored there."

"Italy," said Lizzie, her face mottled and red but otherwise composed. "I'd like to convalesce in Rome."

"If you are a good girl, I'll take you there," said Rossetti, smoothing her hair.

Morris took Lizzie in to dinner and Rossetti took Jane. She held her arm out for him to take, expecting him to grasp it lightly. Instead he pulled her in very close to him.

"You sorceress," he whispered. "I thought I could exorcise this passion I have for you by painting you, but now that you're here, I see that's impossible."

"Shh," said Jane frantically, "they'll hear you."

"Don't tell me that you love Morris," hissed Rossetti, tightening his grip on her arm. "You can't possibly."

Ahead of them Morris laughed at something Lizzie said. Jane could not think of what to do.

"You're not going to say anything?" he asked. "Have you become so timid? So conventional?"

"Gabriel, please stop," Jane begged. They entered the dining room and Rossetti tucked Jane into her place, poured her a glass of wine, and took his seat.

It was all Jane could do to follow the conversation. Rossetti drank champagne. Morris began to describe the scene at Ruskin's.

"And they recited 'Praise of My Lady' to her, right there in the hall. They knew every line!"

"As they should," said Rossetti. "It was the finest work of poetry I've read in many a year. You've completely eclipsed Shelley, in my estimation."

"Don't be ridiculous," scoffed Morris. "In any event, poor Jane was stupefied. I had to rescue her from their clutches."

"Are you sure it was not they who needed rescuing?" asked Rossetti darkly.

"I wish you had come," said Morris.

"We're thoroughly sick of Ruskin," said Rossetti. "Though not sick of his money."

"Well, you know him," said Lizzie apologetically. "He's been very kind to us. But then he's so pompous and controlling that it makes you want to throw the money back in his face."

"Which you will never, ever do," said Rossetti. "We need it too much."

"You're an artist, too?" enquired Jane.

"I draw a little," said Lizzie. "But I hope one day to be really accomplished."

"The sketches she's done of me are remarkable," said Rossetti proudly. "Lizzie's a much better draftsman than I am. If she will only rest and regain her health, I have high hopes for her."

"You know I'll go mad if I can't work," said Lizzie. She turned to Jane. "He and Ruskin want me to stop drawing altogether," said Lizzie. "I can't think why anyone, much less an art critic and an artist, would tell someone else not to draw."

"Because they are worried about you, love," said Rossetti.

"You're not worried about me at all," said Lizzie. "You wish I were dead. It would make things so much easier for you."

"Dearest!" Rossetti gasped. "You know that's not true!"

Lizzie stood up and threw her napkin down on the table. "Someday, Gabriel, you just might get your wish." Her chair knocked loudly against the wall as she ran past it and out of the room. There was a long silence.

"She's not been well," said Rossetti apologetically. "Her lungs are weak and it makes her feverish and tired."

"I'll go to her," said Jane, glad for an excuse to clear her head. Lizzie's volatile changes in mood were not unfamiliar. She had seen and heard much worse in Holywell Street. At least nothing heavy had been thrown, and no one had been injured. But she was still reeling from what Rossetti had said to her.

Lizzie was on the terrace. She had her sketchbook and pencils and was drawing her own left hand. She did not hear Jane come up behind her, so deep was her concentration. Jane saw that the drawing was delicately shaded, fragile and almost tentative but quite accomplished.

"You're shocked," Lizzie said. She put the pencil down and looked sorrowfully at Jane. In an instant Jane saw why Rossetti found her beautiful. "Please know that I'm not as vulgar as that argument makes me seem. It's desperation. If I soften, even for a moment, he'll be gone in a week's time."

"I don't believe it," said Jane. "I think he is besotted with you."

Lizzie patted her hand. "You are not at all what I was expecting," she said. "I hope we can be friends, in spite of everything."

"I'd like to be," said Jane.

"It must all be very strange to you," said Lizzie, returning to her drawing. "Everyone talking, everyone watching. Your name on the society pages."

"It feels as if they are talking about someone else," Jane said. "A character they've invented called Jane Morris."

Lizzie nodded. "After your upbringing . . . well, I got a wonderfully lurid description of the slum that is Holywell Street. It made me feel quite lucky in my millinery."

Jane did not like to think about the past. "Have you always wanted to be an artist?" she asked, to change the subject.

"Not really," said Lizzie. "I never knew I could be anything, other than a shop girl or something worse, until I met Gabriel. But he encouraged me to try, and I found that I liked it."

"Do you ever paint?" Jane asked.

"I've tried a few times," said Lizzie. "But I don't feel my drawing is strong enough yet. I'd be wasting paint. Next year, perhaps, I'll be ready."

Lizzie was so serious and so determined that it made Jane feel very small and inadequate. "Do you hope to be a famous artist?" she asked.

Lizzie laughed, a little bitterly. "Are there any famous artists who are female? Occasionally a poet or novelist, like Mrs. Lewes, but never an artist. So I don't think there's much chance of that. I just hope to be able to sell my work and be independent. Of Mr. Ruskin, and of Gabriel, and whoever else might try to control me and call it support."

Jane did not know what to say. After all, she had chosen to become Morris's wife precisely because the idea of being on her own and all that it meant was too horrible to bear. But perhaps she had been cowardly. Then again, she did not have a talent like Lizzie's, a purpose. For a moment she wished that she did.

"You must meet Mrs. Lewes," said Lizzie. "I think you would like her very much. She never goes out and she doesn't allow many visitors, you know, but she is a very wise woman and she's been very kind to me. I will take you there sometime."

Jane's mother's voice rang in her ears, telling her that her position was precarious enough without visiting the notorious novelist who lived with a man she was not married to. To do so would put certain people and places out of reach once and for all. But Jane shook her head to rid herself of the voice.

"I haven't yet read *The Mill on the Floss*," she confessed. "I wouldn't have anything to say."

"I'll lend you my copy," said Lizzie. She shut her drawing pad and suggested they rejoin the men at the table. The roast beef had just been served and the foursome ate their dinner and pretended nothing was amiss. Morris and Jane described their trip to France and Morris told Rossetti about his next book of poetry. It was quite late when the Morrises went home.

Thirteen

ANE did not know what to do about Rossetti, and she had no one to confide in. She suspected that her new friend Georgie would be shocked if Jane told her what had happened. Of course she could not tell her husband. At last she wrote to Bessie.

You must be very firm with him, her sister wrote back:

> *Tell him, if he tries to make love to you again, that you are appalled and you won't stand for it. Threaten to tell William. Threaten to tell Lizzie. But do not, whatever you do, blush and stammer and give him reason to hope.*
>
> *I have a new beau. He is only a grocer but very rich. You are a lucky girl, Jane Morris. Don't do anything silly and ruin it!*

They had been at Red House two weeks and were measuring the dining room fireplace when Jane looked out and saw Rossetti on the lawn, gazing up at the roof of the house. She had a sudden, foolish urge to hide. Instead she took a deep breath and pointed him out to her husband. They watched as he walked along the side of the house, then disappeared into the back garden.

"Did you know he was coming?" asked Jane.

Morris shook his head. "We won't get anything else done today," he said. "You might as well plan on him staying for dinner, and perhaps the night."

"I'll tell the cook," said Jane, glad of an excuse to flee. She thought the best thing to do was to avoid Rossetti for as long as she could, but she found the resolve difficult to maintain. After she'd gone to the kitchen and satisfied herself that the roast was large enough for three, she went to her sitting room and looked out. Rossetti and Morris were still outside, looking at the house. Jane positioned herself next to the open window, telling herself that the light for sewing was best there.

"It's completely fantastic," she heard Rossetti say. "More of a dream than a house."

"The side entrance faces Canterbury, you know," said Morris.

"Yes, I know," sighed Rossetti. "You've told me. And you'll be putting up pilgrims. I hope you'll start with me."

"Nothing is wrong, I trust?" said Morris.

"Of course not," said Rossetti. "I just felt like taking the country air. Tell me, how does Jane like the house?"

"She thinks it will be cold in winter," said Morris.

"Of what importance are practical concerns like warmth, when such things as the facing of the house toward Canterbury must be considered?" said Rossetti.

"You're teasing me," Morris said, but he was too pleased with his house to take offense. "I've promised her I'll tile the fireplaces. Would you like to help paint them?"

"Of course," said Rossetti. "Just tell me what to do and stick a brush in my hand. I am at your service."

"You can help me hammer out the design program," said Morris. "Janey isn't completely convinced that the entire house should be medieval in theme. Maybe you can help me to persuade her."

When the two men appeared in the dining room for tea, Jane thought she greeted Rossetti very composedly. She did not flinch when he kissed her hand, her skin stayed cool, and her lip did not tremble.

Then, looking straight at her, Rossetti told them that he was to marry Lizzie.

"It's the only thing to do now," he said, looking down into his cup, "now that she may be dying . . ."

"Is she much worse?" Jane asked, horrified.

Rossetti nodded. "The doctors say she may live into the autumn, but no longer."

"I don't believe it," said Morris. "Lizzie is delicate, she needs air and sun, that's all."

Rossetti began to sob. Jane and Morris exchanged alarmed looks. Neither knew what to do. "I've treated her shamefully," Rossetti choked. "I've compromised her, I've made her wait. And now, all I can give her is a few months, not even of happiness, but mere respectability."

"You've been a cad," agreed Morris, somewhat insensitively, Jane thought. "And a fool. You should have done this long ago. But don't give up hope. She may recover yet."

"It's wonderful," Jane said automatically. "That you are to be married," she added quickly.

"It will be a small wedding, only family," said Rossetti. "Given her condition it seems the best thing."

"When?" asked Morris.

"Next week," said Rossetti. "Then we'll go to Rome for a few weeks."

"When you return, Lizzie will be well and we'll have the liveliest party for you Upton has ever seen," said Morris.

"Don't damn our poor party with such faint praise," laughed Rossetti, but he sounded pleased. "And forgive my outburst. My nerves are worn to a frizzle."

"Let's walk into town," said Morris. "The exercise will do you good."

"I must check on the roast," said Jane before they could ask her to join them. "The last one was terribly dry."

"Until dinner, then," said Rossetti.

Jane hid in the kitchen until she heard them leave. Then she went upstairs to her bedroom. The room was almost entirely taken up by a large oak canopy bed. Jane was sewing velvet drapes for it but they weren't finished yet and the bed was still a bare skeleton. There weren't any curtains at the window yet, either, and it was a north-facing room and often cold. Nevertheless she opened the windows that looked out toward the front of the house. The two men were at the gate. Morris ushered Rossetti through it and then closed it behind him. They were lost to Jane's sight behind the high stone wall. Jane looked out toward the town. She could make out the tile and slate and thatch roofs of the houses, and the chimneys. She saw the smoke from the railway train as it passed through town, and heard its whistle.

So Rossetti was to marry Lizzie at last. She had known it was coming, she knew it had to be. And it was conceited to think that it had anything to do with her. But his penetrating look when he told her, the way he seemed to fling the words at her hatefully, made her feel he had done it to hurt her.

And Lizzie was dying! Underneath her shock and grief, an unpleasant inner voice reminded Jane that Lizzie had been "dying" for many years and would probably go on "dying" for many years more. Only now she would be Rossetti's wife.

When the Rossettis returned from Rome, Morris and Jane invited all of their friends to a housewarming party. Everyone came early in the day on Friday and brought their paints and brushes.

"Here is the plan," said Morris when they were assembled on the lawn. "This place is to be decorated in the manner of a thirteenth-century house. Jane and I have already begun painting patterns on the ceiling in the main rooms. Today we intend to plaster the hall ceiling and prick designs into the wet plaster. Ned, you are to begin the frieze in the drawing room. What subject did you decide on?"

"Sire Degrevaunt," said Burne-Jones, holding up a sketchpad filled with scenes from the French romance.

"Very good," said Morris. "Lizzie, we have persuaded you to paint a scene from the Garden of Eden in the bedroom, is that right?" Lizzie nodded. Jane thought that her cheeks glowed more pinkly than usual and that she had gained some weight. Maybe she will get well, Jane thought.

"Gabriel, you are working on the settle, painting scenes from *La Vita Nuova*. Emma, you and Georgie are sewing the embroidered panels for the dining room. What will you do, Brown?"

"Faulkner and I are sketching designs for tiles," he said.

"Don't forget to paint some with my motto on them," said Morris.

"I will if I can," said Faulkner mischievously.

"And Webb has yet to arrive," said Morris. "He's bringing another wagonful of furniture. Well, then, luncheon is on the lawn at one. See you then!"

The artists scattered to begin their work. All through the morning the house rang with laughter and noise. When they were too tired to go on, they left their work and gathered on the grass.

"You must have done something very admirable in another life," observed Rossetti, lying on his back staring at the sky, "to induce all of your friends to slave away for you and call it pleasure."

"Are you saying I've done nothing admirable in this one?" asked Morris, who was tracking a ladybug's progress through the grass.

"Nothing but bring your wonderful wife into our circle," said Rossetti. Jane gasped, but Morris didn't notice.

"Yes, it was my one stroke of genius," he said, taking her hand.

"We wondered at you, bringing a flower like Jane to live here, though she seems to thrive on it," said Brown.

"Of course we wondered about you marrying her at all," said Faulkner. "What was it that Swinburne wrote to you, Rossetti?"

"The idea of marrying her is insane," quoted Rossetti. "To kiss her feet is the utmost men should dream of doing."

"So you are questioning my mental state?" laughed Morris.

"Hubris, my friend," said Webb, "we are accusing you of hubris. Haven't you read your Greek tragedy?"

Jane knew that their incessant praise had little to do with her character or her virtue. She was not even sure it was really her beauty they were praising. The thing had taken on a life of its own. Still, it was difficult not to be flattered.

"How are you doing with your painting?" she asked Rossetti.

"I've blocked in all of the figures and tomorrow I will be ready to begin painting. Georgie's offered to be my assistant, so the work should go quickly."

"I'm no help to Emma," said Georgie. "My sewing is not up to hers. And I can't be any help to Ned either. I make a fearful mess of everything."

"Not true," said Ned. "It's my perfectionism. I wouldn't let Rossetti mix my colors either."

"Tyrant," said Morris.

"Despot," chimed in Rossetti.

"Well, Ned may be tyrannical, but at least he's not slipshod like my husband," said Lizzie.

"She's right," said Faulkner. "You really are very careless."

"Spilling paint," said Burne-Jones.

"Faulty draftsmanship," said Webb.

"Working far too quickly," said Morris.

"Not redoing things nearly enough," said Lizzie.

"I work by inspiration," said Rossetti. "All of the things you mention work against inspiration. They produce heavy, pedantic work."

"Not that you'd know," said Morris, "never having tried it."

"I've seen your work," said Rossetti. Everyone hesitated, wondering if the teasing had gone too far. But Morris only sighed.

"I've begun to consider that I'm not a painter at all. As hard as I work, my drawings never look right and my brushstrokes don't seem to grow more expressive or assured. I've half a mind to give up."

"Don't listen to him," consoled Lizzie. "You can't hope to have Gabriel's style, but I've seen great improvement in your work in the last year."

But Morris shook his head. "Not enough," he said. "Not enough."

"Don't you have anything rude to say about Brown's work?" asked Lizzie.

Rossetti shook his head. "We all admire and try to emulate the old man," he said.

Brown smiled ruefully. "Thank you so much for that."

"And mine?"

"We would never presume to criticize a lady," said Burne-Jones.

Lizzie sighed. "Which is why I never improve," she said.

"Would you like us to come upstairs and criticize your wall painting?" said Georgie. "Because Jane and I don't mind at all, do we, Jane?"

Jane grinned. "Let's go."

Dinner was simple and abundant: roast pork with plum sauce, potatoes dauphinois, peas and carrots, rye bread and sheep cheese, served on the modest Staffordshire blue and white they all loved. There was plenty of red wine. Morris had hoped the enormous oak table that seated twenty would be ready for the party, but it was still being made in London, so half of the party ate in the dining room and half ate out in the hall. The fireplace was heaped with fragrant apple logs that radiated warmth and a gentle light.

Afterward, at Rossetti's suggestion, they played hide-and-seek. At first it seemed absurd to Jane that grown men and women should play games, but Rossetti would not hear of her sitting out.

"Did you never play games as a child?" he asked.

"Not much," she replied.

"Then think of it as a second chance to be a child for an evening. Give it a try."

The first game Georgie quickly found her crouching behind a long bench in the dining room. Jane shrieked with dismay when she was caught, but discovered that she liked to be "it" more than she liked to hide. She enjoyed quietly sneaking up on people who thought their hiding places were safe. Emma Brown got quite a fright when Jane pounced on her in the cellar.

Now Emma was "it" and Jane had crawled into the potato bin to hide. She didn't think timid Emma would venture so far in the dark, so she was surprised to hear the door open. She tried not to shift her position. She heard someone trip over a bag of sugar and mutter a curse.

"Jane," a voice whispered. "Are you there?"

It was Rossetti.

"What are you doing?" she asked. "Do you need a place to hide?"

"Yes," he said. "Is there room in there with you?"

"Not really. Try over there with the apples," she said.

Instead he came closer. He knelt down and she felt his hand grope her sleeve. Then his breath on her neck. Then he was kissing her, passionately, pawing through her hair and tearing at her clothes.

"Oh, Guinevere," he breathed.

She did not like to admit to herself how wonderful it felt. She pushed him away.

"Gabriel, no," she said. He tried to kiss her again, but he was off balance and fell backward into the canned fruits. Several jars smashed. For a moment they sat there, listening to their own breath.

"I think I have cherry jam on my trousers," Rossetti finally said.

Jane laughed, a little hysterically. "Let's go to the kitchen," she said, "and clean you up."

They didn't speak as Jane blotted his pants with a wet rag. What was there to say? When they emerged they discovered that the game had been over for five minutes and everyone was wondering where they were. Rossetti made everyone laugh with the story of his clumsiness.

Fourteen

THEY retired very late: Georgie, Lizzie, and Jane to the Morrises' bedroom, the Browns to the downstairs guest room, and the other five men to the floor of the dining room.

"I wish we didn't have to leave tomorrow," said Georgie as she snuggled into Jane's goose down comforter. "Ned is gone all day, and then when he gets home, he begins directly to work on his painting. I bring him a cheese sandwich for dinner and that's the only time I see him all day."

"Of course you can stay on," said Jane impulsively. "William will be in London every day this week. He leaves early and returns late, so I will be lonely without any company."

"Will you stay, too, Lizzie?" asked Georgie.

"Dinner with Ruskin on Tuesday," groaned Lizzie.

"Another time, then," said Jane.

"Are you sure it will be all right for me to stay?" asked Georgie. "I'd hate to impose."

"Of course it's all right," said Jane, beginning to be excited. "We'll have such a good time, you'll see."

On Monday, after Morris had gone and breakfast had been cleared away, Jane asked the groom to hitch up the cart. As of yet they had only one horse, but he was placid and strong, and Jane was sure she'd have no trouble driving. But Georgie surprised her.

"Oh, let me drive," she begged. "I've always wanted to, but the smallest, youngest person never gets to do anything."

"Are you sure you're strong enough?" asked Jane warily.

"I'm not nearly as delicate as I look," said Georgie, hopping up onto the seat.

Jane soon found that Georgie was right, and they both enjoyed the drive. They got lost following country lanes to even smaller, more remote roads, but neither of them cared. The area was filled with orchards, and as far as the eye could see the landscape was white with apple blossoms. The air was scented with their delicate fragrance.

"It's like heaven, isn't it?" said Georgie rapturously, stopping the cart at the top of a hill to admire the view. "Or how I always imagined heaven. Do you think one of these farmers would mind if we took a few branches home? Apple blossoms are one of my favorite flowers in the world."

"I suppose they won't mind if they don't know," said Jane.

"Is it very wicked?" asked Georgie. "They have so many, and we have none." She pulled a penknife from the pocket of her dress. "We'll just take these branches that lean into the road. They'll have to be pruned back anyway." She filled the back of the cart with the pale pink flowers on their woody stems.

"We'd better turn back then," said Jane. "Those won't last long without water."

"We'll just have to go out driving again tomorrow," said Georgie. "We can follow the trees' daily progress. I can't think of a more lovely occupation than watching the blossoms get pinker and the little leaves begin to show."

"And in the fall we'll have apples," said Jane.

"We must learn to make cider," said Georgie.

On subsequent drives they went to the weekday markets and

the local churches. After only a few days, the local farmers recognized them and bowed as they passed. They often packed a picnic lunch so they could travel farther and farther afield, often not returning to Red House until dusk.

The evenings they devoted to their musical pursuits. For her birthday Morris had given Jane a book, *Popular Music of Olden Time.* She and Georgie soon learned to sing and play many of the songs. Georgie's alto was surprisingly loud and robust. Jane was momentarily shocked the first time she heard the voice, which seemed to come from a person much larger and wilder than Georgie: a banshee, perhaps, or a bushwoman. How could a person so shy unleash a voice like that?

Georgie soon convinced Jane to join in, and Jane was surprised to find that their voices blended nicely. Together they prepared songs to sing to Morris at night after dinner.

The men came down on the weekend and the work of decorating Red House continued. Jane sewed embroidered panels illustrating Chaucer's "Legend of Good Women." Georgie taught herself how to cut woodblocks. Lizzie continued to work on the painting in the bedroom.

At night they stayed up late drinking wine. Jane was too shy to say much, but she enjoyed the lively conversation.

"We are very talented, if I do say so myself," slurred Faulkner one evening. "This house looks good."

"No thanks to you," said Morris, gingerly touching the black eye Faulkner had accidentally given him earlier in the day. "Frolicking all day, hitting people in the face with apples, being a general layabout."

"Poor thing," said Lizzie sympathetically. "You're lucky you didn't lose that eye."

"In my defense," said Faulkner, "you really were lined up perfectly in the doorway. I couldn't not hit you."

"It's true," affirmed Rossetti. "I saw the bull's-eye on your head."

"It's so much nicer to work among friends," said Morris wryly. "You never have to wonder if your colleagues have it in for you. You already know they do."

"I don't remember when I've had so much fun," said Rossetti, reaching for the bottle on the table and discovering it to be empty. "We need more wine."

"I'll get it," said Georgie, rising from the floor near the fireplace where she and Jane were lounging.

"Your injury doesn't seem to have adversely affected the painting on the hall settle," said Burne-Jones.

"Launcelot's castle is the best thing I've done in years," admitted Morris ruefully. "But having you here isn't good for my health, and not just because of Faulkner's deadly aim. My coat is too tight again."

Muffled laughter was heard around the table.

"I'm fat!" moaned Morris. "And you laugh!"

"Should we tell him?" asked Faulkner, winking at the others.

"Tell me what?"

"Faulkner sewed a tuck into your waistcoat," explained Rossetti.

"What!" exploded Morris. "Are you trying to kill me?" Faulkner ran from the table and hid under the stairs. "Don't hurt me," he begged, sliding to the floor. "You know I love you, dear Topsy." He dissolved into a fit of giggles. "You have to admit it's a good joke, though."

"A good joke, when I've denied myself dessert for a week because of it!"

Conversation ceased while Morris dragged Faulkner back into the dining room. The men stood at the sides of the room as if they were at a boxing match. Jane and Lizzie dashed about, gathering plates and glasses so they wouldn't be smashed in the scuffle.

"Pummel him until he apologizes!" shouted Burne-Jones.

"Never!" gasped Faulkner; Morris had his arm bent around his friend's neck.

"Flip him, Topsy!" cried Brown.

Faulkner was too drunk to put up much of a fight, and in five minutes Morris was sitting on his chest. He admitted that it had been a very mean trick to play on a friend and that he would never, ever do anything like it again.

"Faulkner is right, though," said Rossetti when Morris had released his friend and everyone had returned to their places. "We're good at this. We could make money at it."

"How?" asked Burne-Jones. "Some sort of decorating business?"

"Yes!" shouted Morris, leaping to his feet. "A decorative-arts collective."

"It would be a chance to put our beliefs into practice," mused Burne-Jones. "We could paint furniture, make stained glass, weaving, all sorts of things."

"I don't want to work with Topsy," said Faulkner, rubbing his neck. "His temper is too short."

"I don't want to work with you either, you scapegrace," snarled Morris.

"It's true," said Rossetti, "that we would all have to work closely together and there would be disagreements. Some of us might have to refrain from teasing and some of us might have to learn to count to ten."

"It would be a way to support our families without having to work as clerks," said Brown sensibly. "I know it's not a problem for you, Morris, but some of the rest of us would benefit from the extra income."

"Amen to that," affirmed Burne-Jones.

"All in favor of starting a decorative-arts collective say aye," said Morris.

"What about us?" asked Lizzie. "Will there be work for the ladies of the circle?"

"Everyone should contribute," said Morris. "You can draw, Jane can sew, Georgie and Emma can do whatever they like."

"But where will we get the money to do it?" asked Rossetti, pleased that his idea met with such favor but alarmed by the prospect of the work involved.

Morris took out a pound note and laid it on the table. "Everyone put in one pound," he said. "That will be our initial investment." The men did as he asked.

"Now everyone put in their hand and we'll make a solemn vow," said Rossetti excitedly. Jane and Lizzie watched as the men stood with their hands joined in the center of the table.

Just then Georgie walked in with a bottle of wine under each arm. "What is this?" she asked. "The oath of the Horatii?"

With the enthusiastic participation of Morris's friend P. P. Marshall, who had worked with him at Street's office, the fledgling business began as Morris, Marshall, Faulkner and Company, Fine Art Workmen in Painting, Carving, Furniture and the Metals. Rossetti asked that his name not be used.

"I don't have much time or much money to contribute," he said. "And we don't want to prejudice anyone against us with a foreign-sounding name. I'll just be one of the company."

They decided to focus at first on stained glass for churches. Morris was hired to manage the firm and receive a salary. The others were to contribute artistically and be paid accordingly.

Now they had to find a space in London to serve as their workshop and write an advertisement that would appear in the papers. Morris put Rossetti in charge of that.

"You're the most glib," he said. "I've no doubt it will be easy for you."

After a consultation with Jane, Morris invited Ned and Georgie to come to Red House to live. They would build the other wing immediately to make room for them. It would make work on the business easier in addition to being personally gratifying. Ned promised to think about it. Morris also told Jane that because he was contributing the money to start the business, they would have to economize until it was up and running. Jane didn't mind. She was excited by the idea that their friends would come to live at Red House. She would never be lonely.

Fifteen

*J*ANE was going to have a baby. She did not tell Morris at first, not sure how to broach the topic. He was so engrossed in the new business. They had found a workshop and storefront in Red Lion Square and Morris went to London almost every day to oversee things there. Summer turned to fall and Jane's belly grew. Suddenly it dawned on her husband what was happening.

One day at breakfast he looked at her rounded shape and then into her eyes questioningly.

"Yes," she said.

He came to her chair and dropped to his knees, his head on her skirts. "My dear," he said. She thought he was crying. "When?"

"January," she said.

They did not speak of it again.

"Lizzie won't be coming," announced Georgie one day in September as she arrived for a week with Jane.

"What is wrong?" asked Jane, concerned. "Is it her lungs, or something else?"

"I only saw her for a moment," said Georgie. "She looked a little pale, a little languid, but otherwise she seemed herself. She said it was a cough, but I suspect . . ." She let her sentence trail away, but Jane knew what she thought. Perhaps Lizzie was going to have a baby, too.

"Rossetti should take her away again," said Jane. "To the coast, perhaps."

"She doesn't want to go," said Georgie. "Doesn't want to be away from her work."

Jane wondered if Ruskin was right, if the work was keeping Lizzie from getting better. Maybe it would be better for Lizzie to have a complete rest. At the least so that Rossetti would not look so tired and worried when he came.

Georgie left Jane lying on the sofa in her sitting room and went to fetch her a cup of tea. When she returned, she sat opposite Jane in the big wooden chair, which Morris had painted. Her tiny frame was lost in it. She fixed her pale blue eyes on Jane.

"How are you feeling?" she asked.

"Cumbersome," said Jane. "And very tired."

"You needn't exert yourself at all while I'm here," said Georgie. "You know I can manage the kitchen, the servants, anything you need."

"You're such a help to me," said Jane gratefully, reaching out to take Georgie's hand. Georgie's eyes misted.

"You would do the same for me," she said.

Jane wondered if Georgie talked about it with Burne-Jones or whether he was as reticent on the subject as Morris, but she was too delicate to ask such a question. It was hard to imagine the shy couple speaking frankly to each other, but Georgie could be so surprising. What if it turned out that Georgie and Burne-Jones shared their thoughts in an intimate way? Then Jane could not blame marriage, or the unbridgeable divide between men and women, for the silence between her and her husband.

"How is Ned?" asked Jane, pushing thoughts of Morris aside.

Georgie turned pale and the expression on her face was terrified. She seemed to shrink into her clothes and huddled against the arm of her chair.

"What's wrong, Georgie?" asked Jane in alarm. She could not think what could make her friend look so. "Is Ned ill?"

Georgie shook her head. "The air in London isn't good for him," she said at last, "and I wish he wouldn't work so hard."

"Has he made up his mind to accept William's offer?" asked Jane. "Are you coming to live at Red House with us?"

Georgie burst into tears. "I'm sorry," she mumbled, her face hidden in her hands. "I don't mean to burden you, especially now. It's just that . . . I suspect, I mean, I've seen things, and I don't know. It's just nerves, I'm sure. Let's not speak of it."

Jane sat up. "What? What are we not to speak of?"

"Maria Zambaco," sobbed Georgie, pronouncing the hateful name.

"Ned is having an affair," Jane said to her husband that night after Georgie had gone to bed. She was embroidering one of the dining room panels while Morris made sketches for the decoration of St. Michael's Church in Brighton.

He looked up in surprise. "How do you know that?" he said. "Has Georgie said something?"

"I would have thought you'd have told me," said Jane.

"It's not the kind of happy secret one wants to share," said Morris. "I've been trying to convince him to break it off, but he's obsessed. It's making him ill, poor man."

Jane's eyes blazed. "Poor man? What about Georgie? It's killing her, but I don't suppose you care about that."

"Of course I do," retorted Morris. "Why do you think I've been trying to get him to end it? I was hoping I could do it before she found out."

Jane sighed. "They seemed so happy."

"And they will be again," said Morris grimly. "It's a temporary insanity, it has to be."

Jane put down her sewing and went to her husband. She looked down at the drawing he was working on. It was of an angel with its wings unfurled like a peacock's tail. The figure was turned awkwardly to squeeze into an arch.

"It's not easy," Morris said, as if he could read her thoughts. "It has to fit into the space and yet look like there are no constraints, that he is out in the open. And all of the elements—his hands, his face, his symbols—have to read from far away. And then we have to do it in glass!"

Jane thought she might cry. Her heart was heavy for her troubled friend, and she wanted her husband to comfort her but did not know how to tell him. "You wouldn't do that to me, would you?" she finally asked. "What Ned has done?"

"Never," vowed Morris, but he did not look up. Jane waited and watched the pencil moving across the paper. She wanted to wrench it from his fingers and fling it into the fireplace.

The only sound in the room was the rasp of the lead pencil against thick stock.

"Who is this supposed to be?" asked Jane when she had to say something, anything, to break the silence.

"Saint Raphael," said Morris. "The theme is archangels. Each window will be a single figure, which in addition to being relatively uncomplicated for us to make will be striking visually. No muddled Nativity scenes with sheep that look like rocks and camels that look like dogs. No confusing crowds or Giotto-like cityscapes. Very clear and simple and powerful."

"My back aches," said Jane. "I think I'll go to bed."

Morris did stop working then, and insisted on helping her up the stairs and into bed. He procured a hot water bottle and extra pillows and held her hand until she fell asleep.

In January Bessie came to Red House to help. Jane did not want her mother. Most women might be grateful to have their mother there at such a moment, but Jane thought it better if Mrs. Burden stayed away. She wrote a very diplomatic letter explaining that the baby would be more attractive and amusing if they came to Oxford in the summer instead, and Mrs. Burden replied that the summer would be plenty soon enough to see a squalling infant. Mrs. Morris came and Bessie was almost entirely occupied with waiting on her. After a week Mrs. Morris departed, the baby still unborn, saying that the air in Kent was deleterious to her sciatica.

When her time came Jane was frightened; she had seen a girl not much older than herself die in childbirth on Holywell Street. But Georgie was there, and Bessie, and the best doctor in Kent. The delivery was painful but uncomplicated and at the end of it, she had a baby girl named Jenny.

Jenny had a velvety head and bone-white arms and legs. She had round blue eyes and a perpetually worried expression. She sniffed and snorted and rooted at Jane's breast like a little truffle pig.

"She has the Morris coloring," said Bessie, picking the child up from the cradle to inspect her. "But the Burden chin, poor thing." She handed the baby to Jane to nurse.

"I think she's perfectly lovely," said Georgie loyally. "She looks as if she's conducting an opera," she said as Jenny waved her arms while at the breast.

"Yes," said Bessie doubtfully.

"Perhaps she'll be a musician," said Georgie.

"Or a sorceress," said Jane. "I think she looks like she's waving a wand."

"I just hope she'll live," said Bessie. "There's scarlet fever in the village."

"Bessie!" cried Georgie, shooting her a reproachful look.

"Better to be prepared," intoned Bessie. "There isn't a woman in Holywell Street who hasn't lost a baby. Mrs. Ward lost nine, you know, all before their first birthday."

"She will not die," said Jane fiercely.

Having a baby was not what Jane expected. She had not known that the baby would gaze at her with such admiration, as if she was the most important person in the world. And to Jenny, Jane realized, she was. Most of the time she enjoyed the sensation. Sometimes, however, she couldn't stand to have the little thing touching her. It made her want to scream the way it grabbed at her sore breasts and clung to her dress and hair. The way it cried in the night, demanding that she come. Jane hadn't thought she'd be so tired. She hadn't known that one minute she would want to throw Jenny against a wall, and the next minute she would want to hold her and make faces at her. It was very strange. She longed to be away from Jenny but when she was, all she wanted was to return to her.

Morris neglected the office to hang around the nursery, but he could not entirely banish work from his thoughts.

"The Saint Raphael you saw me working on turned out marvelously," he said to Jane, sitting in the rocking chair while she paced with a screaming Jenny. "Rossetti drew the figure and of course did much better than I could have. The angel's hair is as gold as Lizzie's. I drew the face and I realized when I saw it in the window that I'd inadvertently copied it from Rossetti. You know, the heavy-lidded eyes, the small pursed lips. It's strange that as skillful a draftsman as Rossetti makes such disparate women look alike. Clearly he is altering them to suit some fantasy of his own. I wasn't doing that, of course. I just don't have the skill to do better.

"Brown did Saint Michael and it's even better than Saint Raphael. I particularly admire the fish-scaled sword handle and the patterns on his cape and stockings. Above the two in the roundel is another Saint Michael bravely slaying a fire-breathing dragon. All the windows look medieval. Someone who didn't know might think the glass had been there four hundred years."

Jane tried to listen, but her mind could not focus on anything her husband said. For the last several months, he had been working constantly, and it had been difficult to get his attention. Now she saw that when he was there he was just a nuisance. She wished he would go back to work and leave her alone.

"How are you feeling?" he asked solicitously.

"How do you think?" she snapped.

"You should eat a bloody steak," he said. "It will help you to regain your strength."

"But I don't want a bloody steak," protested Jane.

"I will tell the cook to make one for you tonight," said Morris. "You must think of the baby. Jenny wants a strong mother."

Lizzie laughed uproariously when Jane recounted the scene to her. As Georgie and Jane had suspected, she, too, was expecting.

"Perhaps we should exchange husbands," she said, with a devilish smirk. "I think that sounds heavenly."

"You wouldn't say that if you had been forced to choke down half a pound of dripping meat," said Jane. "I nearly gagged at the table. And all the while he smiled encouragingly to me as he stuffed himself with the onion pudding and the carrot soufflé, just the things I most wanted!"

"Poor girl," commiserated Lizzie. "I'll be sure to have some of each the next time you come."

"How are you feeling?" Jane asked sympathetically.

"I've fainted a couple of times, and can't seem to eat anything. Gabriel had the doctor here and he said under no circumstances may I draw, or exert my mind in any way. So here I sit, like a chicken in a coop. I'm glad you've come."

"If I had known I would have come sooner," said Jane.

"I didn't want to disturb you in these first weeks," said Lizzie. "But tell me all about the little one."

When the topics of Jenny's eating and sleeping had been exhausted, Lizzie sighed and pulled the blue paisley blanket up to her chin and lay back against the pillows of her chaise.

"I envy you, Jane," she said. "You came through the birth without difficulty and now you're well enough to come all this way on the train. I'm terribly worried I'll be too weak to have the baby."

Jane, too, had worried about Lizzie's strength, but it wouldn't help her to say so.

"Don't be silly," she said. "Georgie will come and help you as she did me, and Gabriel will be there with the doctor, and you'll get through it."

"Gabriel said he wanted to have a child, and he promised to take care of me while I was having it, but I think every aspect of it terrifies him," said Lizzie. "He's pulling away already."

"He will rise to the occasion," Jane assured her. "When it happens you will be amazed by what a comfort he is to you."

Just then Rossetti came in. "Janey," he said, greeting her with evident pleasure. "I was going to immortalize Lizzie with my chalks, but now you must grace the tableau as well." He sat down on the chair next to hers and they gazed at the expectant Lizzie. Her agate-colored eyes were very large and glowing in her thin, colorless face. She looked restful, serene, and wise.

"My presence would spoil it," protested Jane.

"Nonsense," said Rossetti. "The contrast in your looks is marvelous."

"The compliment is yours, Jane," said Lizzie. "And the reproof mine."

"Nonsense," said Rossetti again. "Neither side of the coin is superior to the other. The dark must have the light, the strong the weak, the sharp angle the soft curve." He guided Jane to a place next to Lizzie on the chaise and went to his easel.

Lizzie closed her eyes. "As soon as the child has come, I will resume my drawing," she said. Rossetti and Jane exchanged a look. Neither of them had thought otherwise.

"I'm composing a new poem," said Rossetti. "For the book of verse I hope to publish next year. It is called 'Genius in Beauty.'" He paused expectantly.

"Will you recite it to us?" asked Jane dutifully.

"With pleasure," he said.

Beauty like hers is genius. Not the call
Of Homer's or of Dante's heart sublime,—
Not Michael's hand furrowing the zones of time,—
Is more with compassed mysteries musical;
Nay, not in Spring's or Summer's sweet footfall
More gathered gifts exuberant Life bequeaths
Than doth this sovereign face, whose love-spell breathes
Even from its shadowed contour on the wall.

As many men are poets in their youth,
But for one sweet-strung soul the wires prolong
Even through all change the indomitable song;
So in likewise the envenomed years, whose tooth
Rends shallower grace with ruin void of truth,
Upon this beauty's power shall wreak no wrong.

When Jane left Lizzie pressed her hand. "Send your irritating, overly attentive husband to visit me," she said. "I'm sure I can find some use for him."

The next time Jane visited, she found Lizzie lying on the sofa, her face white and her eyes wide with panic.

"Something's wrong," she said, the words making her fear concrete. Tears welling, she was frantically pressing her distended belly here and there.

Jane was alarmed. "What is it?" she said.

"It's not moving," Lizzie said. "It hasn't moved since yesterday. I've been lying here listening and feeling for it, but there's nothing."

"Perhaps it's gone to sleep," said Jane. "They do that, you know, just like babies."

"No," sobbed Lizzie.

"Should I call the doctor?" asked Jane.

Lizzie could not speak but she nodded.

Jane ran into the hall and wrote two notes, which she gave to the maid to deliver: one to the doctor, one to Rossetti at his club.

The doctor came and listened. He, too, suspected that something was very wrong. "There's nothing to be done," he said. "We must wait and see."

Jane could hardly bear to look at Lizzie. Rossetti, too, stood at the window looking out, as if he could not face the scene inside.

"So I am to carry a dead baby around inside me?" Her voice was very low and calm now but her eyes were anguished. Then she began to moan, a throbbing, pounding sound that got louder and louder and wracked her entire body. Jane looked at the doctor pleadingly. The doctor's face was impassive.

"You must calm her down," he said to Rossetti. "The hysteria will only make it worse." He gave Rossetti a prescription for laudanum and left the house.

"Shall I go?" asked Jane, feeling that she was intruding on a moment that should be between a woman and her husband. But Rossetti grabbed her arm.

"Stay with her, please," he said. "I'll go fill this." And he ran from the room with the prescription, leaving Jane with the wailing Lizzie.

"My baby's dead," she sobbed.

"You don't know that," said Jane, who felt sure it was true and wished that she, too, could cry. It was agony to sit there with her friend, but she couldn't leave her alone. When Rossetti returned they gave Lizzie the laudanum and soon she was asleep.

Lizzie waited out the next few weeks in a drug-induced stupor. When at last she went into labor, it was very difficult. Jane and Emma Brown held her hands as she screamed. When it was over, it was as everyone expected. The baby was dead, the umbilical cord wrapped around her neck. Jane went to tell Rossetti.

"Is she going to die?" he asked, stumbling toward Jane and nearly falling into her arms. He was very drunk. Jane caught him by the shoulders and stood him upright.

"She's not," said Jane doubtfully. "She's stronger than you think."

"I know she's going to die," Rossetti said. "Everyone I love is being taken from me, and I deserve it." He put his head in his hands and slid slowly to the floor.

Jane would never forget the dead child, perfectly formed, that the doctor brought to Rossetti wrapped in a blanket. Except for a strange bluish cast to its skin it looked as if it were merely sleeping.

"Your daughter," the doctor said. Rossetti groaned and turned away, refusing to take the bundle. Jane led him to a chair and he fell into it.

"My wife?" he asked with dread.

"I've given her a sleeping draft," said the doctor. "She'll sleep for eight or ten hours." He spoke as much to Jane as to Rossetti. "After that, watch for heavy bleeding or signs of fever."

Rossetti began to cry.

"Pull yourself together, man," said the doctor. "For your wife's sake if not your own." He went over the procedures. Rossetti had to sign a form. Then he left.

"What will I say to her when she wakes up?" Rossetti asked Jane desperately.

"I don't suppose you have to say anything," said Jane. "Just sit with her, that's enough."

"I can't," he said. "I'm frightened. I'm frightened of my own wife." So it was Jane who went in to Lizzie. Jane was not sure how much of the ordeal her friend remembered. She took Lizzie's hand.

"How do you feel?" Jane asked. Lizzie turned her sad golden eyes to Jane.

"Is the baby dead?" she asked.

"Yes," Jane said. She felt tears welling up but tried to control them, telling herself that it would not help Lizzie. "It was a little girl."

"Where is she?" Lizzie asked. "I want to see her."

"The doctor took her away," said Jane. At this Lizzie began to howl. Jane heard the door to the next room shut; Rossetti had left, unable to listen to his wife's screams.

"I want to see my baby," she sobbed. "Bring her to me."

Jane told her that it was better, that it would only hurt her to see the dead baby, but in her heart she was not so sure. She thought that if it had been her dead baby, she would want to see it, too.

The doctor returned the next day. Considering what she'd just gone through, physically Lizzie was better than he expected. Her skin was cool and the bleeding minimal. However, the hand he took to feel her pulse was limp. The eyes he looked into were glassy and unfocused.

"You're young," said the doctor impatiently. "You'll have another child."

Lizzie said nothing.

"Many a woman has gone through it," he said, but Lizzie did not seem to hear him. She was staring out of the window, her face turned away.

"You must reason with her," the doctor said to Rossetti. "You must make her want to recover. You artists are so dramatic and self-indulgent. This isn't the end of the world."

There was no funeral. The body was discreetly disposed of. It was as if she had never been.

When Jane came to visit her, Lizzie was always sitting in the same chair, staring out of the window. Her face was expressionless, but Jane could not bear to look into her eyes.

"Beatrice," she said dully. "We were going to name her Beatrice."

"It's better not to speak of it," said Jane miserably. That was what the doctor had said.

"How can it be better?" cried Lizzie. "How can it be better to pretend that she never was?"

"I don't know," said Jane. Being there with her friend was agony, but there was no one else who could visit and nowhere else the Rossettis could go. Georgie was pregnant now, too, and Emma Brown had three little ones. Lizzie could not come to Red House because Jenny was there.

On her next visit Lizzie was in her usual place, but she was rocking her heavy chair back and forth.

"Hush," she said when Jane came in. "You'll wake the baby."

Jane was horrified. She did not know what to say. Had Lizzie lost her mind?

Sixteen

FTER the loss of the baby, Jane did not see Rossetti for several weeks. She knew that he wasn't painting and was spending most of his time walking along the Thames and drinking at his club. Jane thought this brooding was unhealthy, so she was relieved when, one afternoon, more than a month after the baby's death, she got a note asking her to come and model for him. His latest project was a triptych entitled *The Seed of David,* and he had no one to pose for the Virgin. Jane wondered why Lizzie was not sitting for him, but supposed she was still too physically fragile to sit for long periods. It had been some time since Jane had modeled. She had assumed that once she was married, she would not do it again.

"Is it all right if I sit for Rossetti tomorrow?" she asked Morris in bed that night. She half-expected him to voice some objection, tell her it wasn't proper.

"Why not?" Morris said. "If you'd like to. But perhaps you don't want to be away from Jenny?"

"The nurse can manage her for a few hours," said Jane.

"It will be good for you to get out," said Morris. "You should walk to the station. The air and exercise will brighten your spirits." He set his book down and began to massage her shoulders. "Poor Jane," he said. "I know how much you feel the loss of Lizzie's baby."

Jane sighed. There was nothing to do but let him comfort her.

The day Jane came Lizzie was out, visiting her mother. Rossetti draped a gauzy scarf over Jane's head and stretched her neck out in the pose he most liked her in.

Since her marriage Jane had tried hard not to think of Rossetti, and she had mostly succeeded. But now the artist's guiding touch on her throat made her catch her breath. She had forgotten how soft his hands were, how sensual his touch.

"How is Lizzie?" she asked, to keep herself from thinking such things.

Rossetti sighed. "Not very well," he said. "The hallucinations have stopped, thank God, but her spirits are very low. She doesn't sleep at night and then she is listless all day."

"You must try to have another baby," said Jane, practically. It was what everyone had been thinking but was too delicate to say.

"Dr. Branwell thinks so, too," said Rossetti. "When she is feeling better, perhaps."

"She may never feel better unless she has another baby," said Jane. "You shouldn't wait."

"I'm sure you're right," said Rossetti. He stopped drawing and closed his eyes for a moment. "The subject is a melancholy one, do you mind if we change it? What is your ridiculous husband up to these days?"

She could not tell him that the confident way Morris played with Jenny made her feel horribly inadequate. She could not tell him that there were days when she wanted to throw the soup tureen at his head, to get him to shut up about stained glass. She could not tell him that the night before, her husband had made love to her and that she had swallowed her disgust at his increasing girth.

"He is designing wallpaper," she said instead.

"I imagine he will be good at it," said Rossetti, "unless he tries one of those Chinese wallpapers with figures moving across the landscape."

"He's drawing flowers," she said. "Daisies, climbing roses, sunflowers. And fruit. He says that the wallpapers today are too geometric and stiff, that he wants to be reminded of the outdoors when he looks at them." It was not so much that she objected to his making wallpaper, or that she thought his ideas were wrong. Mainly she resented his preoccupation. It was obvious not only that he was quite happy and content but that he had no idea how miserable she was.

"So much industry!" Rossetti said. "The man has more energy than three other men. And yet less inspiration than almost anyone."

It was just what Jane felt, and she was relieved to hear Rossetti say it. But Jane knew she was being disloyal and tried not to give in to the temptation to speak ill of her husband.

"Why is Lizzie not modeling for the Virgin?" Jane asked instead.

"I'm going to use her for the adoring angels, but I'm working from old sketches. She has no interest in sitting for me. That would involve spending time with me." Rossetti sounded petulant and hurt.

"You must be patient with her," said Jane. "Think of what she's been through"

"That is just what I can't allow myself to think of. When I do I want to throw myself in the river. It is all my fault."

"You are too hard on yourself," said Jane.

"Besides," said Rossetti, "you have a more earthy quality, which is what I need for Mary, and more Semitic coloring. Despite what the Renaissance painters did, we both know that Mary wasn't blond."

"But the angels were," said Jane.

"Aren't the angels and the gods always blond?" said Rossetti.

The Firm was going to move its headquarters from Red Lion Square to Red House. Georgie and Ned had agreed to come and live with Jane and William. Georgie had just had a little boy, Philip, and Jane was already expecting another child. The two women could watch the children together, or take turns to give the other some leisure time.

"It will be such a relief," said Georgie. "For Ned's health, I mean," she added quickly. Since the day she had broken down, she had not so much as hinted at the affair.

"Yes, our husbands will be very happy," said Jane wryly. Georgie's reticence was very frustrating because Jane longed to unburden herself to her friend, to confide her feelings about her husband. But even if she could, Jane knew that Georgie would be shocked and grieved to hear how Jane felt. She would counsel patience, and forgiveness, and she would make Jane feel horribly guilty. If Georgie would only admit the troubles in her marriage, Jane felt that she would be more understanding.

"I only wish that Lizzie could have the benefit as well, but Rossetti refuses to leave London," said Georgie, with a little frown.

Lizzie looked tired and worn when Jane went to see her. "Our arguments are terrible," she said. "You wouldn't believe the things I find myself saying. You don't think I'm a horrid person, do you?"

"Of course not," said Jane reluctantly. She wished she could think Lizzie a horrid person; it would make everything so much easier.

"Because I really am horrid to him," Lizzie said.

"Are you working again?" asked Jane, knowing that talking about drawing was the one thing that made Lizzie smile.

"No," said Lizzie. "I'm still forbidden. I think if he would let me draw again, I could stop hating him for what happened."

"When your health is better," said Jane. Each time she visited, she hoped Lizzie would tell her she was expecting again, but she never did.

"My health won't be better until I start drawing again," said Lizzie. She glanced over at Jane and her eyes lit up with an artist's delight in beauty.

"The way the light is hitting your face, you look like a goddess in some Roman wall painting. No wonder my husband loves to paint you!"

"He loves to paint you, too," Jane said.

"I've been usurped, in art and in life," Lizzie said sardonically. "The only thing for me now is a lingering and romantic death by consumption."

"Don't be ridiculous, Lizzie," said Jane. She turned the conversation toward Roman wall paintings. She knew little about them, but it was a much safer subject.

A week later Jane and Morris were awakened by the insistent ring of the bell. Hastily they threw on their dressing gowns and went downstairs. It was a telegram from London. Jane waited with dread while Morris paid the messenger and scanned the message.

"We're wanted at Rossetti's," Morris read. His face was grim.

"What is it?" said Jane fearfully. She realized that she couldn't bear it if anything happened to Rossetti.

"It's Lizzie," said Morris. "She's not expected to live until the morning."

Jane was not supposed to be seen in public so visibly pregnant, but she went back upstairs and began to dress. Morris did not try to stop her, but found a loose coat for her to wear.

On the way to the train station, Jane tried to think what could have happened. Lizzie had been ill much of the time she had known her, it was true, but it had never seemed life threatening. She was thin, and her lungs were weak, but she had muddled along with that for years. Was it a pregnancy, perhaps such an early one that they had not told their friends of it yet? Had there been some horrible complication?

I just saw her, thought Jane in anguish. She was perfectly well. But then she thought of the fights with Rossetti, and Lizzie's tone when she spoke of being usurped, and her heart lurched.

"Poor Rossetti," said Morris, and with horror Jane thought of him. How must he be feeling now?

Maybe she'll live, thought Jane. Maybe it's not as bad as the telegram made it sound.

When they arrived at the house, Rossetti's brother William was there. The doctor had just left. Ford Madox Brown had been sitting with Rossetti but had gone to alert the Burne-Joneses.

William Rossetti shook his head in response to their anxious, questioning looks. "The doctor said there's nothing more to be done. He's injected her stomach with water, but if enough of the stuff is already in her blood . . . we must wait and see."

Jane went into the room where Lizzie lay. Jane's eye immediately went to the vials on the bedside table, eight or nine of them, lined up in a row. Rossetti sat at Lizzie's bedside, holding her hand. There was a stain on the front of her dress, which the meticulous Lizzie would never have allowed. Otherwise she did not look as if she were dying, only as if she were asleep.

"Feel how cold her hand is," said Rossetti.

Jane sat across the bed from him and took Lizzie's other hand. It was indeed ice-cold.

"She breathes very seldom," said Rossetti. "I think she's gone and then I'll see the faintest movement. It's been like this for hours."

"What happened?" asked Jane. She thought she knew, now, at least in part, but wanted to be sure. Rossetti dropped Lizzie's hand and buried his head in the bedclothes.

"I murdered her," he said.

Jane gasped. "What do you mean?" she asked.

"We went out to dinner. She was very tired. And then in the carriage home we quarreled," Rossetti said. "I went out. I was angry. I didn't come home until very late. And I found her like this"—he pointed to the unconscious Lizzie—"with empty bottles of laudanum everywhere."

Jane, who had been imagining Rossetti imprisoned in gaol, where he was chained to a wall and where his hair grew long and gray and his body became filthy and wasted, sighed with relief. Whatever else he was, Rossetti was no murderer.

"How did you come to have so much of it in the house?" Jane

asked, not able to completely conceal her shock at the number of bottles.

"The doctor gave it to her," said Rossetti, "to help her sleep. Lately she'd been taking more and more of it. But she never had any trouble."

"It must have been an accident," said Jane.

"She did it to punish me," said Rossetti.

When Jane left Lizzie and Rossetti and went back into the sitting room, she found her husband deep in conversation with William Rossetti.

"My God," she heard her husband say, "this can't be known."

"What is it?" she asked.

Morris held out a scrap of paper to Jane. "When he arrived home tonight, Gabriel found this."

It can't go on, the note read:

I've tried and I've tried but I can't make things better and I don't see any way out, except this. I'm sorry. My love to you.

So it was true. Jane folded the note and handed it back to her husband. She hardly knew what to think or feel.

"But to destroy it," said William Rossetti. "It's so disrespectful."

"It's the only way. It's Lizzie I'm thinking of. If there's no saving her life, we must at least save her reputation. She must have a Christian burial. And Gabriel . . ."

"It would ruin his life, if it got out," said William Rossetti.

"Exactly."

Bolstered by Morris's opinion, William Rossetti burned the note that Lizzie had written to his brother.

The shops were opening when Lizzie took her last breath. The doctor agreed to ascribe her death to accidental laudanum poisoning. Suicide was a cause of death to be avoided at all costs. And as she had left no note, who was to say that it wasn't an accident?

Lizzie looked very beautiful in the mahogany casket lined with white silk. Her hair still glowed like a precious metal. She wore the lace dress in which Rossetti had married her, and a locket he had given her. Jane looked into Lizzie's empty marble face for some clue as to where she was now, but there was none. Her expression was neutral. Wherever she was, it was far away from her body and her friends. Jane saw that Rossetti's knees were buckling as he walked toward the casket. He would have fallen if his brother had not been supporting him. She saw that he held a sheaf of papers in his hand and she could not think what they were. Then, in horror, she realized what he was going to do. She wanted to stand up and scream at him to stop, but it was already too late. The papers fell from his hand and into the casket.

They were Rossetti's poems. Jane prayed that they were only copies.

When she visited him the next day, alarmed by the gesture of the poems and by his pallor and stumbling, she found him on the sofa where Lizzie had spent much of her pregnancy, holding one of her shawls and drinking Irish whiskey. Jane took one look at his slumped posture and bloodshot eyes and stopped the decanter. She carried it back to the sideboard and hid it inside, on a low shelf, behind a stack of dessert plates. She sat in a chair opposite him but could not now bring herself to touch him. Now he was a widower, and etiquette had to be observed.

"I had to do penance," Rossetti said. The words seemed to flow from him, like blood from a stab wound. "At first I thought that Lizzie would not want me to destroy my life for her sake. Then I realized that of course she did. Why else did she . . . and anyway, I deserve to be punished. I don't know how my punishment serves

Lizzie, but it must. She must be able to see me from wherever she is. She must know what I've done."

Jane put a hand on his arm to stop him, but he shook it off and went on.

"It was my only copy, you know. At the last minute I almost couldn't do it, but I had told my brother I was going to and I knew what he would think if I didn't. That's Gabriel, he would say to himself. Full of noble thoughts that never translate into action. I wonder what other people must be saying about me now. Do you suppose they think I'm mad with grief? Do you suppose they think I'm a tragic figure?"

"Gabriel," Jane said, "you can't go on like this. You have to take care of yourself."

"If they knew," Rossetti said. "If they knew the truth about me, they would not think I was a tragic figure or that my gesture was fine. They would know, and you would know, that I'm a monster."

"You're not," said Jane.

"I didn't tell you all," Rossetti said. "The other night, I didn't tell you everything."

"Is there something you want to tell me now?" Jane asked. Rossetti wanted to tell her about the argument. The thought of hearing the ugly words they must have hurled at each other was disturbing, but if it would help him to tell her . . .

"I kept secrets from Lizzie. I've kept secrets from you. I thought if you knew, you'd despise me."

"I could never despise you," said Jane, shivering involuntarily. He had been lying to her as well as to Lizzie?

"Lizzie left a note. I gave it to my brother. Did you see it?" asked Rossetti, getting up and walking to the sideboard. He knelt on the floor and rummaged inside until he found the decanter. He brought it with him to his chair and began to drink directly from it.

"Yes," said Jane. "I saw it. She was never right after she lost the baby." It was the received opinion of everyone they knew, even those who thought the laudanum poisoning was an accident. She wouldn't have been taking laudanum at all if it weren't for that.

"It wasn't the baby," moaned Rossetti. "I . . . I was seeing someone else."

Jane felt as if she had been doused with cold water. "After the baby was lost?" she asked. Rossetti buried his head in his hands.

"Before?" she asked. Rossetti nodded, his face still hidden from her.

Jane felt a rush of anger. And yet, she reflected, she was not at all surprised. Of course it was something like that.

"The night she . . . we had an argument about it. She said it must stop or she would leave me. I taunted her, I dared her to leave. Then I went to see Fanny. I was with her all night. And Lizzie did leave me, didn't she? She was true to her word."

Fanny Cornforth, one of Rossetti's models. Jane had met her several times: a buxom blonde who seemed dim-witted but good-natured. Entirely unworthy of Rossetti, Jane thought. And entirely unworthy of being the cause of Lizzie's death.

"How could you do it to her?" asked Jane bitterly. "Did you love Lizzie at all?"

"I did once," said Rossetti. "But we should never have gotten married. It was already too late by then. But of course I had to marry her. It was the only moral thing to do. Perhaps if the baby had lived, things would have turned out all right."

"But you said yourself that you were seeing Fanny before the baby died. You think if it had lived, you would have stopped?"

"I'm a monster," agreed Rossetti, burying his face in the silk cushions.

"I see now why you put your poems in the casket," said Jane.

"Don't reproach me, Jane, I can't stand it!" Rossetti cried. "Don't you think I'm torturing myself already? I can't sleep at night, Lizzie's face is always before me. The last thing she said to me was, 'You're not worthy of me.' Of course she was right. I wasn't worthy of her love and I'm not worthy of your friendship, but if you see fit to take it away, I just may go to join Lizzie. Please, Jane." Now he looked up and Jane saw tears in his eyes. She relented.

"Do you love Fanny?" Jane doubted it was so, but stranger things had happened. After all, Morris had fallen in love with her, and she had not had much more to recommend her than Fanny.

"Fanny's a wonderful girl," Rossetti said. "But I won't marry her, if that's what you mean. She knows I won't, and she doesn't care. She's very independent and she likes it that way. I never meant for Lizzie to find out about her, you know. I never meant to hurt her."

"You hoped your lies would never become public," said Jane severely.

"I swore to myself that when the affair with Fanny ended, there would be no others."

"Which others? Annie Miller? Alexa Wilding?"

Rossetti groaned. "I'm so ashamed," he said.

Jane struggled to compose herself. It wouldn't do to scream, or to run at Rossetti and beat him with her fists. Her anger on behalf of her friend could not justify such behavior.

"Whatever you have done, Lizzie knew you loved her," she said, although she was not sure if it was true. "Maybe she meant to scare you, but I don't think she meant to . . ."

"Kill herself?" said Rossetti. "I think she knew exactly what she was doing. She knew what this would do to me."

Jane made Rossetti some tea and managed to convince him to drink it and to eat some roast chicken and jelly. He would not go to bed; he said only children went to bed in the afternoon, but he promised not to drink any more that night. She couldn't tell if he was saying it just to humor her, but she left feeling that she had improved things, if only slightly and temporarily.

On the train Jane sat unseeing as the dismal wintry landscape passed in a blur of frozen fields and trees drooping with ice. She did not know how to feel. She had thought it was Rossetti's commitment to Lizzie that had kept him from her years ago, but apparently it was not.

It's just my pride, she thought to herself. To have lost out to Fanny Cornforth, it does sting. But I would not have wanted to be what she is, little better than a harlot, living alone in rooms he's paid for.

For the first time in years, she gave thanks that she had married someone as transparently honest as Morris. She could not imagine him going out at night to meet another woman. And yet, didn't that make him dull and predictable? He had no passion left for her, but he hadn't transferred it to someone else, he had just let that part of himself go dormant. Wasn't it better that Rossetti was passionate, even if his feelings were misplaced?

That night at dinner Jane told Morris of her visit.

"He's brooding," Morris said. "It's very bad for him. You shouldn't encourage it." The servant girl came in with a tureen of beef broth and they waited silently while she served it.

"He needs to unburden himself to someone," Jane said when the girl had gone. "He feels responsible."

"It's not good for you either," Morris said, stirring his soup complacently, seemingly unconcerned at the thought of Rossetti's distress. "You'll get overwrought yourself."

"Well, why shouldn't I?" said Jane. "My friend is dead, my other friend is calling himself a murderer and drinking himself to death; I think the situation warrants a little bit of upset." Her voice was twisted with sarcasm.

Morris sighed. "It's terrible," he agreed. "Poor Lizzie. The girl was absolutely driven to do it."

This made Jane even angrier. She put down her spoon, her appetite quite gone. "Gabriel is suffering deeply," she said.

"And no doubt enjoying every minute of it. That business with the poems was the most self-pitying thing I've ever seen."

"If I died I doubt you'd do the same," said Jane.

"No, I wouldn't," said Morris, "because I'd have the knowledge that I'd treated you well in life to comfort me, and not a heart full of guilt."

Rather than listen to Morris's indictment of Rossetti, Jane muttered something about the squab and went to the kitchen. The cook was surprised when Jane took the bowl of cake batter from her hands and beat it until it frothed. When she returned to the dining room, Jane sweetly asked her husband about the stained-glass program for All Saints Church in Selsley, and they did not speak of Rossetti and Lizzie again.

As she lay sleepless that night, though, listening to Morris grinding his teeth while thinking about Lizzie lying cold and motionless in the bed she and Rossetti had shared, Jane was filled with doubt. Had Lizzie been angry enough to kill herself to spite Rossetti? And ultimately, did it matter? She could turn her brain inside out searching for the truth, and at the end her friend would still be dead.

Stubbornly, the more everyone blamed Rossetti for what had happened to Lizzie, the more sympathetic Jane became. Though Jane agreed that he had behaved badly, she began to suspect that Lizzie had managed to win the argument. She had made sure that Rossetti would never be free of her, that he would always be haunted by guilt and regret. One was not supposed to speak ill of the dead, but at times Jane found herself very angry with Lizzie.

A month later, Jane gave birth to her second daughter, May. She was very busy, and though she wrote faithfully to Rossetti, she did not see him for quite some time.

Seventeen

ORRIS, Marshall, Faulkner and Company won two gold medals at the International Exhibition in South Kensington in 1862. They sold a painted cabinet and received two major church commissions. It appeared that the business would soon be a success.

"I thought it would take five years at least to turn a profit," marveled Morris to Jane. "But now I think two or three years at the most." He picked Jenny up and whirled her around until they both tumbled to the floor of the nursery in a heap.

"That's wonderful, William," said Jane, trying to sound as encouraging as possible.

Chastened by the terrible outcome of Lizzie's battle with Rossetti, Jane attempted to rededicate herself to her husband. Accordingly, she spent a week instructing the cook as to Morris's favorite dishes. She made sure that a very good roast of beef or pork was on the table each night, along with a potato pudding or a vegetable pie. Unfortunately, at the moment that Jane decided to shower her husband with the affection she did not feel, he was having a difficult time at the loom he had built in the basement of Red Lion Square. Consumed by learning ancient weaving techniques, he hardly glanced at the food. He automatically shoved it into his mouth and then immediately retreated to his studio to read a sixteenth-century French treatise on weaving he had bought at an antiques store in London. After three days of special dishes that were ignored, Jane gave up.

Next she cleaned the house from top to bottom with her own hands and the help of the housemaid. They washed the windows and the floors. They scrubbed walls and ceilings; they washed all of the linens in the house. They polished all of the furniture, the silver, they washed all of the china. Everything smelled of lemon and sandalwood, but Morris did not notice.

Jane bought a piece of striped silk in peacock blue, made it up into an evening dress, and wore it to dinner with a new amethyst brooch affixed to her breast that brought out the blue in her eyes, but Morris scarcely glanced at her. He did not notice when she pinned her hair in a new way, or when she spritzed her neck with a new lilac eau de toilette. She had to admit that unless she could tell him how to increase the density of his weaving or help him perfect his half stitch, her husband was inaccessible.

In the brief moments he was in the house, Morris was happy to complain about aniline dyes or explain the difference between tapestry cartoons and other drawings, but she found it difficult to pay attention. Her mind kept wandering to the butcher's bill and the tooth that Jenny was cutting; should she apply a cold compress to the gums, or give her a sugar cube wrapped in cheesecloth? He showed her eleven drawings of a pomegranate and wanted her to tell him which was the best, but she had trouble distinguishing between them. Why couldn't he just appreciate a good roast, like other men?

One afternoon Morris came home unexpectedly early. Jane was sitting at the table with May in her lap, attempting unsuccessfully to get her to eat some mashed carrots. Most of it had ended up in May's hair and on her dress. Beside her, Jenny was trying her best to handle her soup spoon, but could not keep it level. Chicken broth spilled on the tablecloth and on the floor. Jane did not have the energy to reprimand her. When the meal was done, all three of them would need baths, and fresh clothes. It wearied her to think of it. Morris stood in front of her waving a sheaf of papers.

"Look what I have!" he shouted. "The wallpaper prototypes have come!" He placed them next to her elbow and waited for her to look at them.

"I'm afraid I'll get carrot on them," Jane said. "Can I look at them after we're done?"

"I suppose," said Morris, disappointed. "Or I can turn the pages for you." He sat down next to her and showed her each sample. "Do you like the color schemes?" he asked. He had asked her when he had made his first drawings, and she had responded positively. But that was a hundred compliments ago, and Jane's energy was flagging.

"They're lovely," she said with as much enthusiasm as she could muster.

"Which do you like, Jenny?" asked Morris hopefully, holding them in front of his daughter.

"Blue," she said, pointing with the hand that was holding the spoon. Jane flinched.

"Eat your soup," she said.

"I fear that the blue is a little childish," fretted Morris. "The yellow is more subtle."

"Just because a child likes it doesn't make it childish," snapped Jane. "I like the blue. Does that make me childish?"

"What is the matter with you?" asked Morris. "Are you ill?"

Jane didn't answer, she just kept spooning carrots onto May's face. Morris moved to the end of the table and began to eat his lunch.

The bell rang and soon Georgie, heavily pregnant, lumbered in holding two-year-old Philip by the hand.

"Soup!" she said brightly, easing herself carefully into a chair and pulling her son onto the one next to her. "Is it chicken? Chicken is my favorite. And I see we're having wild blueberries for dessert. How lovely."

"Which do you like, Georgie?" Morris asked, standing up again with his sheets of wallpaper.

"Oh, I'm not qualified to speak about things artistic," Georgie said, blushing.

"Nonsense," said Morris. "You have two eyes."

"Two nearsighted ones, you know. But if you insist." She scrutinized the samples for several minutes before declaring the yellow her favorite.

"But I wish you had made one with a pale green ground," she said. "I can't wear it, but pale green is my favorite color."

"The next one will be green," promised Morris. "What is your favorite flower?"

"White star jasmine," said Georgie. "Such delicate flowers, but with the scent of the gods, don't you think, Jane?"

"I know it's common, but I like roses," said Jane. She wished that she and Morris could speak so cordially about color and flowers, the way he did with Georgie, and she knew it was at least partly her fault, but it seemed that everything that came out of her mouth now was terse and angry.

"Yes, you are very common," said Morris, standing up. "I can't stay, I have a meeting with the rector of a church in Scarborough to go over the installation schedule." He bowed to Georgie. "Pale green jasmine. I won't forget."

He kissed Jenny on the forehead and patted May's head. He said nothing to Jane as he left. Jane and Georgie listened to his footsteps on the flagstone floor as he walked down the hall. The heavy front door banged shut and he was gone.

Georgie took May from Jane and wiped her face and hands with a napkin. She rang for the nanny and asked her to take Philip and Jenny into the garden. Then she took Jane's hand.

"He has never spoken to me that way before," Jane said, almost to herself.

"He's working very hard," consoled Georgie. "He's not himself."

"I wonder if we have any laudanum in the house," Jane joked bitterly. "That would show him."

"Don't say that!" gasped Georgie in horror. "Don't even think it!"

"Let's not talk of it," said Jane. "When May has her nap, let's have a picnic in the orchard."

That evening Morris was remorseful.

"I should not have spoken to you that way," he said. "Forgive me."

Jane knew that she, too, should apologize for her snappishness, but she found she could not.

"I'm not feeling well," she managed to say, by way of explanation. Morris was immediately solicitous.

"Is it a cold? Is it your head?"

"My back aches," she said. Morris found a pillow to put behind her. He had the cook make a hot compress scented with lavender. He brought a blanket for her feet, and a cup of tea with lemon and two sugars. He offered to call the doctor; he offered to carry her to her bedroom. It made Jane sorry she had said anything.

Jane and Morris were eating a silent breakfast in the dining room. She was considering visiting Georgie and wondering whether a molded jelly would travel safely on the train when a telegram arrived from Burne-Jones. Morris scanned it quickly, then stood up so violently he knocked over his chair.

"What is it?" asked Jane in fright. Morris thrust the telegram at Jane.

Georgie scarlet fever, it said. *House quarantined.*

All at once Jane's problems shrank to unimportance. All she could think was that Georgie might die.

"I must go to her," she said, rising from the table. Morris held her wrist.

"You know you can't," he said. "That's what a quarantine is. You can't risk infecting yourself, or Jenny and May."

Jane sat back down in her chair and put her head on the table.

The courier was waiting for the telegram's reply. Morris began to pace the room as he tried to think of ways they could help. "Perhaps they need money. Perhaps I could send Dr. Briggs over there."

It was agony, waiting to hear what would happen. Jane was sure that Georgie would die. She had never had real friends before she knew Lizzie and Georgie, and she had already lost one; of course she would lose the other now. She tried to pray, but it seemed hopeless. Morris did pray, every morning, on his hands and knees, despite the fact that he no longer believed in God. They went through their daily tasks in a fog.

Georgie was still dangerously ill when her son Christopher was born. Weakened by his mother's illness, he lived only three weeks.

If I were Georgie, I would certainly give up now, thought Jane when she heard.

But Georgie lived. She was made of strong stuff and she had her boy Philip to raise. When it was finally safe for Jane to visit her, she brought small, thin-skinned russets and dark red grapes, and the last dahlias from her garden.

"These must have been so expensive," said Georgie, scooping the seeds from a grape with a small spoon. "You should not have spent so much, not for me." Her hands were so shaky Jane was worried none of the fruit would make it to her mouth. But Georgie would not let Jane help her.

"You need to eat good things to get strong again," said Jane.

"I'm sorry to have worried you so much," said Georgie. "But you see, I am well."

Jane thought that Georgie, with her wasted frame and pinched, peaked face looked far from well, but she only smiled and said she planned to spoil her friend as much as she could. To herself she thought that she must bring pears, and filberts, and the very best dates from Persia.

"The doctor's bills were much more than we could afford," confessed Georgie. "And of course the funeral cost money. I don't know what we shall do."

"William will help," said Jane. Georgie looked alarmed.

"You mustn't tell him! Edward will be angry with me if he finds out I've told you. He is determined that we shouldn't appeal to our friends. He is very stern on that point."

"Can I do anything?" said Jane.

"Just sit with me," said Georgie plaintively. "And tell me about the doings at Red House. It seems ages since I was there."

"William has had rheumatic fever, you know," said Jane.

"Yes, Ned told me, how selfish of me not to ask after him!"

"He is better," said Jane. "But he is a terrible patient, always trying to go down to his office and refusing all attentions." The truth was that with Morris ill, without Georgie and Ned, without Lizzie and Rossetti, Red House was rather dismal. But Jane comforted herself with the fact that it would not be long before her friend lived at Red House with her.

When a letter came for Morris from Burne-Jones, Jane thought nothing of it. The two men were in constant contact. So when she heard her husband crying behind the door of his study, she could not imagine what it could be. All she could think was that someone had died. Had Georgie taken a sudden turn?

The tears were still on his face when Morris came into the sitting room to tell her that the Burne-Joneses had sadly decided that they could not move to Red House after all. They could no longer afford to pay Morris what he needed to keep the place going.

"Perhaps in another year, when they've recovered, they will come," said Jane, who was deeply disappointed but felt that Morris's tears were excessive. It's the fever, it makes him weepy, she thought to herself.

"You don't understand, my dear," said Morris. "We have to leave Red House."

Jane fell into the window seat heavily, and Morris rushed to her to make sure she had not hurt herself. She brushed him away. She could not believe it. Red House was the first place, the only place, she'd ever lived that she truly loved.

"Is there no way?" she cried. She had not meant to blame him but Morris looked stricken.

"It's my fault," he said. "I miscalculated how long it would take the Firm to turn a profit. And, as you know, the copper mines have been steadily decreasing in productivity. Every year the income is less. Fairly soon we won't receive any income at all, and by that time the Firm had better be on its feet."

Jane reflected that, if anything, Morris loved the place more than she did, and that if there were a way to save it, he would have thought of it.

"Where will we go?" she asked bitterly. "Somewhere nearby? That cottage on Finch Street in the village?"

"No," said Morris adamantly. "If we have to leave Red House, I don't want to live anywhere near it. I don't want to pass it on my daily walk. I don't want to see how the new owners destroy it or have to speak politely to them."

"Where then?" asked Jane, feeling helpless.

"London," said Morris. "We can live over the shop," he said with a hard laugh. "It will be better; I can keep a closer eye on things there."

"London," repeated Jane bleakly. "Over the shop."

"Don't reproach me, Jane, I can't bear it," he said, and fell into her lap. It seemed to Jane that the men in her life were desperate for her good opinion but did very little to secure it.

Jane oversaw the packing with a heavy heart. She tried to console herself with the thought that she would have friends close by. Better that they had come to Red House, but what mattered was that they would be together. They could play tag in anyone's house. They could drink wine and play charades anywhere. With a shiver she remembered the night Rossetti had kissed her.

Morris stayed in London as much as possible. He could not bear to see things in boxes or being driven away. Jane wanted to console her husband, but the truth was, she did blame him. How had he managed things so poorly?

Their new house was not as nice as Red House, of course. It was not even as nice as the place they had lived when they were first married. She had enjoyed London then, but she had not been encumbered with two children, a very small kitchen, and a husband who worked constantly. She had forgotten how sooty everything was, how hard it was to keep things clean. She had forgotten that London gave her a cough and made her back ache even more. Jane knew that Red House had spoiled her, and she told herself that things would improve. After all, she had not lost a child. And Morris was sure he could make his business a success. Sometimes, though, she wondered what would become of her.

Five years into her marriage she was married to a tradesman who kept a shop, a man who scarcely looked at her, though he had once been entranced by her beauty. She examined her face carefully in the mirror, but she did not think her looks had gone. At least, they were much the same as they had been.

Eighteen

*J*ANE was sitting in the garden of Rossetti's new house, petting the lemur he had just acquired. It was a twitchy, active thing and kept squirming out of her hands. Rossetti was stage-directing as his friend John Robert Parsons attempted to photograph her holding it, but every time he found the right light and the right pose, the lemur would escape into the trees and have to be coaxed down with apple slices.

"What about the wombat?" said Jane. "Would he make a better portrait subject?"

"Top?" asked Rossetti, who was perched on the lowest limb of the tree in case the lemur wriggled free again. "He is heroically good-natured, but about the least romantic-looking creature I've ever seen. Like his namesake."

"Perhaps one of the parrots," mumbled Parsons from underneath the camera curtain.

"I don't like birds," said Jane. "They're so dirty."

"Not my red-tailed Polynesian parrot!" exclaimed Rossetti. "I assure you he is as well-groomed as any dandy in London."

It was wonderful to see Rossetti smile, and joke, and climb trees, and take photographs. For nearly two years he had been a virtual recluse. Even Morris had to admit that his grief and depression were genuine. He had found that he could not stay at the flat where he and Lizzie had lived. She haunted him there, he said. For several months he had stayed with his family and then, with a loan from Ruskin, he had taken the house at 16 Cheyne Walk, with a view of the Thames. Several boats were moored in the river just below, and across the way was a green glimpse of Battersea Park.

The house itself was spacious, a welcome contrast to Jane's own cramped abode, and though other houses crowded close on either side, the back garden was expansive and filled with plane trees, and the fence that separated it from the others was covered with climbing roses. Rossetti called it Tudor House.

Early on he seldom left Tudor House and received very few visitors. For months he could not paint, and when he began again, the only thing he was interested in was an apotheosis of Lizzie entitled *Beata Beatrix*. Jane was not sure if this canonization of Lizzie was morbid or not. He worked on the painting relentlessly, drawing and painting many versions of it to the exclusion of anything else. In his mind Lizzie became conflated with Dante's Beatrice, and he developed a fervent belief that Lizzie had been a saint.

When Jane visited they talked about Lizzie. She seldom discussed her own isolation and loneliness. She felt that by comparison she had nothing to complain about, and Rossetti was too preoccupied to ask her about herself.

Then one day Rossetti wrote to Jane and asked if she would like to come to his house to be photographed.

If I had my wish, he wrote, *you would always be nearby so that I could always look at you, but as that is impossible, I hope that the photographs will serve as memory aids to me when I wish to paint you and you're far away.*

Despite herself, Jane was flattered. It had been so long since her husband had wanted just to look at her. Even when they were in the same room now, he barely seemed to see her. She missed being someone's muse.

She did not inform her husband of her plans, telling herself that he would not care anyway. Jenny and May could spend the afternoon with their nanny.

So there she was, in the lavender silk dress Rossetti had specifically requested. Laid out on the table were various shawls and sashes and parasols to be used as props. Rossetti had contributed a large black silk umbrella to block or direct the light, and of course his menagerie. Hanging up inside were two other dresses that she had brought just in case, one the color of the chalk cliffs at Dover, the other a watery green.

When she had asked him what she should bring, he had given her a list and then said, "Most of all, my dear, you should bring yourself, with all of your movements and gestures, all of your expressions and moods, all of your thoughts and ideas, for that, after all, is what will make the photographs stunning, and not any of the props."

Jane colored a little as he said it, and hoped that he did not notice.

Though she had had her photograph taken several times before, Jane was rather excited about it, even though the lemur had muddied her skirt and scratched her hand.

"When will I be able to see what you've done?" she asked the photographer, as Rossetti stood behind him to see what he was composing.

"The plates have to be developed while they are still wet," Parsons answered. "You'll see them this afternoon."

"I don't think I can wait that long," said Rossetti. "In fact," he said, leaping down and heading toward the house, "perhaps I can sketch each one as you're making it. That will give me something to do until they are ready."

The photographs had turned out well; at least Rossetti thought so. Jane was alarmed to see how very dark and thick her eyebrows looked; they almost touched in the center. She thought her nose looked very large and her forehead did look uncommonly low, but Rossetti assured her that they were perfect.

Several days later Jane went with her husband to a party at John Everett Millais's. She wore a new dress with some trepidation. She knew that there would be at least one reporter at the party to make notes on "Mrs. Morris's latest bed coat" and that—no matter how lovely her attire—a caricature of her, looking stooped and witch-like, would appear in the papers in the morning.

Her gown was lovely. It was of pumpkin-colored velvet with trailing devoré sleeves and a wide belt of peacock blue satin. She hoped that she had stayed one step ahead of her imitators and that there would be no one else at the party in a similar dress.

When Jane walked through the door of Millais's London town house and removed her coat, she was aware of many eyes upon her, judging her. They made note of the foulard print of her Indian shawl, and its colors of saffron, gold, and peach. Some ladies tittered when they saw her sleeves, but Jane was used to it by now and could sweep past without much embarrassment or self-consciousness.

At parties many people asked to be introduced to Jane. It was not so acute as it had been when she first arrived in London, but there were still plenty of curiosity seekers: writers from America, painters from France, soldiers' wives who had been in India and were just returning home. They all wanted to meet her. At first, worried that she would be a disappointment to them, she had tried to be a good conversationalist, to ask them about their country or their travels or their work, but she soon found that the less she said, the more they liked her. So after a time she gave up trying to charm anyone, and sat laconically while they gazed at her. It was somewhat tedious, but she was used to it.

Tonight it was an English explorer who had been in Papua, New Guinea.

"You compare very favorably to the native women," he said. "They are not very tall there, but they have coarse hair, like yours. Their skin is somewhat darker, and not quite so sallow."

"How interesting," she said.

"Of course, being heathens, they wear only skins, which they have treated and worked to the thinnest, softest leather imaginable. And feathers. They wear the most vibrant, colorful feathers, from birds no white man has even seen." The explorer gazed at her, shining-eyed, as if he were imagining her in such an outfit.

"I hear it is very hot there," said Jane. "I imagine they would not be comfortable in a velvet gown such as mine."

At this moment Rossetti thankfully appeared before her with a plate of strawberries.

"If you will excuse me, sir," said Rossetti. "We must not allow the lady to become hungry and faint."

"Of course," said the explorer, and stood up to find his friend the cartographer and tell him of his conversation with the curious dark lady.

Rossetti sat down beside Jane.

"Enjoying yourself?" he inquired.

"I feel like a bearded lady," said Jane. "That man will probably write pages in his journal tonight about my low forehead and the odd cast of my skin, as if I were a Hottentot to be studied."

"There, there," said Rossetti. "Have a berry." He picked one up by the stem and solemnly shook the cream from it; Jane did not like cream. When it was bare and red, he held it to her lips. Obediently Jane opened her mouth and took in the sweet fruit. "You know you are the most beautiful woman that silly man is likely to ever meet," he said, sounding serious suddenly. "No wonder he said foolish things to you. His mind switched off at the sight of you."

"I think he wants to have me stuffed and put in the British Museum. Or perhaps he'll take my pelt back to Borneo and show it to my kinswomen there," said Jane.

"How dull it would be if the room were full of English roses, with no Dark Lady in sight," said Rossetti.

"I sometimes wish I were as blond as Fanny Cornforth," Jane sighed.

"Perish the thought!" Rossetti cried. "The explorer has bewitched you. He must be punished. We shall write about him in *our* journals tonight." The man was still in their line of sight, chattering away to poor Georgie. "I will say that with that high color, he almost certainly drinks. And might there be a touch of madness in him, from spending too much time with the native women to whom you compare so favorably?"

To even hint at syphilis was shocking and enlivening. Jane already felt better. "I will say that he lacks imagination," she said.

"The cruelest cut of all," said Rossetti. He held up another berry and again she parted her lips and took it in.

"What are you two whispering about over here in the corner?" said Georgie, approaching them, "and may I join in? I've just had the most horrid conversation with that red-faced man about"— she sucked in her breath as she attempted to say the words— "female nudity! Can you imagine?"

Rossetti and Jane looked at each other and then burst into gales of laughter.

"We've been casting hoodoo curses on him," said Jane, making a place for Georgie next to her. On her other side, Rossetti held up another strawberry, cupping his hand underneath it to catch its juice, and she took it into her mouth.

Georgie fidgeted uncomfortably. "Did he say something rude to you, Jane?" she asked.

"You have spilled cream on your velvet, you messy girl," said Rossetti, pulling out his handkerchief. He pretended to dab the shoulder of Jane's dress, but she knew it was just an excuse to touch her. She tried not to gasp with pleasure and desire.

"I'll just go find Ned," Georgie said, standing up quickly, her eyes resolutely fastened to the crowd in front of her and not the couple beside her.

"Tell him we're forming a Hottentot Society," called Rossetti as Georgie hurried away. "Ask him if he wants to join us!"

Jane knew she was behaving outrageously, and for a moment she flushed with shame. She knew she was allowing Rossetti to lure her into a compromising position, but she couldn't help herself.

"Is something wrong?" asked Rossetti, concerned. "Are you not enjoying the party?"

The truth was, Jane had never had so much fun in all her life, and like an addict, having tasted her poison she could not give it up now. She reached over and touched Rossetti's shoulder and felt him shudder under her hand.

"I am perfectly happy," she said.

When Morris came to collect her, the bowl of strawberries contained only pale pink, seed-flecked cream and Rossetti was stroking Jane's wrist under the guise of arranging her hands in a pose.

She was nervous on the carriage ride home, waiting for Morris to say something, to chastise her for her behavior.

"Did you have a good time?" he asked. He was looking out the window of the carriage, so she could not see his face, and his tone was neutral.

"Yes, it was a very nice party," said Jane.

"I thought you must be very bored, to sit in the corner with Rossetti all evening," he said.

"I was just trying to avoid the explorer," she said quickly.

"I was thinking about the font for the text in the All Saints window," said Morris. "I copied it from the book of hours in the Bodleian, the one I told you about. But now I think it may be too rounded, too feminine. I think something more square and unabashedly Gothic is needed. I wonder if they have anything else that would be useful there. I may have to go to Oxford on Monday. Or maybe I'll call at the British Museum." He spoke to her but Jane knew it did not matter to him whether she was there or not. It did not matter whether or not she replied. He had not even noticed Rossetti stroking her wrist. She should have been relieved but instead was furious. Morris obviously paid no attention to her at all.

The next week she went to Rossetti's to sit for him. She wore a new dress of aubergine wool. Her belt was a thick piece of geranium pink dupioni silk with an orange chrysanthemum pinned to it. One glance in the mirror as she left the house told her that if she had lost her looks, they had returned. Her eyes were clear and bright and her skin had a golden sheen.

Rossetti greeted her at the door in his dressing gown and carpet slippers, something no other man would have dared to do. He seemed not to be the least bit self-conscious.

"My dear!" he said, taking both of her hands. "That is a wonder of a dress. The colors are magnificent on you."

Jane smiled. She had been nervous about seeing him again after the party, but she realized she needn't have worried. Being with Rossetti always put Jane at ease. "I'm glad you like it," she said.

"Like it!" he said. "I adore it." He led her by the hand through the sitting room. "Let's have tea in the garden. I must tell you about the séance I attended Wednesday night."

The table was laid with a Syrian printed cotton cloth and blue Chinese porcelain vases filled with pink peonies. There was hardly room enough for the faience cups and plates and the silver trays of scones and sandwiches.

"You must try the plum jam," Rossetti said. "Someone or another's mother made it. Swinburne, I think. It's very tasty." He handed her the scallop-edged, gold-painted bowl and Jane thought, not for the first time, that Rossetti had exquisite, almost feminine taste. Morris would have smashed such a piece within minutes.

"How was your husband after the party?" he asked lightly. Though his tone was unconcerned, Jane knew he was asking if Morris had noticed anything.

"Preoccupied," she said. "Something about fonts." Jane did not particularly want to talk about her husband, though she preferred the topic to hearing about the séance. Rossetti was sure to bring up Lizzie, and Jane did not want hear about her.

"Baptismal?" asked Rossetti teasingly. He cut a piece of apricot tart and put it on a plate for her. "I thought your husband had lost his faith."

"Typographical," she said.

"Ah," said Rossetti. "He has replaced his faith in God with his faith in script, has he?"

"Copperplate Gothic," said Jane. "That's his religion now. That and Bookman and Caslon old face and Garamond."

"Does he believe it is wise to bore his lovely young wife with such esoterica?"

"He doesn't care," said Jane flatly. "If someone were to spirit me away, I doubt he'd even notice."

Rossetti smiled—Jane could not guess the meaning of the smile—and then returned to the subject of the séance.

"I know what you think of these things, but I really think you would have changed your mind if you had been there. I truly felt Lizzie's presence."

Jane surrendered reluctantly to the tale.

"It was held at Mrs. Gorham's. Frightful house, stuffy and close, all lace curtains and smelling of rose petals and orange peel. The old lady still in weeds for her daughter who died six years ago."

"In childbirth," recalled Jane.

"Yes. But she was very cordial. Meredith went with me; he's a complete skeptic, found it hard to keep a straight face, at least at first. We all gathered in the dining room; there were five or six others there; I didn't know them. A Mr. and Mrs. Paul, young couple whose son drowned, two silly young ladies who seemed to be there for the thrill of it, and an old fellow wanting to speak with his wife. And the medium, of course. Not so much of a crone as you would expect. Middle-aged, no nonsense, more like a governess than a mystic. She had us hold hands and close our eyes."

"And did the spirits come?" asked Jane wryly.

Rossetti ignored her tone.

"Not at first. She had Mrs. Gorham put out the lamps and open the windows. It was a chilly night and quite uncomfortable. Then she had us all concentrate our minds on the person we wanted to communicate with. After a bit there was a series of raps on the table, which the medium interpreted. The first visitor was the little drowned boy. Mrs. Paul fainted when the medium told her that little Robert was safe and well in heaven. Mr. Paul had to carry her out. That distracted us all for a few minutes."

"And then did Lizzie come next?"

"No, one of the silly girls had a brother who died in the Crimea and he came next. Then Lydia Fitzwilliam, Mrs. Gorham's daughter. Then Lizzie. The taps were a little different with each one. Lizzie's were quite peremptory."

"What did she say?" asked Jane.

"Just that she was happy, that she was in heaven, that she hoped I would forgive her and myself and be happy again."

Jane did not think that sounded much like Lizzie, but she did not say so.

"And you say you felt her?"

"It was the strangest sensation. I felt something lightly touch my shoulder, and then it was if she passed through me. I'm not ashamed to say I cried like a baby."

"And the others?"

"The brother said not to worry, that he hadn't been in much pain when he was shot, and Lydia Fitzwilliam said the baby was with her in heaven and was the most darling baby anyone could want."

"So they all appeared," said Jane.

"Not the old fellow's wife," said Rossetti. "The window opened and shut of its own accord, and the medium said that she was try-ing to speak. She expressed great hope that the next time Molly would talk."

Thereby necessitating another séance, thought Jane. "Will you go again?" she asked.

"I think I'll have one here," he mused. "I imagine her presence would be even stronger in a place filled with things she loved."

"Perhaps I'll come," said Jane, thinking that if it gave Rossetti comfort, it did not much matter if the medium was a fraud or not.

The lemur dropped onto the table from the tree above and snatched the scone off Rossetti's plate.

"I'm thinking of getting an elephant," he said gaily. "I shall teach it to wash windows and when people pass by and see the elephant, they will ask, 'Who lives in that house?' and when they find out it is Rossetti, the painter, they will say, 'I should like to buy one of that man's pictures.'"

"Won't it be expensive?" said Jane. "And how will it fit in the garden?"

"It will be a very small elephant," said Rossetti. "They have a pygmy variety in Africa that a friend of mine is going to bring back for me. Hardly bigger than a draft horse. There will be plenty of room."

Jane smiled at the ridiculous image of Rossetti riding around his garden on a horse-size elephant. "Will you paint me on it?" she asked.

"Most certainly," he said. "Though my next painting of you is to be *La Pia de Tolomei*, from Dante."

"The pious wife?" asked Jane.

"Imprisoned by her cruel husband," added Rossetti signifi-cantly. "You must come and sit every day. The photographs aren't enough. I need you here."

Nineteen

'VE noticed you seem preoccupied lately," said Morris one evening during a typically quiet supper. "Is something wrong?"

Jane could not believe what she was hearing. After all this time it had occurred to him to notice her mood. "I seem preoccupied?" she sputtered. "Preoccupied is hardly the word for it."

Morris seemed surprised by the anger in her voice. "Distant, then. As if your mind is far away."

"That's very funny, coming from you. The only time you even glance in my direction is when the children are with me."

"I've been working very hard," Morris said reproachfully. "You know how important it is that the business become a success. I don't do it for my own pleasure, you know. It's for you and Jenny and May, your security, your future."

"You know that's a lie," hissed Jane. "You do love the work, the drawing and the dyeing and the glass blowing. You love it much more than you have ever loved me." She knew she was being petulant but she couldn't help herself.

"I'm sorry you feel that way," said Morris stiffly. "I will try to do better."

Jane realized that she didn't want to reconcile with Morris. She didn't want him to pledge to do better, to try harder. She wanted to be the wronged wife and to feel sorry for herself and feel justified in her grievances.

"You should never have married him," Rossetti said when she confided in him. "But he had the audacity to think that a grace could become his wife. You were meant to serve as man's inspiration, not fetch his dinner."

Rossetti was sketching Jane as La Pia and she was looking down at the floor, her head tilted in an uncomfortable way. He didn't see her eyes narrow with irritation.

"That's all very well," she said, "but I couldn't serve as an inspiration if I was working as a chambermaid, now could I?"

"I would never have allowed that to happen," said Rossetti, gallantly and falsely. They seldom alluded to their meeting or the weeks that followed, and it seemed Rossetti had almost come to believe that it was he and not Morris who had rescued her. "You were always meant to shine on the great stage of life. Already yours is the most famous face in London, and I will make it the most famous face in the world."

"I owe him a great debt," said Jane, feeling a twinge of remorse.

"And haven't you repaid it a thousand times over?" said Rossetti. "You have borne his children and kept his house and listened to his endless monologues. You have been a pattern wife in every way. It's time for you to think of yourself."

"Perhaps," said Jane, uncomfortably. She didn't know whether Rossetti was speaking generally or referring to something specific. After the admission he had made following Lizzie's death, she was careful not to expect too much from him.

"This composition is gorgeous," said Rossetti, stepping back from his paper and eyeing it with satisfaction. "The curve of your jaw, the length of your neck . . . but in the full-scale painting you should wear a smock, like an altar boy. Silver white silk, with a purple sash. Can you sew something like that?"

"I know just what fabric to use," Jane said. "I'll bring it with me the next time I come."

When the drawing was finished, Jane thought it was the best

likeness of her that anyone had ever made. He had captured the pain in her eyes, the melancholy that enveloped her. Though it was only siena and umber chalks on paper, it was the most herself she had ever looked.

When Jane arrived for the painting's third sitting, she found Rossetti in a black mood. He was silent through tea and she was afraid he might be angry with her. When they were finished, she put on the smock and sat as she had for the drawing of La Pia, head tilted, hands folded together. She was careful to weave her fingers exactly as they had been the day before. They worked in silence for some time, until finally Jane couldn't stand it any longer.

"Gabriel, what's wrong?" she asked.

Rossetti scowled. "Ruskin's been hounding me," he said. "He says my work has become monotonous."

Jane's heart plummeted. "Is it me?" she asked.

"I told him that you are all that I am interested in painting, and that you have as many shades and moods and expressions as a thousand women, but he said it was bad for me to focus so exclusively on one person."

"Perhaps he's right," said Jane reluctantly. "You must think of your patrons, and your livelihood."

"Livelihood be damned!" said Rossetti, throwing down his pencil. "Don't you know that you are the only thing that matters to me in the world?"

Jane broke her pose and looked at him. His expression told her that the moment had come.

"You've never painted better," she said, in case she was mistaken.

He came and kneeled beside her. "I'm not talking of painting," he said, disentangling her hands and holding her right one to his heart. "And you know I'm not. I can only hope that you feel the same."

"You know that I do," breathed Jane. Their lips met, and any doubts Jane had about Rossetti's feelings or her own fled completely. They had to be together. There was nothing else to be done. She clutched at his coat as if she were drowning.

"I've imagined this moment so many times," he murmured into her hair. "Even before Lizzie died; I knew it was wrong but I couldn't help it."

He kissed her slowly and deliberately, lingering over each part of her. He kissed her eyelids, her nose, her neck. He unfastened her smock and pulled it over her head. He unpinned her amethyst brooch and pulled her linen collar free.

Jane had imagined herself back with Rossetti on the scaffolding of the Oxford Union so many times it had come to seem like a dream, or an especially lovely story whispered late one night at Red House. Now he was there, real and warm, and it was the last nine years that were the dream, and being with Rossetti was her life. She forgot that she had had two babies and that perhaps her body was not what it had been. She forgot the unsatisfying gropings of her husband. She forgot everything but Rossetti.

While he kissed her he fumbled with the buttons on the back of her dress until Jane couldn't wait any longer. She ripped the dress open and threw it aside. Her shoes, stockings, chemise, and crinoline were gone in seconds. Then she began to strip Rossetti. She surprised both of them with her ardor.

Rossetti was suddenly uncertain. "Should we . . . someone might come in?"

"Everyone knows not to disturb you here," said Jane.

When they were undressed, their bodies tightly bound by heat and sweat and years of waiting, neither of them could speak, but only move. He teased her, flicking her breasts with his tongue, running his hands over her body, breathing in her ear. When he finally entered her, the sensation was of lightning striking her down and she was overcome.

When they were finished they lay stunned and panting on the cool silk carpet. Jane thought that she should be ashamed, ashamed to have broken her marriage vows, ashamed to have experienced so much pleasure, to have lost control. But she found that she was not.

Jane turned to look at Rossetti and found that he was crying.

"This is the most wonderful moment of my life," he said.

Twenty

ANE was afraid to go home. She thought it must show on her face, in her walk. She could hardly bear to sit at the dining room table with her husband.

"You and Rossetti are awfully chummy lately," he remarked. "You sat for him again today?"

"What's that supposed to mean?" she said, immediately on her guard.

"Nothing at all," he said mildly. "Just an observation of fact."

"He is quite lonely," Jane said. "His other friends are too busy to visit."

Morris did not seem to notice the jibe.

"Does he do any work, or does he only make sketches of you?" he inquired.

"You don't think that my sitting for him constitutes work?" bristled Jane. "You think it's frivolous and pointless?"

"I didn't say that," Morris protested. "I only wondered if he was doing any new history paintings."

"He is more interested in portraiture right now," she said. "Allegorical portraits."

"Of you," said Morris.

"Yes," said Jane. "Do you think I am not worthy of such attention, that my image is a waste of a great artist's time?"

"Don't be silly," said Morris. "I'd like to see these paintings sometime. Perhaps I'll go with you the next time. But now we must go over the menu for the dinner next Thursday. I thought we could order a goose."

The guests were due to arrive any minute and Jane had a terrible toothache. She suspected it was because Rossetti was to come to her house, and sit across the table from Morris, making a mockery of her unsuspecting husband. She had never felt sick with guilt before. This is how Rossetti felt when Lizzie died, she thought to herself. No wonder he drank himself to sleep.

Jane lay on the sofa with a warm compress on her face. She did not get up to greet the guests as they arrived, and she did not try to take part in the conversation swirling around her. She resolved that when Rossetti arrived, she would be reserved with him. After Millais's party Jane feared that Georgie suspected something; she had to make sure that her behavior was above reproach.

Unfortunately Rossetti had made no such vow. When he saw her reclining on the sofa, he rushed to her in dismay.

"Mrs. Morris, are you ill?" he cried.

She tried to calm him. "It's nothing," she said, glancing around nervously. "A toothache."

The other guests looked surprised by Rossetti's disproportionate alarm, but Jane realized they would attribute it to emotions triggered by memories of his wife. She reflected that he must have played this part with Lizzie many times.

"May I bring you anything? Can I help in any way?"

Jane shook her head. "I just need rest, and quiet."

"I am at your service," Rossetti said as he moved away.

Morris was late arriving from the workshop and Faulkner, as usual, contrived to play a joke on his host. When Morris entered the drawing room, a large volume fell from the door top onto his head.

"Are you trying to tell me something?" Morris asked as he picked the volume up from the floor and checked to make sure none of the pages was torn or bent. "Do you think I need a knock on the head?"

"You said it, not us," said Faulkner.

"Thackeray," observed Morris. "Always hated him. Such a mincing, simpering way of writing." He walked across the room to replace the volume on the shelf.

"I quite liked *Pendennis*," said Jane.

Morris glanced over at his wife.

"Not feeling well?" he asked carelessly. "I'm sorry to hear it. Now, then, who would like to hear an excerpt from a marvelous poem after dinner?"

Burne-Jones pretended to fall asleep.

"I assure you it's very thrilling," said Morris.

"Did you get my order yesterday?" asked Rossetti with a grin. "The one for thirteen bugles and a two-ton head of cheese?"

"So it was you," said Morris. "I suspected as much. Of course the whole thing was illegible, so there was no way to tell who it was from, not even to contact them and ask them what in the world it said."

"Exactly," said Rossetti. "Did you tear your hair out when you saw it?"

"Well, not entirely, since I still have some, as you see. But I did throw a vase or two."

"None of mine, I hope," said Burne-Jones.

"No, I believe they were Webb's," joked Morris.

Webb picked up the decanter and pretended to hurl it at Morris.

"Now we must be quiet and good," said Rossetti. "We have a sick lady present."

Jane sat languidly across from her husband at dinner, listening as he told the others about the antics of a ridiculous prelate who was a client. Occasionally she went into the kitchen to check on things, or brought a fresh dish of nuts or a plate of cheese, but the evening seemed empty, colorless. Rossetti did not approach her, which was what she wanted, she told herself. It would not do to make a spectacle of themselves, in her house, in Morris's house. But she felt left out and ignored. Now I have two men to neglect me, she thought petulantly.

After dinner Morris read from his poem, "The Life and Death of Jason":

And now behold within the haven rides
Our good ship, swinging in the changing tides,
Gleaming with gold, and blue, and cinnabar,
The long new oars beside the rowlocks are,
The sail hangs flapping in the light west wind,
Nor aught undone can any craftsman find
From stem to stern; so is our quest begun
To-morrow at the rising of the sun.
And may Jove bring us all safe back to see
Another sun shine on this fair city,
When elders and the flower-crowned maidens meet
With tears and singing our returning feet.

Their longing eyes beheld a lovely land,
Green meadows rising o'er a yellow strand,
Well-set with fair fruit-bearing trees, and groves
Of thick-leaved elms all populous of doves,
And watered by a wandering clear green stream
And through the trees they saw a palace gleam
Of polished marble, fair beyond man's thought.
There as they lay, the sweetest scents were brought
By sighing winds across the bitter sea,
And languid music breathed melodiously,

Steeping their souls in such unmixed delight,
That all their hearts grew soft, and dim of sight
They grew, and scarce their hands could grip the oar,
And as they slowly neared the happy shore
The young men well-nigh wept, and e'en the wise
Thought they had reached the gate of Paradise.

Morris swayed a little as he read; his voice was strong and loud and he unconsciously flourished his hand at the parts he thought were the best. He is so happy, thought Jane, watching him. When he had finished, there was enthusiastic applause.

"It's so sad," observed Jane. "For of course they were mistaken."

" 'Gleaming with gold, and blue, and cinnabar,'" quoted Georgie. "That is my favorite line. How do you think of these things?"

Morris blushed with pleasure. "Not easily," he said. "Through much toil and trouble."

"I've recently finished a poem," announced Rossetti. "Would you like to hear it?"

"Yes, of course," said Morris, surprised. "I didn't know you were writing again."

"The muse has returned," said Rossetti. He leaned against the mantel, gazed directly at Jane, and began:

O Lord of all compassionate control,
O Love! let this my Lady's picture glow
Under my hand to praise her name, and show
Even of her inner self the perfect whole:
That he who seeks her beauty's furthest goal,
Beyond the light that the sweet glances throw
And refluent wave of the sweet smile, may know
The very sky and sea-line of her soul.

Lo! it is done. Above the long lithe throat
The mouth's mould testifies of voice and kiss,
The shadowed eyes remember and foresee.
Her face is made her shrine. Let all men note
That in all years (O Love, thy gift is this!)
They that would look on her must come to me.

Jane thought she might die of mortification right there in her own living room. She could not believe how reckless Rossetti was being. She tried very hard not to let anyone see how she was affected by the poem, but she knew the color was in her face and that she was trembling.

It was a vague poem, she told herself. It could have been about Lizzie, or about Fanny Cornforth. The poem could have been about portraiture in general, or about the act of painting. But it was not, and Jane knew it.

Everyone was very complimentary of Rossetti's poem, too.

"That's the kind of poem I like," said Webb. "Short and full of feeling."

"Rossetti is in love again," teased Burne-Jones. "Is it the elephant who has inspired these lines?" Elephant was Rossetti's pet name for Fanny.

"A gentleman never reveals the name of his muse," said Rossetti.

Morris was staring at Rossetti as if he'd never seen him before.

"What did you think, Top?" asked Rossetti. "You're the eminent poet I have to live up to."

Morris shook himself from his stupor. "The rhythm is good," he said. "And the depth of emotion, of course, which is always your strong suit."

"Thank you," Rossetti bowed.

"If there are no more poems, I suggest music," said Morris abruptly. "Will you play, Georgie?"

"Of course. Come turn the pages for me."

Rossetti sat down in the chair opposite the sofa where Jane was reclining. "May I adjust your wrap, Mrs. Morris?" he said. "I fear your shoulders are cold."

Jane was vexed and pleased and worried and sorry and besotted all at the same time. She hardly knew what to do or say.

"Thank you," she said at last, "but I am very comfortable."

"I hope you liked my poem," he said.

"The lady in question is very fortunate," she said.

"It is I who am fortunate," he replied.

"Will you sing, Jane?" Georgie called to her.

"No thank you," Jane said. "I intend to retire early."

Twenty-one

THE Firm had been commissioned to create a dining room for the South Kensington Museum. Morris was very excited about it.

"Just think how many people will see our work there," he said. "This will mean more commissions, more attention, less worry. We must celebrate."

"Oh, William, I don't think I feel well enough," protested Jane.

"Nonsense," he said. "We're going to the Dorchester hotel for dinner."

Jane wore a jade green dress and several strands of gold, jade, and amber beads. She tried to ignore the twinge in her back and the pain in her head every time she looked at her husband's pink and beaming face. The crab-stuffed sole in white sauce and the new peas were not as delicious as they should have been.

"The onion tart is sublime," said Morris.

As she ate Jane concocted a story in which Morris died suddenly of apoplexy. After the suitable mourning period, she and Rossetti were quietly married at the Catholic church in Bexleyheath. With the money Morris left her, she purchased Red House from the people they had sold it to, and she and Rossetti took Jenny and May there to live. Rossetti was on a scaffolding, painting the ceiling of the bedroom with angels, while she lay faceup on the bed, eating cherries from a bowl and watching him.

Morris reached over and took her hand. Reflexively, she shook it off.

"Is my touch so repulsive to you?" He sounded annoyed that she was spoiling his pleasant evening. She had not planned to tell him so soon, or in this way. But suddenly she could wait no longer.

"William," she said, and stopped.

"Hmm?" said Morris, his knife shrieking across the plate as he cut his ham.

"I have something I must tell you," she said.

"What is it?" he asked, his eyes still on his plate.

"I no longer love you," she said. She did not know how to say it in a gentler way. And even if she could, Morris had an endless ability to ignore or discount the subtle ways in which she had let him know that she did not care for him anymore.

They sat in silence for several minutes. Morris sawed at a spot on the tablecloth with his knife; he appeared stunned.

"How long have you felt this way?" he finally asked. His voice sounded strange; the words came out slowly and calmly, quite unlike his usual quickly tumbling speech.

"Does it matter?" she asked. She had hoped, foolishly she now realized, that since Morris apparently had lost interest in her as well, he would take this news with some measure of calm.

"I know I've neglected you," he said. "The business has sucked all of the energy out of me for too long. But now things will be different. Now that we have this commission, success is more or less assured. I'll be able to spend more time at home. More time with you and with the kiddies."

"It's too late, William," she said sorrowfully. "It might have made a difference two years ago, but not now. I don't love you."

Now he looked at her, incredulously, his eyes full of pain. "You stopped loving me years ago, but you kept it to yourself until now? Why tell me, then? Why not let me go to my grave thinking I had a loving wife, a family?" With horror she saw that he might cry, but there were other people dining nearby and though his voice had become thick and hoarse, he managed to keep the tears in check.

"It seemed dishonorable to continue living a lie," she said.

"Have you fallen in love with someone else?" he asked sharply, catching Jane off guard. She had hoped to ease her conscience by disengaging herself from her husband, but she could not tell Morris about Rossetti. Not yet. In a few months, when they had accustomed themselves to the reality of their loveless marriage, then she would tell him. He would find someone else, too. But now she was frightened.

"This does not concern anyone else," she said, her heart pounding.

Morris seemed to accept this.

"Is there any way your feelings might return?" he begged. "If I change?"

"I don't mean to reproach you," she said, "but no, I don't believe they will."

"But there is a chance?" he said. He got up from his place and came to kneel before her. He took her hand, which she tried, successfully, not to draw away.

"If there is anything I can do to make you love me again, you have only to say it. For I love you more than anything and your happiness is my only concern."

"Get up, William." Jane felt guiltier than ever. "Don't make such a display." Other diners were frowning at their hands to avoid staring.

"I don't care," he said. "I will do anything."

At home he paused awkwardly in the doorway of their bedroom. For years now he had worked late in his study and come to bed when she had been asleep for hours, but now he hesitated.

"Would you like me to come to bed?" he asked.

"It doesn't matter," she said wearily.

"I'll just check on May," he said. "Then I'll come."

She submitted to his clumsy, desperate attentions that night because it seemed to be the only way to appease him. She felt no disgust, only pity. Afterward he tried not to let her see that he was weeping.

At breakfast Morris stared at her dolefully and it made Jane unable to eat.

"I think we should take a trip," he said as Jane aimlessly stirred her tea. "We've never been to Italy together."

"William," she said pityingly. After that he quickly finished his toast and went down to the shop.

At Ruskin's party the next night, by prior agreement Jane and Rossetti greeted each other cordially and formally, spoke to a few people, and met after an hour or so in the darkest corner of the drawing room. There they would lounge for the rest of the night.

"I've withdrawn from him," she whispered, clutching Rossetti's hand. "I've told him I don't love him."

Rossetti put her palm against his lips. "Thank you," he said. "But you didn't tell him? About us?"

"How could I?" she said. "If he didn't kill *me,* he might kill himself, or you. And it's not as if there has been any talk of separation."

"Not yet," said Rossetti. Jane's eyes were drawn, unbidden, to her husband. He was waving his arms about wildly as he talked to a small fair-haired man. The man's face was very pink and he was laughing at whatever Morris was saying.

"Who is that?" she asked.

"That's Eirikr Magnusson," said Rossetti. "A man of the cloth. From Iceland, I believe. He's come to England to supervise the printing of an Icelandic New Testament. He's also working on a Norse dictionary and a series of translations of Icelandic legends."

"William is obsessed with Icelandic legends," said Jane.

"I know," said Rossetti. "When he lived at Red Lion Square, he used to read them out loud in the evenings, and he invariably complained that there isn't a reliable English translation."

Georgie came and stood next to the sofa upon which Jane and Rossetti were lounging.

"Have you learned any good gossip out there, Georgie?" asked Rossetti merrily.

Georgie didn't smile. "Could I speak with you, Jane?" she said.

"Well, if you must go, try to find out something shocking to tell me when you get back," said Rossetti.

They left the drawing room. As they passed into the hall, Georgie turned and gripped her hand.

"Is it true?" Georgie hissed. All at once Jane felt faint and sick.

"Did he tell you?" she gasped, reaching for the wall to support her trembling legs.

"I received the most terrible letter," Georgie said. "Full of curses and self-recrimination and so much pain! I know that you would not deliberately be the cause of your dear husband's torment."

"If I've hurt him, I'm sorry," said Jane. "I don't know what else to do." She could not look at her friend. She gazed over Georgie's shoulder into the room they had just left. William was still gesticulating at the Icelander. Rossetti had joined a group that included Ruskin and a young woman with copper-colored hair. She wore it in an intricate style and Jane wondered whether the hair was entirely her own, or a fall. There was so much of it, and it curled so beautifully. Rossetti was staring at it as if he wanted to touch it, and it gave Jane a pang.

"You know, when we married, we took a sacred vow," Georgie began. She was not used to giving lectures and she instinctively fell back on the sermonizing she had grown up with. "We said that we would love, honor, and obey our husbands, and they promised to love, honor, and cherish us."

"I know," said Jane miserably. How could she explain it all to Georgie, who was faithful to Ned despite Maria Zambaco?

"I understand that sometimes marriage is difficult," Georgie rasped, the tears she was trying hard to suppress nearly choking her. "I wish you had come to me when you began to have doubts. Together we could have figured out how to help you."

"I don't think there is anything to be done," said Jane.

"Sometimes people turn our heads. They make us forget our duty and the things we hold most dear," said Georgie. "But if we gave in to temptation, we would be very sorry afterward that we had forgotten ourselves."

"I have not forgotten myself," said Jane heatedly. "Quite the opposite."

When Georgie left her to find Burne-Jones, Jane did not have the heart to return to Rossetti. But neither could she join her husband and the Icelandic minister. Instead she wandered about Ruskin's house, picking up seashells and fossils and examining portraits of his parents until she heard the other guests departing.

"I met the most interesting man," said Morris on the way home. "He is going to teach me Icelandic. We are to meet next Thursday afternoon."

"That's wonderful, William," said Jane. She was staring out the window of the carriage, trying not to cry.

"At last I will be able to learn all of the great stories," said Morris. "Perhaps we can translate them into English together."

"You can write some poems of your own, based on the stories," said Jane.

"My poor poetry isn't worthy of the stories," said Morris, taking her hand. "But I'm touched that you think so."

Jane's sobs now became audible but she told her husband it was the backache again.

It was very disconcerting to Jane, how hard Morris tried to win her love. He came home earlier from work. He attempted to engage her in conversation that interested her. He seldom droned on about the minutiae of his business now; he was more likely to ask her what she was reading, or what she thought of a new book of poems. He began refusing dessert at dinner. He trimmed the beard she disliked and bought a new suit of clothes. Jane did not have the heart to tell him that these gestures were hopeless.

One evening Morris hesitantly entered her sitting room. Jane was embroidering a design of heart's ease onto a dress for Jenny and did not look up.

"A nice pattern," he said, touching the starched pink cotton fabric.

"I was thinking of making one for May, in yellow, with green floss," Jane said.

"What about willow leaves?" he said. "Or fern. I can draw it up for you."

"Did you want something?" asked Jane.

"I have a surprise for you," Morris said eagerly. "I've commissioned Rossetti to paint your portrait."

Jane could not believe it. "Are you sure?" she asked. "It would mean even more time sitting."

"I figure if you are going to spend so much time modeling for him, I might as well get something out of it. And I want a portrait of my wife by the best painter in London. And as Millais is abroad . . ."

Jane smiled at his joke but did not think it very funny.

Rossetti grumbled about painting Jane for her husband instead of solely for himself. He had wanted to say no, but could not think of a legitimate excuse for doing so, and, as usual, he was short of cash.

"He wants to play Medici to my Michelangelo, does he?" he said to Jane at the first sitting. "He cannot tell me how to paint you, at least. It won't be one of those horribly tasteful portraits that fill the drawing rooms of London, where the lady is softly pretty, perhaps holding a spaniel in one hand and a fan in the other."

"It would be funny, though, if you did that," said Jane. "He's expecting a Rossetti and you give him something proper and horrible."

"You are a cruel woman, Jane," Rossetti said. He left the easel and came to sit beside her. "Do you really want to wear this dress?" He stroked the sleeve of the brown velvet gown.

"William asked me to," Jane said. "It is his favorite."

"I should have known!" exclaimed Rossetti. "You are drowning in it. It hides your light entirely. You must wear something else."

"What would you like?" asked Jane.

"I like the idea of blue," he said. "The Virgin Mary, the sky, the ocean . . . Something vivid. Peacock, with that iridescence."

"I don't have anything like that," said Jane. She knew that Rossetti, who paid close attention to dress, remembered her gowns perfectly.

"Then you'll have one made. I'm sure we can find the fabric I'm thinking of if we scour the shops."

She did not ask why she could not wear the dull dress and have him paint it blue. He wanted her to have an iridescent blue dress and so she would have one. Instead of sitting for her portrait, she and Rossetti left Tudor House and went to Oxford Street. There, in the third shop they visited, they found what they were looking for, a crisp blue silk with the sheen of a gem. Jane bought twelve yards of it.

She worked on the dress in every spare moment.

"It's very pretty, Mama," said Jenny one day, touching a corner of the material hesitantly.

"Do you like it, May?" asked Jane.

May nodded. "It's rustley," she said.

"Mr. Rossetti says I should wear it a few times at home before I come to sit for him, to take away the stiffness of it," said Jane.

The girls were excited to see it on her.

"Will you wear it to our tea party?" asked Jenny. "I think Flora would like to see it." Flora was Jenny's china doll.

"Of course, darling," said Jane. "When it's finished, we'll have a tea party."

Morris was disappointed that in the portrait she would not be wearing the dress he chose.

"It's my picture," he complained. "I paid for it, you should wear the dress I want."

"This is the palette he's working in right now," explained Jane. "Bright, oriental. There's a red curtain behind me and the contrast would not be so arresting without this shade of blue."

"Artists," muttered Morris. "So cantankerous and particular and obsessed."

"I don't know anyone else like that," said Jane.

"Yes, I suppose I am," admitted Morris ruefully. "If I could paint you, I would put you in the other dress. As I can't, I suppose I will just have to give in gracelessly."

"You do it very well," Jane said, smiling.

When it was finished the dress had a full, voluminous skirt and dropped shoulders in the dolman style Jane favored. It was ornamented with delicate gold thread at the throat and wrists.

"Mama's a princess," breathed May when Jane appeared in the nursery for the tea party, and Jenny and Flora agreed.

Twenty-two

ORRIS published the first volume of *The Earthly Paradise* in 1868. It was an immediate success. Even Rossetti had to admit that it was very good.

"I don't like sagas much," he said sulkily, brandishing a brush slick and wet with lapis. "I'm more for single poems, perhaps about a beautiful woman. But it's the best of its kind."

Jane thought sadly about the time in Oxford when Morris had brought her his poem, apprehensive and shy. And of the poems he'd written about her when they were first married, announcing his love and declaiming her beauty. He no longer read his poems to her. It was her own fault. She had taken her love from him; she could not expect him to share his poetry with her.

Rossetti was hard at work painting the folds of her dress. The underpainting was almost black, the next layer the color of the deep sea. Where the light reflected off the seam attaching the arm to the bodice and the sleeves he wove threads of hot, Caribbean blue.

"It's rather melancholy," said Jane.

"I'd be melancholy, too, if I were Topsy. Of course he does nothing about it, just composes mournful lines."

"But as you said, his poems are good."

"I can write good poems, too," Rossetti snapped. "I just happen to think that painting is more important."

Jane knew he was annoyed because Morris's book was receiving so much attention and selling so well. "So do I," she said soothingly.

"I'm very nearly finished with this," he said, stepping back from his canvas and squinting at it critically. "I could do more, but it would just be overpainting and it would get mucked up and ruined."

"I hate to give up these afternoons," said Jane. "They are the happiest moments of my days."

"Who said these afternoons should end when the portrait is finished?" Rossetti asked, wiping his hands carefully on a clean rag. "We must start in immediately on another. I was thinking Mariana, from *Measure for Measure.*" He came to where she was sitting and picked her up, chair and all.

"Gabriel," she shrieked. "What are you doing?"

"I am conveying you to the boudoir, my sweet," he said. "You see, I can use fine, poetical language if I want to."

Rossetti thought of Titian, Tintoretto, and Veronese while he was painting Jane's portrait, and in the finished product Jane's hair shone very brightly against the red curtain behind her, and her dress glowed like sunlight on water. At the bottom of the canvas he wrote: "Famous for her poet husband, and famous for her face, may my picture add to her fame."

"What a talented painter Rossetti is," said Morris when he saw it. He spoke apparently without jealousy. "He was right about the color of your dress. I like the vase of white roses against that dark background. But I don't like the pink carnations. The color is insipid. Why did he put carnations in anyway? Such an ugly flower."

"I like them," said Jane.

Rossetti had written a declaration of love into the painting, using the language of flowers. He knew that Morris thought it silly and would not know what any of the flowers meant. Jane, however, knew that the pink carnation in her belt, and on the book open in front of her, symbolized her love. The large vase of white roses meant "I am worthy of you." Rossetti was telling her he was a different man from the one who had driven his wife to suicide. There were no other women now, no Fanny or Alexa. Only Jane.

Morris hung the finished portrait in the parlor above his customary reading chair. Jane thought it odd that he did not place it where he could look at it. Instead Jane faced herself while she sewed, which she found unsettling. Still, she liked to look up at it every now and then, and a little thrill went through her each time she thought to herself, *He loves me.*

In January 1869, Burne-Jones got into an argument with Maria Zambaco outside Robert Browning's house. When he said that he would not leave his wife, she tried to drown herself in Paddington Canal. The police were called and Burne-Jones was nearly arrested. Morris agreed to go with him to Rome to escape from the scandal and from the hysterical Maria.

"I'll be gone at least a month," he said to Jane as she packed his suitcase. "I am so sorry to leave like this, but you know I can't abandon Ned. The man is wretched."

"What of Georgie?" asked Jane hotly. "I'm sure she is completely serene about it all."

"Don't talk to me of Georgie," snapped Morris. "She is the dearest friend I have in the world, after Ned. I am only trying to help both of them."

Jane said nothing, but continued to fold his shirts. She would be relieved when he was gone. Think of all the extra hours she could spend with Rossetti.

"I do have one favor to ask of you," said Morris. "I would prefer that you not sit for Gabriel while I'm gone."

Jane, startled, glanced up at her husband, but he was looking out the window at the passing carriages.

"If that is what you wish," said Jane angrily, unable to think of an argument against it.

"It is," said Morris.

Georgie appeared the next morning in traveling costume, her eyes very red.

"I can't stay," she said. "The children are in the carriage."

"You're not going after him?" said Jane, alarmed.

"Oh, no," said Georgie. "We're going to Oxford. I've rented some rooms there. I can't stay here, not with . . . not with all that's happened. I'll lose my mind, I really will. Some time in the country will be good for me. Shall I visit your mother while I'm there?"

"Not unless you really want to suffer," said Jane.

Georgie smiled the smallest possible smile. "I expect to be gone at least a month, perhaps longer," she said.

Jane embraced her friend. "I will write to you," she said.

Morris and Burne-Jones went as far as Dover before Burne-Jones demanded that they return to London. He did not retrieve his wife and children immediately, but within a month the family was reunited.

Morris began illustrating a large book of his verses for Georgie, painstakingly imitating the techniques of medieval illuminated manuscripts.

Jane was nearly sick with relief that she did not have to forgo her time with Rossetti. He was making sketches for the painting of Shakespeare's Mariana, and he would have been annoyed at the interruption and infuriated by its cause.

But whether it was because of Rossetti's love or in spite of it, Jane's backaches became excruciating. She found that no matter how much she wanted to go to Tudor House, there were many days when she could not rise from bed. Morris was very concerned and made arrangements for the whole family to go to a spa in Germany for the summer. Jane was heartbroken at the idea of being away from London and Rossetti, but the pain was too great for her to pretend any longer that she was all right.

Twenty-three

London, August 1, 1869

My Dear Mr. Morris,

I hope that by the time you receive this you are settled in nicely and that Jane is resting comfortably. I'm sure the train journey was very trying but it is all in the interest of making her well and strong again and one could bear anything if one could make that happen!

Ned misses you horribly, of course. On Sunday he wandered the house aimlessly, from dining room to hall and back again, from sitting room to studio to kitchen, as if he were a dog that had lost its master. Twice he put on his coat and hat as if to go and meet you, and twice I had to gently remind him that you were away until at least the end of September. At last he went into his studio and began to paint but he said his work that day was a complete failure. I don't know what he shall do without you!

Philip fell out of the oak tree and for a while we feared he had broken his elbow but it turned out to be only badly bruised. At times like this I think you are fortunate to have girls!

Ever your,
Georgie

Fortuna Bad-Ems,
August 1, 1869

My Dear Gabriel,

Today I have drunk four glassfuls of cloudy, tepid water and had a steaming hot bath that smelled of sulphur, followed by a freezing-cold bath that smelled of mud. This evening I will repeat the entire process again. I cannot say that my back throbs any less or that my head has ceased to ache, but it is certainly different. There is a little lake here with strange-looking ducks with red tufted heads. Yesterday William poled me about in a gondola, with more energy than skill, I must say, and we had a little picnic of pork sandwiches and cold potatoes. I gave most of my sandwich to the birds, and they seemed to enjoy it much more than I.

Your Jane

Fortuna Bad-Ems,
August 4, 1869

My Dear Gabriel,

I feel very hopeful that I will return from this journey much better than when I left. Whether or not you will be able to stand me in my altered state remains to be seen. We went for a drive in the countryside today and I was jounced around quite a bit. It was extremely wet but the country is very green and wild—like Millais's painting of Ruskin, with the giant granite rocks and the cold rushing stream. William occupies himself tramping about for several hours a day, and working on his poems—right now it's Acontius and Cydippe. He seems dissatisfied with what he has, but then he often is. He is reading me Vanity Fair and it's quite a sacrifice, I assure you, as he loathes it absolutely. In your last letter you wrote that you had a cold. A summer cold is dreadful. I hope by the time you receive this you are much better.

Your Jane

Fortuna Bad-Ems,
August 9, 1869

My Dear Mrs. Burne-Jones,

How funny it looks to write your name that way! To me your husband will always be Ned Jones, no matter what gewgaws he affixes to his name!

I was sorry to hear of Ned's condition. I advise brisk walks and plenty of shortbread. Tell Philip to keep his feet on the ground. We cannot afford to lose any of you.

Janey appears to be better. I don't know if it is the water she drinks or the water in which she bathes, the clean air or the chilly sleeping quarters, but the circles under her eyes are not so purple and she may have gained a pound or two. I find the spa somewhat stifling, but I just go on my way with my notebook and pen my silly verses and am as happy as can be.

William

Fortuna Bad-Ems,
August 12, 1869

My Dear Mrs. Burne-Jones,

Forgive my audacity in writing to you this way, but my heart is too full to remain silent and you have been so kind in the past in listening to my ranting and raving. My last, cheerful letter was a lie. I thought perhaps that leaving London and coming somewhere restful we might have a chance to quietly reform our battered and bent marriage. And she is kind—so very kind! She kills with kindness, because it is so formal, and distant, like an angel on high. But she is so far away from me I begin to despair that she will ever return. What am I to do? At night I dream of death, sometimes hers, sometimes my own. During the day I try to remain cheerful, for the kiddies if for no other reason, but at night I cannot stop the gruesome nightmares. Tell me what to do. Tell me how I am to bear it!

William

Twenty-four

WHEN they returned from Germany, Jane did not feel much better, but she tried to pretend that she did. Morris worked furiously to finish the second and third volumes of *The Earthly Paradise,* and one day Jane found a brand-new copy of the second installment on the table in her sitting room. She opened it and began to read:

Time and again, he, listening to such word,
Felt his heart kindle; time and again did seem
As though a cold and hopeless tune he heard,
Sung by grey mouths amidst a dull-eyed dream;
Time and again across his heart would stream
The pain of fierce desire whose aim was gone,
Of baffled yearning, loveless and alone.

It was too painful to go on. So he was still writing poetry about her, just a different kind. Nearly every verse was about her and the loss of her love.

Yet that evening she had to return to the book. Her husband was at a meeting with the other partners of the Firm, but when he got home, he would want to know what she thought.

Look long, O longing eyes, and look in vain!
Strain idly, aching heart, and yet be wise,

And hope no more for things to come again
That thou beheldest once with careless eyes!
Like a new-wakened man thou art, who tries
To dream again the dream that made him glad
When in his arms his loving love he had.

Jane fell asleep with these reproachful words still echoing in her ears.

She woke in the night to find Morris out of bed, sitting at the window.

"I'm sorry," she said.

"You can't help it," he said, "any more than I can help still loving you."

The next morning, in a deceptively cheerful voice, he told her that he was moving his things into the spare bedroom.

But not everything was so bad. His book was selling well and receiving critical praise. He was becoming known as a poet.

"I have something to tell you," Rossetti said nervously one afternoon at tea. "I fear that you will think me horrible, but I can't keep things from you. You have to know what I am thinking of."

"Whatever it is cannot be as horrible as you're making it sound," said Jane. "Just tell me."

"Well, as you know, I buried my poems with Lizzie," began Rossetti.

"A foolish thing to do," said Jane. "I'm sure you regret it now."

Rossetti nodded. "My volume of poetry is almost finished, but it is incomplete without those poems. So I'm going to have them dug up."

Jane nearly choked on her toast. "Have Lizzie exhumed?" she said, her horror growing as it dawned on her fully what he meant to do.

Rossetti would not look at her. "It's gruesome, I know, but it's the only way. Those poems must be in this volume. I can't reconstruct them, I've tried. Jane, you must understand."

Jane shuddered. "How is such a thing done?" she whispered. She had a sudden, terrible vision of Rossetti clawing at the dirt with his bare hands. Of opening the casket and finding—she didn't want to imagine, but her mind went on anyway. Rotted lace, crawling with parasites. Golden hair hanging from a delicate skull. Dust, desiccated flesh and bone.

Rossetti grabbed her hand beseechingly. "My brother is handling it, as he handles everything. The coroner will do it, I imagine. I don't know if the pages will be salvageable. Who knows what has become of them while underground?"

Jane drew her hand away.

"You won't tell your husband?" pleaded Rossetti. "I know he will judge me for it."

"Of course I won't tell him," said Jane.

But word reached Morris through other channels. He mentioned it to his wife the very next evening.

"It's ghoulish," said Morris. "And after making such a show of burying them with her, to change his mind and decide he wants them back. So like him." He waited a moment for Jane's reaction.

"You don't seem very shocked," he said.

"It's horrible," said Jane unconvincingly. "Shocking."

"You knew!" said Morris, standing up and coming toward her. For a terrifying moment Jane thought he was going to hit her. "He told you!"

"Yes," Jane admitted. "He asked me not to say anything to you, for fear you would judge him."

"He was right to fear it," said Morris, and he left the room without another word. Jane was left with the uneasy feeling that Morris had discovered more than she would have liked about her relationship with Rossetti.

Rossetti's poems were published to fair acclaim. Of course it was true that his friends wrote most of the reviews that appeared, and they were uniformly generous. Rossetti's public profile rose. He was invited to more and better parties. His name appeared in the newspaper frequently. Patrons who had shown no interest in him before were suddenly eager to come to his studio. And when they did, they invariably found a tall, dark-haired woman with him. She did not say much, but the prospective buyers got the impression that she was very much at home there. People had begun to talk of Rossetti's fixation on Mrs. William Morris. For there were now many parties where the two of them were observed in a dark corner, their heads very close together. They were seen walking together along the Thames, giggling like schoolchildren.

Georgie took Jane with her to George Eliot's one Sunday afternoon. Jane had wanted to meet the novelist for years, but Eliot was very cautious with people she didn't know. However, she was very fond of Georgie and respected her opinion. If she approved of Jane Morris, then Jane Morris could be received.

The woman who took her hand was not as ugly as Jane had imagined. She was dressed very well, in gray striped silk, and a lace mantilla covered her face. It was only when she drew it back to greet Jane that she saw Eliot's hooked nose and pointed chin. The two curved toward each other in a most witchlike way.

"I am honored to meet you," said Jane, recovering herself. "I admired *Felix Holt* very much."

"And I am honored to meet you. I have heard tales of your beauty, and you can imagine how that piqued my interest, since it's something I know nothing about."

"Jane is also a talented seamstress," said Georgie. "She has designed many beautiful articles for the decorative arts collective."

"Indeed," said Eliot, in a way that made it clear she did not think Jane's talents were worth much. "You are a fine specimen of comeliness, aren't you? Sit by me and tell me about your life."

"I am going to play your adorable piano and let you two get acquainted," said Georgie. "Is there something you would like to hear?"

"Berlioz," said Eliot. "Did you ever see him? Such a brilliant man. He died too soon."

Jane perched herself on the corner of the pink chaise where the author held court. Eliot fixed her with a gaze of terrifying intensity.

"Tell me about your husband," Eliot said. "I admire his poetry very much."

Jane shrugged helplessly. "He is very industrious," was all she could think to say.

Eliot rapped the table in front of her with impatience. "Come now, you can do better than that," she said. "Is he amusing to live with? Does he slurp his soup? Do you have terrible disagreements with regard to salvation by works versus faith?"

Jane found herself telling the novelist everything. Eliot was not a warm, sympathetic listener, but her keen interest was irresistible. When Jane began to speak of the failure of her marriage and her love for Rossetti, the other woman stopped her.

"I am not against marriage, contrary to popular opinion," said Eliot. "In fact, I consider myself married to Mr. Lewes in every way that matters. No, if you came to me expecting me to sanction leaving your marriage, you were wrong. Marriage is a sacred commitment."

"But in your case—," began Jane.

"In my case," said Eliot icily, "Mr. Lewes's wife left him for another man."

"But if they had been free to divorce, then you could marry."

"These laws are in place for a reason. Imagine the social upheaval if everyone had leave to divorce at will."

"What about love?" said Jane desperately.

"Love is for poetry," said Eliot. "Love is for children and for pets. We are grown women and we live in society. Love is a luxury we cannot afford."

Jane looked around the room and saw that except for herself and Georgie, the company was composed entirely of men. Ladies who called upon George Eliot were still risking their own reputations. It must be a very lonely life, thought Jane.

Twenty-five

ANE noticed that Morris had asked the cook to pre-pare his meals separately and have them sent to the study. When she asked him about it, he replied blandly, but without looking her in the eye, that his translation work was grueling. He hoped to finish *The Volsung Sagas* by the spring, which meant he must translate many pages a day. In fact, he almost never left the study now when he was at home. When Jane cleaned it one day while he was in the workshop, she realized from the blankets piled on the divan that he had been sleeping there.

He knew.

That night Jane lay awake, counting the hours as the grandfa-ther clock in the hall beat them out. She couldn't sleep knowing that Morris was downstairs, tossing and turning on the uncom-fortable sofa, torturing himself with thoughts of her with Rossetti. She got up, put on her dressing gown, and went downstairs.

Morris was sitting at his desk, his back to the door. He did not appear to hear her. In his hand, she saw with horror, was a pistol. It gleamed in the yellow lamplight. She saw an empty box of shells next to it and realized that Morris had just loaded it. Perhaps he was going to leave the house, go to Rossetti's, and shoot him. At least as likely was that he was going to shoot himself. The third possibility, she realized with dread, was that the bullets might be meant for her. If that were his intention, her best course of action would have been to turn and leave before he noticed her. But her instinct compelled her to try and get the gun away from him. If he meant to shoot anyone, she must stop him.

"William," she said. He nearly leaped from the chair. It was a miracle, she reflected, that his hand was steady enough not to inadvertently fire the weapon. Inwardly she cursed herself for startling him.

"What are you doing up?" he said, not turning around. She observed with relief that he placed the gun in his desk drawer.

"Why are you sleeping in the study?" she said. "If it's to avoid me, that's silly, you have your own room."

"I can't be that near you," he said in a choked voice. "On the same floor, just a few steps away. Even being in the same house is like torture to me. At least here I don't feel as if my skin is turning inside out. I don't sleep, but at least my mind is a little bit quieter here."

"Why do you have a pistol?" she asked.

"I'm not sure," he said. "I bought it at a pawnshop. The gentleman there said it had been Colonel Fawcett's. He used it in the duel against Lieutenant Monro. Of course, he was killed. I would have been better off buying Monro's pistol, but I assume he still has it."

"Were you planning on dueling?" Jane asked.

"It had occurred to me," said Morris. "Though I was never much of a shot. I used to hunt squirrels as a child, but I so loathed killing them that I usually missed on purpose."

"Whom were you going to duel?" asked Jane, though of course she knew.

"The blackguard, my former friend, whom I loved like a brother." At this Morris laid his head on the desk and his shoulders began to shake. Jane walked over to the desk and put her hand on his head. Violently he shook her away.

"I know you never loved me," he said. "I always knew you loved him. I know that you married me to have a better life and that you were grateful but that your feelings never extended beyond that."

"William . . . ," she cried.

"Don't try to deny it," he said. "I always hoped that as the years passed and we made a life together your feelings would deepen, but I see now how naive that was. Your choices were intolerable and I was the least onerous of them, but that's not the same as making a free choice."

"I do love you, William," she said.

Morris laughed bitterly. "I am so dear to you, I know. So dear that you have made a cuckold of me before all of London. And if you could, you would leave me and live with Rossetti as his mistress."

"I don't know what I would do if I could," said Jane, in anguish. "As you said, I've never been free."

"Get out," he said. "I have to think."

"What will you do?" she asked.

"That is for me to decide. When I have made up my mind, I will call for you." He stood up and shut and locked the door behind her.

Jane longed to go to Rossetti and tell him of the situation, but she didn't dare. Such a flagrant provocation might inflame an already volatile situation.

So she waited. She wrote Rossetti a cursory note, telling him that she was ill and unable to sit for the foreseeable future. The note she received in return was so kind and solicitous that it made her cry. She found being confined to the house nearly intolerable. She had not realized how many hours of her day had been spent with Rossetti. Though her own house was enlivened by two pretty little girls and their games, Jane could hardly look at them without crying. Morris could choose to send her away from them, not let her see them at all. She didn't know if he was angry enough to do it. Her thoughts were agitated and she couldn't read, or sew; all she could do was pace from room to room, looking at her things, wondering if she would be leaving them soon.

In the afternoon Morris came into her room. He was very calm, though he still could not look at her.

"This could ruin us, you know," he said.

Jane nodded.

"I don't think you would be happy with Mrs. Lewes's life, though that is of course for you to decide. But there are the children to think of."

"Don't take them from me," she begged.

"I have no intention of doing such a thing," said Morris disdainfully. "But we need a plan. I will tell you what I am thinking, and you tell me if it is acceptable."

Morris outlined a strategy that would save all of them. Jane could not believe what she was hearing.

"It's more generous than I deserve," she said.

"Yes, it is," said Morris, "and certainly better than what Gabriel deserves, but it's all I can think to do. Does it meet with your approval?"

Jane assented.

"Then I'll write Rossetti a note and ask him to come to my office."

"I thought it was about the business," said Rossetti. He stroked her hair and she felt her breathing slow. Being with him could always calm her. "How could I have known? I thought he looked tired, and he was very terse when he greeted me, but I attributed it to the ridiculous hours that he works. Another man would turn over day-to-day operations to someone else and return to the life of a gentleman of leisure."

"He doesn't want to," said Jane. "There's nothing he would rather do than supervise the design and installation of stained glass in a new church, or attempt to learn the old ways of weaving."

"It's his calling, I know, he has a laborer's heart. Anyway, I thought he might have a commission for me, a piece of painted furniture or a sketch for a tapestry. But then he said he called me to talk about you. 'I called you here to discuss my wife, Jane,' he said. When he called you his wife, I knew that he knew. I scanned the room and noted with alarm that he was between me and the door. It would have been the most ridiculous melodrama if Morris were to kill me, and most unlike him, but such things have happened."

"Don't joke, Gabriel," Jane said.

"It's no joke, I assure you. I did not want to lose my life in such a humiliating and sordid way. So I tried to keep my tone light and pretend that I didn't know anything. Then he said that it had come to his attention that you no longer loved him, and that you love me."

Jane touched the hand that was at her forehead. "And then?"

"Well, I was struck dumb. His candor took me completely aback. It was as if he was discussing a business transaction, he was so matter-of-fact. I wasn't sure if I should deny the statement or agree with it, so I waited. He laid out the options: divorce, separation, and why neither of them suits him."

"You know I can't," said Jane. "Because of Jenny and May."

"I don't see why," said Rossetti peevishly. "Why should you lose all right to them?"

"It's the law," Jane said.

"Damn the law," said Rossetti. "We could go to Italy for a year or so, until people have stopped talking. I could show you Florence, and Venice. Then we could quietly return to London. You could live with me at Tudor House. Or, if you prefer, we could take another house, one that we both like. I could paint and you could do just as you pleased."

"And the children?" she asked.

"I'm sure Morris would let you see them when you returned."

"I couldn't be away from them for a year," Jane said.

"Then we'll take them with us," said Rossetti carelessly. "I'm sure it would be educational."

"I didn't like to agree not to see you as much in London," sighed Jane.

"Well, he wants to avoid a scandal, and I suppose he's right. It wouldn't be good for business, either for him or for me. The papers would be merciless. But leasing a house in the countryside is the perfect solution."

"I can't believe he proposed it," said Jane.

"Neither can I," said Rossetti. "In his place I wouldn't be nearly so magnanimous. I asked him why he was doing it and he said it was for you, because he wants you to be happy. So I agreed. Just think, we can be alone together, away from gossiping tongues and prying eyes."

I have spoken to him, Morris wrote to Georgie.

I found him to be willfully stubborn and far too blasé about what is after all a solemn matter. I fear he does not love her as he should. Of course if he did love her he would take her away from me, which would be too much to bear. Now I have the unwelcome task of finding the house. Gabriel showed little interest in looking with me, which in some ways is a relief as I can hardly stand to be around him.

Of course it is wrong to complain. The children are healthy and the business is doing very well. And my plans for Iceland are proceeding apace. Your husband has volunteered your back garden as a place where I can learn to cook over an open fire, which I will have to do for weeks. I hope I do not burn your house down, but that is the risk that must be run.

Twenty-six

"THE Fleshly School of Poetry and Other Phenomena of the Day,'" slurred Rossetti. He had drunk too much wine with lunch. "Accusing me of immoral desires. As if the senses are immoral. Weren't they given to us by God?"

"It's only one review among many," said Jane.

"But of course one must discount the positive reviews as so much bunk, and believe the scathing critic as the only honest one in the bunch."

"If he were honest wouldn't he identify himself?" said Jane. "I am sure Thomas Maitland is not his real name."

"Always so practical," said Rossetti. "Can't you let me wallow in my irrational ravings?"

"No," said Jane.

"That is why I cannot do without you," he said.

"And the book is selling so well," she said. "The controversy probably helps it."

"I will put it from my mind," said Rossetti, "and concentrate on painting, which is what I do best, after all."

But he continued to drink. At dinner he didn't stop drinking until he fell asleep. Sometimes he fell asleep at the dinner table, sometimes in the sitting room afterward. Sometimes he fell and hurt himself trying to climb the stairs to bed. Sometimes he became maudlin and cried that he was being persecuted. Sometimes he gave long, self-pitying speeches that usually ended with glass breaking and furniture being knocked over.

Then Rossetti found out that Thomas Maitland was the pseudonym of Robert Buchanan, whose poetry Rossetti's brother had criticized some years earlier. To Jane that made the criticism personally motivated and not worthy of consideration, but Rossetti didn't see it that way. He began working out a response. They all thought it was unwise. Jane advised him to let the matter drop. People quickly forgot about such things. But Rossetti could not forget. His response was titled "The Stealthy School of Criticism."

All through the winter, when he wasn't at the workshop or down in the showroom, Morris was looking for a house. He was very particular about what he wanted, and it took many trips to the countryside before he found Kelmscott Manor, in Gloucestershire. He sent a note to Rossetti, who went to see it several days later and agreed that it was perfect.

"It's a large stone manor house," Rossetti wrote to Jane. "The original part was built in 1571 and has a medieval plan, while the addition, from 1670, gives it a pleasing asymmetry. There are stone barns and large gardens and orchards that lead down to the Thames. It's near Lechlade, a charming village, but not too near, and lovely old trees shield it from the road. I think you will be happy there."

Jane wanted to ask Morris what he thought of it, but he seldom spoke to her about anything but the quotidian. he worked late every day, and most weekends he went to the country to supervise the renovation and decoration of the house. At the same time, he prepared for his trip to Iceland.

At last it was June. Everything had been packed and the carriage was waiting downstairs to take them to the train station. The girls were fearfully excited and were running up and down the stairs, shouting to their parents to hurry. May tripped over Jenny and began to cry. Somehow they all made it into the carriage. Husband

and wife had not been so close to each other in many weeks. They had Jenny between them and Jane held May on her lap. Still, the proximity was alarming. The children kept up their excited chatter, but whereas in the past one or both of them would admonish the girls to be quiet and behave, now they secretly welcomed the din. It meant that they did not have to speak to each other.

"Will I have to buy a ticket?" asked May. "I only have fourpence. Is that enough?"

Jane smiled. "The tickets are already bought, sweet pea."

"Good," said May. "I was concerned. I've never been on a train before, you know."

"Yes you have," corrected Jenny. "When we left Red House we went on a train, didn't we, Papa?"

"Yes, you did," said Morris, "but I'm surprised you remember it. You were very little."

"I remember it was very dirty. And loud. And a man dropped his suitcase on Mama's foot."

"You do remember!" exclaimed Morris.

"As do I," said Jane. "My foot was bruised and swollen for a week. Remember, I had to wear that ugly slipper?"

Once on the train the girls did not want to stay in their seats but ran up and down the aisles annoying the porters. Morris called them back and pulled them both onto his lap.

"Let me tell you a story," he said.

"Is it about ponies?" asked May, who was besotted with them.

"It's about the house we are going to," Morris said. "It was built long ago, in 1557, in fact. Do you know who was king in 1557?"

"Henry," guessed Jenny.

"Not quite," said Morris. "It was a trick question anyway, because Bloody Mary was queen in 1557."

"Why do they call her that?" asked May.

"Because she liked to chop off people's heads," said Morris, drawing his finger across her throat.

"William," said Jane. "They won't sleep tonight."

"In any case, the house we're going to was built for a prince, who was a Protestant and loyal to Mary's sister Elizabeth, who was in the tower. The house is full of secret passages he used to sneak out to meet his friends, and bring them into the house without being seen. For they were being watched by Mary's spies, and our prince was very attached to his head."

"I thought it was built by a yeoman," said Jane.

"Shhh," said Morris.

"What was his name?" asked Jenny.

"Lord Pomfret," said Morris. "Arthur Pomfret. And when Elizabeth became queen, he left Gloucestershire and went to Greenwich."

"Was his head ever cut off?" asked Jenny.

Morris winked at Jane. "No, because Elizabeth ruled for forty-five years. He died when he was ninety-two, in bed, of influenza."

"It's too bad," said May. "I like the stories where the heads are chopped off."

After that Jenny pulled out a book and began to read. May fell asleep in her father's arms. Jane gazed out of the window at the passing countryside. The way was familiar; it was the way she had come to London for the first time after she had married Morris. It was the end of the time for violets, but the snapdragons and hollyhocks were up in the cottage gardens, and the climbing roses were blooming. It made her a little sad, to think that in the thirteen years since she'd left Oxford she had never once gone to the fields to pick violets, not even when they lived at Red House. Things were changing along the road; new houses were being built, a factory that had not been there before belched steam in the distance. But the fields looked the same as they had when she was eighteen. It was she who was different.

After her experience at Mrs. Wallingford's, Jane was worried that Kelmscott Manor, which was not many miles away, would be gloomy, but she was charmed by it immediately, as Rossetti had said she would be. Morris had seen to it that the inside had been repainted and was bright and clean. Her room and the room the girls would share had been decorated with Morris and Company wallpaper and bed hangings: Willow Boughs for her, Blackthorn for the girls. The housekeeper had placed an earthenware jug of hot pink peonies on her bedside table. She had a balcony that over-looked the river.

Morris brought in her bag and set it down beside the bed. He seemed reluctant to leave, and stood by the window, rearranging the folds in the curtains.

"What do you think of the house?" he asked.

"You know it is magic," she said. "You have a knack for finding it, and making it, too."

"You mean Arthur Pomfret?" he said, smiling. "John Turner the yeoman was just too prosaic a man and does not lend himself to tales. What do you think of your room?"

"The fabrics are lovely," she said. "And the view."

"The room gets quite a lot of sun," he said. "I know that's what you prefer."

"Thank you," she said. She said it to encompass everything, not just the room or the house but all he had done for her. It made him think of Rossetti, and his smile faded.

"When does he arrive?" Morris asked, as if he could not bear to say the name.

"Tomorrow," she said. "His train is due at four o'clock."

"I'll return to London the following morning, then," Morris said. "It wouldn't do to leave before he arrives, but I have to be at Granton on the Firth of Forth in three days' time."

"And you sail from there for Iceland?" she asked. He had only spoken of his trip to her in the vaguest terms, which, considering how he used to tell her everything, was painful.

"If all goes well, I'll be back in London September fifteenth, give or take a few days. If we are trapped by storms or ice, I could have to winter over there, though it's not something I want to do and I'll make every effort to avoid it. They say the winters are very difficult. But don't worry. Reykjavik is a town of some size. If we have to wait there for the weather to clear, I'm sure we can find comfortable accommodations." He caught himself. "Not that you're worried, of course. I'm just telling you so that if anything happens, you can contact me. I'll leave you my forwarding address, though once we head for the interior and the north, I'll be unreachable. But my letters will be waiting for me there."

"You'll write to me?" said Jane, feeling inexplicably forlorn.

"If you like," he said. "Of course I'll write to the girls."

"Of course," Jane said.

The following afternoon Jane sent the girls to their room to read and one of the servants to meet Rossetti's train. Then she went upstairs to find an appropriate dress to wear. They were in the country, so it could not be too formal. On the other hand, it had to signify the momentousness of the occasion. The jade green velvet was too sumptuous, the camel-colored wool with yellow braid too ordinary. In the end she put on the bright blue silk he had seen a thousand times before. It might send the message that nothing had changed, but on the other hand she did not want to seem like a stranger.

"You've worn our favorite dress," observed Jenny when she came downstairs. Jane winced.

"It's Uncle Gabriel's favorite as well," Morris said wryly.

"I don't suppose it matters to him what dress you wear," said May.

"That's true," said Jane. "But we want to show good manners and make him feel welcome, and that means putting on nice clothes."

"I have on my new dress," said May, lifting the skirt of her pink-and-white-striped pinafore.

"And very nice it looks," said Morris. "Uncle Gabriel will be pleased."

"Papa, your vest is very dirty," said Jenny. "Shouldn't you change clothes as well?" Morris and Jane's eyes met and they very nearly burst into hysterical laughter.

"I am the lord of the manor," said Morris, winking at Jane. "I can do as I like."

Jane heard the rattle of the carriage wheels before she saw it. And then the door opened and he was there, and she could barely look at him. The girls threw themselves into his arms, but Jane greeted Rossetti primly. Despite the fact that the three adults were under no illusions about the situation, it still seemed improper for Jane to show the joy she felt at seeing him.

"How was your journey?" Morris dutifully asked.

"Frightful," Rossetti said. "I've a splitting headache. Do you suppose I could retire to my room until dinner?"

"Of course," Jane said. "I'll show you."

Rossetti's bedroom was on the first floor, next to the Tapestry Room, which was to be his studio. Jane's bedroom was directly above. The children were in another wing and would not notice any comings and goings. Morris had made sure of that.

They had a quiet meal and retired early to their separate rooms. Morris left after breakfast the next day. He hoisted both of the girls into his arms in an expansive bear hug. He shook Rossetti's hand and pecked Jane on the lips, but it was for show and they all knew it. Then he was inside the carriage and it was pulling away. May burst into tears and tried to run after him, but Jenny pulled her back.

"Don't be a baby," she said. "Father's coming back."

Jane was not so sure. It seemed to her, too, that they were saying goodbye forever. Perhaps this is a premonition, she thought. Perhaps he is going to die in Iceland. Or perhaps he is going to leave me, and the Iceland trip is just a pretext, a way of lessening the blow when it comes. She felt that May was right to cry.

"Who would like to introduce me to the river?" said Rossetti quickly. "I've been here twelve hours and no one has shown it to me."

"I will!" shrieked May, forgetting her father immediately. Taking Rossetti's hand she led him through the garden and down toward the water. Jenny lagged behind.

"Will you come too, Mummy?" she asked.

"Yes, I will," said Jane, collecting herself. "I want to see this heron you've been telling me about."

Twenty-seven

THE house seemed very big and dark at night. Jane waited in her bedroom. She had plaited her hair and dabbed on the rosewater scent she had used since the night she met Rossetti. She felt it in her breasts and in the wetness and ache between her thighs. She needed him to come to her.

But an hour passed and then another and still Rossetti did not come. She unbraided her hair and let it fall to her shoulders. She went to the dressing table and brushed it out. She changed from a peach-colored pelisse to a violet one. But where was Rossetti? Finally she put on a scarlet satin dressing gown and went in search of him.

His light was on and his door was ajar. She slipped through the opening and into the room. He was asleep on top of the bedclothes, fully dressed. When she sat on the bed beside him, he smiled but did not open his eyes.

"I thought you'd never come," he said.

"I was waiting for you to come to me," said Jane.

"I thought you might not want me to," said Rossetti. "With Morris just left, and the children here." Jane leaned down and kissed him, softly at first and then fervently. He slipped the dressing gown over her shoulders and it slid to the floor.

Rossetti seemed content to kiss her and stroke her back. It was she who finally began to take his clothes off him, first his tie and then his shirt. Rossetti laughed at her.

"Aren't you a bad girl," he said. "I think you need to be punished." He rolled onto her and pinned her beneath his weight. Then they were both pulling at her clothes and flinging them to the floor.

"The lamp," she said.

"Leave it," he said. "You think that now we are going to play husband and wife, I will become prudish and stodgy like Topsy? Blow out the lamp, indeed."

He pinned her wrists with his hands and kissed her hard. In her struggle to free herself, Jane flung out a hand and knocked a bottle on the nightstand to the floor.

"What's that?" she asked.

"It's nothing," he muttered. "Chloral. To help me sleep." With a feathery touch he brushed her lips with his thumb. Slowly he worked his way down the length of her body, and when he reached her most sensitive place, she clamped a hand over her mouth so as not to scream and wake the servants or the children.

They slept late in the morning. The children had already eaten and were by the river collecting wildflowers by the time Jane came down to breakfast. The cook, who had come with the house, was excellent and her strawberry jam and plum preserves were the best Jane had ever had. The currant scones, lemon curd muffins, and Irish soda bread, too, were all delicious, and Jane ate heartily. Rossetti devoured so many eggs that the cook came out to scold him. As they quietly read the newspaper, they would look up every now and then, as if on cue, and Rossetti would smile at her or touch her face. How different it was from when Morris read the articles aloud to her whether she wanted him to or not.

"What shall we do today?" she asked when the dishes were cleared away.

"I hope to set up my studio this morning. Perhaps after that we should have a picnic," said Rossetti. "We can row down the river until we find a nice spot."

"Can you row?" she asked.

"Of course," he said. "I may not have been to Oxford, but I know a thing or two about boats."

"Who will look after the children?"

"They'll come, of course," said Rossetti. "They can pick berries or make daisy chains or whatever it is little girls do on picnics."

While Rossetti organized his things and commandeered the gardener to help him move some tables and chairs, Jane conferred with the cook about the picnic lunch, and saw that the maid knew how to clean their rooms properly. Then she went in to tell the girls about the picnic and to make sure that they wore their oldest boots and brought rain slickers.

At half-past one the little group left Kelmscott Manor. Jane carried the enormous basket.

"How many meals are in there?" teased Rossetti. "Are we spending the night on the river?" They walked down to the boathouse while the girls skipped ahead and then doubled back, urging them to hurry.

"We only have four and a half hours of daylight!" wailed Jenny.

"It will be enough," promised Rossetti. "And if it isn't, we have forty-two days left in summer to have another picnic." Rossetti pulled the boat from the boathouse and dragged it toward the bank.

"What about the oars?" asked May.

For a moment Rossetti looked confused.

"For rowing?" prompted Jenny.

"The oars, yes," said Rossetti. "May, do you think you can carry them?"

They put in at a sandy spot just in front of the house. Jane went in first while Rossetti held the boat. Then Jenny stepped in, then May. At last Rossetti leaped in and nearly capsized the boat with his weight. The girls shrieked in excitement, but with a heroic effort Rossetti managed to steady the boat. May handed him the oars and he began to pull with them, but they spun in circles for several minutes.

"Use the left one alone to turn the boat," instructed Jane. "When you set a course, use both with equal strength and we should go straight."

"You think I don't know how to row?" growled Rossetti.

"It doesn't seem like you do," giggled May.

"Would you like a turn?" Rossetti pretended to be very offended. May shrank back in her seat and shook her head, laughing.

"Would you like me to get us away from the bank?" said Jane.

"You three are my ladies and I am your knight," said Rossetti. "You are not to do any work today, but to sit back and enjoy yourselves." Just at that moment they crashed into some weeds and cattails on the bank, startling a family of ducks. The ducks honked indignantly and flew away with a great commotion. Rossetti pushed away from the bank with his oar, and at last managed to turn the boat in the right direction. They made their way downstream, "toward London," Rossetti said.

The area around Kelmscott was stippled with fields of barley and corn. They passed a farmhouse built of sandstone, with a pretty cottage garden on one side. A boat was tied up at a rickety wooden dock on the bank below the house. A beagle saw them approach and began to bark furiously, racing toward the water.

"Do you think he can swim?" asked Jane, a little nervously.

"Not as fast as I can row," said Rossetti.

"I'd like to have a dog like that," said Jenny, as she watched the little dog recede. They glided past a few black cows drinking at the bank. The cows lifted their heads and looked at them curiously.

"I see a castle up there!" shouted May, pointing toward a distant hill.

"I believe that is the home of Lord Farnsworth," said Rossetti. "We must be coming very close to the village."

Now the farmhouses were closer together, and there were boats on the water ahead of them.

"Be careful," warned Jane, "and stay close to the bank."

"I am counting on the other boatmen to be much more experienced and to steer away from us," laughed Rossetti. They were so close to the bank that the willow trees slapped their faces as they passed. Ahead they could see a long row of buildings on either side of the bank, and a pretty stone bridge.

"We must come to town soon," said Jane. "It looks charming."

"Good day to you, sir!" called Rossetti to a boy on the bridge with a fishing line as they passed under him. "You girls should learn to fish," said Rossetti. "Think of all the money we could save at the butcher's!"

"I shouldn't like to be caught by the mouth with a hook and dragged into a boat, if I was used to water," May said.

"Yes, that's true," agreed Rossetti, winking, "but a fish is not the same as a girl. A fish's brain is very small and very primitive, like an ant or a grasshopper, and I've seen you step on them many times."

"I would never step on a grasshopper!" said May, horrified. "But you're right about the ants."

"Well then, just think of a fish as a kind of ant," said Rossetti. "A large, clammy ant."

"Silly!" giggled May.

Half an hour past the village they found an idyllic spot under a group of weeping willows and landed the boat there. Jane laid a cloth in the sun and spread out the lunch. There was cold chicken, smoked salmon sandwiches, corn salad, sliced tomatoes, and chocolate cake. They ate until they were thoroughly stuffed. Afterward Rossetti took out his sketchbook and began to draw Jane while she read. Jenny and May asked if they could explore the woods.

"Put on a sweater," said Jane, pulling one for each of them out of the basket.

"It's such a warm day," said Rossetti, "do they really need them?"

"Take them," said Jane. "And take care not to lose them." The girls disappeared into the bracken.

"It reminds me of my own childhood," said Jane. "No doubt they'll collect a lot of acorns and insist on bringing them back."

"Is that what you used to do?" said Rossetti.

"More like walnuts, to keep us fed," said Jane. "They'll never know that kind of life, thank God."

When the girls returned, with twigs in their hair and their pockets full of acorns, they cuddled next to their mother while Rossetti told them a tale of an inquisitive frog. Halfway through they were both asleep, and Rossetti and Jane took a little walk into the woods where they could steal a few kisses. When the sun got low, they packed up their things, jumped into the boat, and rowed home.

Each morning Rossetti spent in his studio, sometimes sketching or painting Jane, sometimes drafting his response to "The Fleshly School of Poetry." Even at Kelmscott, even when mixing colors or walking along the shore or skipping pebbles with Jenny and May, even when making love to Jane, Buchanan's criticism was never far from his mind. In vain Jane tried to distract him, to soothe him, to make him laugh at the whole silly incident, but even Jane wasn't fully aware of how much the article had wounded him.

If she was not modeling, Jane sewed or read until Rossetti was finished working. The girls spent most of their time out of doors. Their favorite activity was roof riding, climbing the house's many steep gables. They made friends with a few local children and went, with the nurse Jane engaged the second week of their stay, to visit them often. It was only when the girls were gone that she allowed Rossetti to embrace her openly. She was adamant that they think of Rossetti only as the friend of her parents, and that they not suspect anything. She hoped that if gossip reached them someday, through one of their friends in London, perhaps, they would be able to honestly and innocently say that there was no romance between her and Rossetti. But when she was sure they were alone, Jane made no effort to hide her ardent feelings from the servants. They may have disapproved, but they were too well trained to say anything.

During the first days it was difficult for Jane to keep her mind on anything, so conscious was she with every nerve fiber of Rossetti's closeness, and so aware was she that she could reach out and touch him if she felt like it.

In the afternoons they walked along the Thames. Jane found that her back no longer ached and that she could walk five or six miles without feeling weak or faint.

If the weather was inclement, there was always something pleasant to do in the house. It was so enormous that they spent the first week just exploring its many wings and shut-up rooms. It was the ideal place for hide-and-seek, and the games could last several hours. They all enjoyed charades, and tag. In the evenings they roasted apples in the fire and told stories. Rossetti's were often scary, Jane's romantic and sentimental, Jenny's laced with duels and poisonings. May's most often involved a pony named Roy.

Sometimes Rossetti gave the girls instruction in drawing, but it was never regimented or strict. Instead, he gave the girls paper and oil crayons and told them to draw whatever they felt like. Jenny was serious and tried to copy from life, and Rossetti encouraged her as he pointed out things she had not seen. May drew imaginative renderings of ponies and the people in her family, and Rossetti was as excited about these as he was about the work of his friend John Everett Millais.

Jane found that with Rossetti she was something of a child herself. There was none of the dour quiet of her London home. Nothing was serious at Kelmscott, nothing was urgent or upsetting or alarming. If the groceries did not arrive when they were supposed to, they ate bread and jam for dinner. If it rained, they put on galoshes and walked by the river anyway. If May fell on the stairs and bumped her head, Rossetti made faces at her until she laughed instead of cried. Jane had never laughed so much. She had never enjoyed herself so much.

"It is time to go fishing," announced Rossetti solemnly one day.

"Finally!" exclaimed May. "I thought you had forgotten. Shall we put on our boating dresses?" These were simple gray cotton pinafores that Jane had made. They were impervious to mud, brambles, brackish water, anything the girls might find themselves dirtied by.

"Go on," said Jane. "And wear your second-best boots."

Rossetti was now quite skilled at rowing, and they glided down the river sedately.

"A gentleman in town told me about a spot where the fish are always biting, just across from the sheep meadow," he said. "It will take about twenty minutes to get there."

"I think it's going to rain," said Jane.

"So much the better," said Rossetti. "The fish bite better in the rain."

"Is that true?" asked Jenny skeptically.

Rossetti raised his hand. "I swear it is."

When they reached the appointed spot, it was indeed drizzling. Jane passed out the mackintoshes and helped May put her worms on the hook. Rossetti helped Jenny. Then Rossetti baited his own hook and they tossed the three lines into the water.

"Don't you like to fish, Mama?" asked May.

"I never did," admitted Jane. "Though my brother was expert at it and my sister Bessie once caught a trout as big as you are."

"Now that's a fishy tale," said Rossetti. Jane splashed him with water until he begged her to stop.

They caught eight gudgeon, small bony fish that were good only for soup, but Jenny caught a perch and Rossetti an enormous pike. He made a great show of difficulty with it, rocking back and forth and threatening to tip over the boat, pulling at his line with all of his strength.

"His eyes are very big," observed May. "Is he looking at us?"

"I don't think he can see out of the water," said Rossetti.

"How shall we cook him?" Jane asked the girls.

"Oh, we can't," said May, beginning to cry.

"The best way is to fry him," said Rossetti. "With potatoes and salad."

"Doesn't that sound delicious?" said Jane, and even May had to admit that it did.

Twenty-eight

THAT afternoon the light rain became a downpour. It rained all through the night and all the next day. The girls looked forlornly out the window, but there was no going out that day. Rossetti watched their disappointed faces.

"We should put on a play," he said. Jenny and May turned away from the window in surprise.

"A play?" said Jenny doubtfully. "We don't know how to put on a play."

"We could do Shakespeare," said Rossetti, undaunted. "*The Tempest* would be appropriate."

"I thought I saw a *Plays for Children* on a shelf somewhere," said Jane.

The book was found and Rossetti and the girls pored over it until they found a play they all liked and that did not have too many parts for their small company. It was an adaptation of "The Franklin's Tale." Jenny was to be both the husband Arveragus and the suitor Aurelius. May was to be the faithful wife Dorigen and Aurelius's brother.

"And I suppose I will have to be the sorcerer," said Rossetti.

"How appropriate," smiled Jane.

"Now, Jenny," continued Rossetti, "as you are the better seamstress, I think you should be in charge of costumes. May will be in charge of props. I will help you both with the scenery this afternoon, after you have learned your lines and can say them perfectly without the book. We'll rehearse tonight and put on a show for your mother tomorrow evening at eight."

"Where is our theater to be?" asked May.

Rossetti thought for a moment. "In the parlor, in front of the fireplace," he said finally. "We can move all of the furniture back to create an open space. Now off you go."

The girls went off to their room to learn their lines, excited about their new project.

It was fortunate that Rossetti had thought of putting on a play, because the rain did not let up all day, and without their new pastime Jenny and May would have been very bored. On the other hand, Rossetti got no work of his own done that day. By covering some small tables with pillows and draping them in tan cotton velvet, he managed to create a couple of plausible horses. He moved the dining room table into the parlor and gathered up mismatched china from the pantry. The "pilgrims"—pillows tied together with string and dressed in Jane's and Rossetti's clothes—would gather for their meal and to hear the tale.

"We need a castle," said Rossetti, "and some rocks. This empty space next to the pilgrims will do for the castle. We can put one of the carved armchairs in there and drape some velvet on the wall. For the rocks we can arrange some pillows. They will be easy to move when they have to disappear."

"What about the sorcerer's house?" asked Jenny.

"We'll build a tent," said Rossetti. "Out of blankets. And we'll make a red paper shade for the lamp. It will look very eerie."

"Jenny needs breeches and a coat for Arveragus," said Jane, turning to the problems of costume.

"Yes, of plum velvet!" said Rossetti. "And a hat with a plume. I wonder if we can figure out how to make chain mail for Aurelius?"

"What about me?" asked May.

"I will pin a dress of mine for you," said Jane.

In the afternoon Rossetti heard the girls' lines and helped them block out the play. He would not let Jane in to watch.

"This is all to be a surprise for you," he said. "You can't see it in its rudimentary form."

Instead Jane sat in her room, pretending to read but really just watching the rain. The garden had become completely saturated and pools had formed everywhere. She observed that many of the smaller pools were being absorbed into the bigger ones, threatening to turn the entire garden into one large lake. I wonder if it will ever stop, she thought.

Thoughts of Morris came to her unbidden. What was he doing now? Iceland was hazy in her mind; she only saw stone cliffs and black, forbidding skies, but it was easy enough to imagine Morris in such a landscape, frying sausages and sharpening his pencils with a knife.

The next day they had a dress rehearsal in the morning. Jane brought the costumes she had been working on and went to the kitchen to check on things. She found the cook in a bit of a panic because no one had been able to go to town to do the shopping in three days. They were low on meat and vegetables. And now a thunderstorm was raging outside, making a trip to town even more forbidding. Jane told her not to worry, that they would eat anything, toast and cheese or stewed apples, and the cook said grudgingly that she thought she could put together a chicken stew.

It was hard for the girls to be heard over the claps of thunder. Rossetti said it was good practice in teaching them how to project their voices. Each time they saw lightning, they were apt to jump and shriek, but Rossetti commanded them to concentrate, and soon they paid no attention to the storm. By nightfall the thunder and lightning had passed, but the rain had not.

"We should have done a biblical play," said Rossetti, as he sat next to Jane and waited for the performance to begin. "It certainly feels like the Flood."

Rossetti had covered Jenny's chin and cheeks with bootblack. Jane had sacrificed a velvet cape to make the duke's suit, and given her one of Morris's swords to carry. Rossetti had taught her to affect a rolling swagger and Jane was amazed by how much she resembled an arrogant nobleman. May wore rouge and lipstick and her hair was piled on top of her head. Her crying and lamenting were very realistic. When Jenny, as Aurelius, arrived to woo her sister, wearing a coat of chicken wire, carrying a box of chocolates and a bouquet of peonies, Jane laughed until she choked.

Rossetti made a very sinister sorcerer. When he waved his wand with a flourish, Jenny held a sheet in front of the rocks and there was scurrying behind it. When Rossetti lowered his wand, and Jenny lowered the sheet, May was still carrying pillows into the hall.

When Aurelius had renounced Dorigen and the sorcerer had released him from his financial obligation, Jenny and May bowed to their mother, who rose from her seat and clapped as loudly as she could.

"Wonderful," said Jane.

"And though it was written four hundred years ago, it's still a timely tale," said Rossetti. " 'Love is a thing as any spirit free; Women by nature love their liberty, And not to be constrained like any thrall, And so do men, if say the truth I shall?' "

"I thought the play was about faithfulness," said Jenny innocently.

"It's very late," said Jane. "Help May out of her costume, and into bed with both of you."

The next morning Jane awoke to find that the Thames had completely flooded its banks, and was seeping toward the house. By midmorning the water submerged the garden; by midafternoon it was up to the front step.

"What shall we do?" said Jane.

"Make the best of it, I suppose," said Rossetti. "Roll up the downstairs carpets and put things of value up on the second floor. I'll take the girls out in the punt and we'll see what's what."

"Are you sure it's safe?" asked Jane.

"Oh, Mama, please," begged Jenny. "It is no fun being inside when everything out there is underwater."

"All right," said Jane. "Though if it goes on much longer, I wonder what we will eat."

"We'll try to make it to town," said Rossetti. "We'll see if any shops are open."

When they returned they were soaking wet and Rossetti was carrying the neighbor's dog.

"I found it clinging to a large tree branch," he explained. "I managed to steer the boat toward him and pull him into it, but he sprayed us all with water and then bit me. I'm beginning to regret rescuing him."

"Were the shops closed?" asked Jane.

"We never found the shops," said Rossetti with a grin. "With everything underwater there were no landmarks. You would think that would have occurred to me, wouldn't you? We got lost immediately."

"It was very exciting," said Jenny. "To see all that floated by."

"Yes, we saw fence posts, and road signs, furniture, even a wagon."

"Why are you crying, May?" asked Jane, taking the child into her arms.

"Drowned chickens," said Rossetti.

"Poor things," said Jane.

That afternoon the baker came by in a boat and tossed three loaves into the second-story window with his pitchfork. The postman delivered their mail by boat as well. Four days later the water had receded enough for them to go downstairs and begin to clean up. Jane hoped it would never happen again, the mud and debris made such a mess, but the girls considered the flood one of the best things that had ever happened to them and referred to it for years.

Rossetti was lying on his stomach on the rug in front of the fire, reading Browning. Jane was in her chair, sewing a nun's habit for Jenny, who had written a play about an Italian convent and was to be Mother Superior. Occasionally she would stop her work and gaze fondly at the boyish figure on the floor. Sometimes he would catch her and smile. At one of these pauses he spoke.

"Don't go back to London," he said, looking up at her soulfully.

"We still have three weeks," Jane reminded him.

"You know that's not enough," Rossetti said. "You know we have to be together. You can't go back to Morris."

"You know I have to," she said. Still, her heart was beating wildly.

"I can't get along without you," said Rossetti. "I know you think I'm being dramatic when I say it, but I'm not. Without you I will go mad."

"Don't say things like that, Gabriel," said Jane.

"I mean it," he said. "Stay here with me."

"You mean divorce?" asked Jane. She hated even saying the word. "Would you and I marry?"

"I don't care," said Rossetti. "Divorce or not, marry or not. Imagine, Jane, if we could be like this all of the time, with no Morris, no scolding gossip in the papers, no enemies. If we could live alone, together, just the two of us."

"Enemies?" said Jane. " "You mean Buchanan? He's a nuisance, but I'm not sure he's sinister enough to be an enemy."

"Oh, but he is," said Rossetti solemnly. "He's been intercepting my letters, you know. When they come to me, the seals are already broken."

"Really?" said Jane. "I'm sure it's just one of the girls trying to be helpful."

"The birds jeer at me," he said darkly. "I hear them when I'm out walking. 'Sinner!' they caw. 'Sordid sensualist! Sorry sap! Your poetry is trash. Trash! Trash! Trash!'" His voice rose to a piercing shriek.

There was a pit opening up before Jane's eyes and she would not look into it, she would not. "You've had too much to drink," she said. "Perhaps you should go to bed."

"Say you'll think about going away with me," said Rossetti. "And then I will be your obedient boy and trot off to sleep."

Jane slid off her chair and crawled along the floor into Rossetti's arms. "I will think about it," she said.

"Say you will," said Rossetti.

"I will," she said, tears running down her face.

July 17, 1872

Dearest Jane,

We left Reykjavik yesterday. Almost immediately I lost my penknife. Of course I brought two others, so I unearthed one of them from the immense pack my poor horse has been burdened with. Feeling quite pleased at my own foresight, I attached the knife to my belt and went on. When we stopped for dinner I looked down and saw that it was gone.

Well, I cursed then, as you can imagine. But I still had one other, which I tied to my waist with a thick rope. I was sure that no force on earth could wrest that penknife from me. We went on our way, fording three torrents before stopping for the night. I won't be able to adequately describe the terror of stepping into that icy rushing water, the horse up to its withers, me clinging to the poor beast for dear life, it slipping on stones and scrambling toward the bank, our guides Eyvindr and Gisli shouting, me screaming probably.

We stopped for the night at a pleasant homestead. I dismounted, gratefully stretching my stiff muscles, and reached for my knife.

Of course it was gone. Faulkner and Evans were in hysterics but now I am without my most useful implement and no one will lend their knife to me.

Please tell the girls to write as often as they can. I miss Jenny's funny stories and May's silly drawings so much. I ache with missing them.

Your William

Jane folded the letter and put it back into its envelope. She uncorked her ink bottle and took out a sheet of thin stationery, but for a long time she sat at her desk without raising her pen. She had no idea what to say to her husband. She could not tell him that she hadn't thought of him in weeks, or that she feared Rossetti might be losing his mind. She could not write that Rossetti had asked her to run away with him and that she had told him she would, or mention that sometimes when the post came, the children were enjoying Rossetti's company so much that they did not look up. Even describing the flood necessitated naming Rossetti. He had taken the girls out in the boat and he had dreamed up the idea of the play. He had taught Jenny to play chess, he had put a poultice on May's sprained ankle. That very day he had matched in oil paint the exact color of the azure sky and had joined the girls on the roof and fallen into the yew, sustaining minor injuries.

No, unless she wrote a letter that contained only the blandest of generalities, it would be difficult to write to her husband at all. She put the cork back in the ink bottle and left her desk.

July 30, 1872

Dearest Jane,

We have come to the place known as Woden's tomb. It is a huge stone monolith. The stone is different from the volcanic rock, and different from any of the other stones in the area. It does look as if it had fallen from the sky and landed in this place. From a distance the area all around looks completely barren, but up close you can see that the ground is covered by millions of tiny flowers. The most abundant of them resemble phlox. Most of them are white, though a few are pink. There are also clumps of yellow blossoms like yarrow root. The stone is covered with colorful green and orange lichen, so that the overall effect, instead of being one of emptiness, is one of teeming life.

The vista from up here, needless to say, is breathtaking.

You will be pleased to learn that I have lost quite a bit of weight on the heavy exercise and Spartan diet. It's hard to say how much, but I can tell you that I bored a new hole in my belt just yesterday.

Tomorrow we will enter the mountains at last. I have been taking very copious notes and have almost used up my supply of journals. When I run out I am afraid that I will have to use my writing paper and won't be able to correspond as frequently. Know, however, that I am thinking of you just as often and that you are always in my heart.

Your William

Twenty-nine

THE day came, early in September, when word arrived that her husband had landed in Scotland. It would take him three days to reach Kelmscott.

"Have you thought about what we agreed?" asked Rossetti that night after the girls were asleep and the fire had burned down to glowing embers.

"You want to do it now?" she asked, trying to keep the panic out of her voice. As much as she was dreading Rossetti's departure and the arrival of Morris, she was terrified at the idea of taking such a step. Could she really count on Rossetti? Would he be able to take care of her?

"Is there a better time?" Rossetti asked. "The girls will be all right with their nanny until Thursday. Morris will come back and find us gone. You can even write him a long letter if you like, though I'm sure explanations won't be necessary."

"Are you sure this is the right step?" said Jane. "Are you sure you won't get tired of me, that we won't quarrel and you won't leave me at the foot of Mount Olympus or something?"

Rossetti smiled and patted her cheek. "I will never be tired of you as long as I live, no matter where we go or what we do."

They were to leave in the morning. Jane stayed up very late packing her things. She was not asleep when Jenny came in the night to tell her that May was moaning in her sleep and seemed ill.

Jane went to her and found her tossing and turning, bathed in sweat.

"She has a fever," said Jane. "Wake Nanny and tell her to bring a basin of cool water and some towels." Though she was worried about May, she felt dizzy and light-headed with relief. She could never leave the girls now. Not even Rossetti would expect her to.

The doctor came to examine May and did not think her seriously ill, but left some medicine and told her to keep a careful eye on the girl. He did not have to encourage Jane, who hovered over the bed all day, arranging pillows, bathing her with cool compresses, and feeding her anything she agreed to eat. After several hours of it, May became churlish.

"You'd think I was dying," she grumbled. "I heard the doctor, I'm going to be jumping rope by the time Papa comes."

Then Jane began to cry, thinking of how close she had come to leaving them, perhaps forever.

"I'm not dying, Mama," said May, touching her hand. "I promise." They both looked over at Jenny, who was reading on her bed.

"It's because Papa's coming, isn't it?" said Jenny, wisely.

They were all in the garden when Morris arrived. The girls ran to the drive when they heard the carriage and squealed with delight when they caught sight of the thick-coated pony trotting along behind. Jane and Rossetti watched quietly as they threw themselves on the man who emerged from the carriage, hurling questions about the pony.

"His name is Mouse," Morris said. "I bought him in Reykjavik and a very reliable traveling companion he was. Never stumbled."

"Is he ours to keep?" asked Jenny.

"Can we ride him?" asked May.

"Yes, and yes," said Morris. He lifted first Jenny, then May onto the pony.

"Grab hold of the mane," he instructed. "You won't hurt him." He handed the lead to the carriage driver and turned to face his wife and her lover.

"Did you enjoy being up to your neck in ice, Top?" asked Rossetti, shaking his hand. "It certainly seems to have agreed with you." He was indeed thinner, as he had said, and his face was tan.

"Thank you," said Morris. He was not looking at Jane, or at Rossetti, but at the girls on the pony. "I'm quite exhausted actually. The train journey was much worse than any hardship I endured on the trail."

"You'll want some tea, I suppose," said Jane finally. She had hoped that she could behave warmly and naturally, but she found she felt awkward and that as a result, her voice was colder than she would have liked.

"Just have someone bring a tray to my room," said Morris. "I'm worn out. I may fall asleep in the middle of eating and I think that would set a bad example were I to do it at the table in front of the kiddies."

"I'll bring it," said Jane.

"There's no need," said Morris. "Katie can do it just as well."

Rossetti and Jane ate a rather silent supper.

"I'll go tomorrow," he said. "Now that appearances have been preserved."

"Don't go," Jane begged.

"There's nothing to stay for now. Everything is spoiled when he is here. No, I'd rather go back to Tudor House and draw and imagine that we are back here, alone together. That is how it must be, apparently, until next summer."

"Aren't I coming to sit for Proserpine next week?"

"Yes, but don't you remember your promise to your husband? In London we must be friends only."

Jane felt that she might dissolve at any moment into a weepy mass of despondency, but she tried to remain composed.

"Unless . . . ," Rossetti said. "Unless you change your mind and leave with me tonight."

"I can't," Jane said. "The girls . . ."

"Of course," said Rossetti, not looking at her. He stood up from the table. "My train is very early tomorrow. I'd better say good night."

"Gabriel," she pleaded.

He bowed and walked away.

When Jane awoke, Rossetti was gone. Everything seemed drained of color: the bed curtains in her room were dingy; the sky outside her window was hazy and gray; the face in her hand mirror was pallid. She went to the garden to read but the blush roses were white and wilting.

She had been staring at the same page for an hour when her husband emerged.

"Did you sleep well?" she asked, feeling ridiculously polite and formal.

"Like the dead," he said. "I hadn't realized how much I missed a feather bed. Though I must be careful, now that I've toughened up, not to go soft. I may have to sleep out here, or perhaps in the boat. That sounds chilly and uncomfortable."

"When are we returning to London?" she asked. Morris frowned.

"Are you so eager to leave? Do you not enjoy it here?"

"I love Kelmscott," she said. "I was only thinking the girls must resume their lessons."

"In three weeks," Morris said. "But if you are set on leaving, we'll go tomorrow." He paused. "I hope that the summer was satisfying?"

"It was lovely," said Jane.

"You didn't write to me," Morris said.

"I didn't know what to say," said Jane.

"It's a shame that everywhere I look, I see you and Gabriel together," he said bitterly, "because this really is a wonderful house. So elegant in its Tudor solidity."

"It's been idyllic," said Jane. "Thank you."

"Where are the girls?" he said, standing up.

"Down by the river," said Jane. "They have run completely wild this summer. They will be sorry to go back to London."

"I think I'll go to them," he said. He left her there alone.

Thirty

HE fall and winter had passed quietly. Morris had been busy with the Firm and came home only to sleep. Jane and her husband had seldom gone out together because it was too awkward to pretend. As a result she had seen Rossetti socially very infrequently, though she still modeled for him regularly. But through all of the gray days, when the icy winds blew the rain against the parlor glass and Jenny practiced the piano and May sang slightly off-key, Jane had thought about Kelmscott. She thought about Rossetti's touch, and about the peonies in the garden, and the willow herb and mugwort that grew on the banks of the river. She thought about the neighbor's dog that had been rescued in the flood, and about the cook's strawberry preserves. Sometimes it seemed impossible that she could wait out the days and the months until it was time to return.

Now it was May, and the summer was only a few weeks away. Jane went to Tudor House to model, as usual, but Rossetti did not answer the bell.

Finally she pushed on the door and discovered that it was not locked. She went inside, calling his name, but there was no answer. At last she found him in bed, an empty quart bottle in the covers with him, a glass of whiskey on the bedside table. For a moment her heart stopped. Had he decided to join Lizzie? Then he groaned and jerked his head. Jane removed the bottle, covered him properly, and went downstairs to wait.

She paced the studio and examined Rossetti's work. He was about to begin his painting of her as Proserpine and there were sketches pinned everywhere of her holding a pomegranate. There were drawings of the pomegranate alone, its flesh open to reveal a cross section of seeds. There were several drawings of just her hand holding the pomegranate. There were pastel drawings of just her eyes, and of the ivy that was to curl behind her head. Jane reflected that it was strange she could find these studies so compelling, when looking at Morris's sketches never failed to bore her.

After an hour she went back to Rossetti's room. His eyes were open but he had not moved.

"What has happened?" she said, sitting on the bed beside him and taking his hand. He gestured toward the table. She had not noticed, in her horror at the sight of the chloral, the pamphlet that was lying there. It was by Buchanan. Jane flipped through it and saw that it was an expanded version of the original article attacking Rossetti.

"You see he will not rest until I'm destroyed," Rossetti said. "He and the others."

Jane was afraid. "That's madness, Gabriel dear."

"Is it? Or are you in league with them?" He clutched her wrist tightly and pulled her to him. Her face was very close to his and she smelled his sour breath.

"I love you," she said, kissing the hand that held her fast.

"I know," Rossetti said mournfully, releasing her. "It's just that I didn't sleep last night. That's why I took the chloral. The words of the pamphlet kept ringing in my head, attacking me, mocking me, laughing at me for my poor pathetic poetry, which isn't good for anything. I should have left it to rot with Lizzie."

"You need to sleep," said Jane. "I'll go."

"Sit with me," he said. "I'm afraid to be alone. It's the voices."

She stayed until he was asleep again, and went home with a heavy heart. She wrote to William Rossetti, but he didn't reply.

Two days later she visited Rossetti again and found him with his head bandaged. He had accused his brother of being in league with Buchanan and had tried to physically remove him from the house. In the process he had fallen down the front steps and cut his head badly on the iron railing.

It was terrifying to see him in such a state. When the doctor came to examine his head, Rossetti screamed at him and had to be restrained. Several of the servants left. Jane was afraid to go to see him but also afraid not to. She could not abandon him when he was so obviously suffering, but neither could she talk him out of his delusions. He had an answer for every argument, whether it made sense or not. If she told him he was unreasonable or that his accusations were nonsense, he accused her of being Buchanan's whore. Once he threw her from the house and locked all of the doors.

Then came the day when her letters went unanswered. For three days she tried to reach him but could not. Finally, in a panic, she asked Morris to go to Tudor House and find out what was wrong.

"His brother is there," said Morris when he returned. "Gabriel's raving. William's keeping back your letters."

"But why?" cried Jane.

"They blame you," Morris said. "William and the doctors. They think the stress of your liaison has broken him down."

"But it's the chloral," said Jane helplessly. "And Buchanan. You know it's not my fault."

"You triggered the change in him," said Morris coldly.

"No," said Jane, "it can't be."

"I don't know," said Morris wearily. "Perhaps the passion you inspire in him has unhinged his mind. He's always been a little bit wrong, and then Lizzie's death."

"But they have doctors there?" asked Jane. "He will get well?"

"I don't know," said Morris.

The next day she received a letter from Rossetti, asking her where she had been and why she had not written. They returned to their usual routine without acknowledging what had occurred.

A month later she again went to Tudor House to model, but there was no answer. This time, however, when Jane went inside, Rossetti wasn't there. Panicked, she went to William Rossetti's house, then the doctor's. No one was home at either place. In tears, she went home to Queen Square and found Burne-Jones having tea with Morris. It was he who told her what had happened.

"They've taken him to Roehampton," Burne-Jones said. "A doctor's house there. For a change of air and scene."

"And company, I suppose," sobbed Jane.

She wrote Rossetti letters, telling him to be strong and to think of his painting and of the time they would spend together in the summer, but she never received a reply. She knew William Rossetti was confiscating them, yet she continued to write. It was the only thing she could do for her lover.

She began to have nightmares. One night she dreamed that Rossetti had died and that his ghost had come to her and was standing next to the bed. Some days later she learned that he had swallowed an entire bottle of chloral and had been unconscious for thirty-six hours. It made her wonder whether his interest in séances was so foolish after all.

Morris took her to see Rossetti in Roehampton, before he was taken to Scotland to the home of his patron William Graham. When she went in he was very groggy. His body was slack from inactivity and very pale from spending all of his time indoors. At first he seemed not to recognize her. She spoke to him in a too loud, too cheerful voice about what she had been up to in London while he had been gone and how sure she was that he would be better soon. At last he took her hand and murmured, "My sweet," and she began to cry. No one but Rossetti saw the tears. She went into his room calm and composed and that is the way she exited, leading his brother to remark that her heart was as cold as a cinder.

But she didn't care what the others thought. They didn't know her. Only Rossetti mattered.

A few days later Morris accompanied her to Kelmscott Manor and returned to London for the summer. May chose to go with her and Jenny chose to stay with her father.

The cook had made plum jam and ginger scones, and the garden was riotous with apricot foxglove and sweet peas and cornflowers, but neither Jane nor May could enjoy it.

"It's quiet," said May. "I remember it being noisy. And the house seems gloomy. Without Jenny here I won't be able to put on any plays. Monologues are no fun. And I suppose you won't let me go down to the river by myself, so I'll be stuck in the house."

"I'll go with you," said Jane, thinking that she, too, found the house gloomy and would be better off outside.

The very next day she took May canoeing, and they went to the spot of that first picnic, but although they saw a family of foxes, it failed to cheer them up. The next day May spent with her friend Alice Turnham and seemed to forget her complaints. But Jane did not have a friend to visit and the days continued to be sad and lonely.

Jane knew that Rossetti was doing his best to convince his doctors that it was safe for him to come to her, but she didn't know if he would be able to. She had no letter from him in June or July. She began to suspect that he was dead and no one was telling her. But Morris had promised that whatever happened, he would let her know. All she could do was wait.

In early September Morris came down to take them back to London.

"Any news?" she asked her husband.

"He is better," Morris said. "They think he is out of danger. He still wants to come here, and his brother is thinking about giving in and letting him. You'll be back in London, of course. William still thinks it best that you not see each other."

"I'm not leaving here until I see Rossetti," said Jane. "I don't care what William thinks is best."

"All right," said Morris. "I'll take May back, and you can write to me when you are ready to return home."

When the carriage pulled into the drive, she ran out to meet it and could hardly believe that the man who emerged was her lover. He moved slowly, and needed help getting down. He was bundled to the eyes but she could see that he was very, very thin. His face was very pale and clean shaven, making him look much younger. But it was his eyes that alarmed her. They were empty. They did not shine with joy when he saw her. His face did not change.

"My dear," he said flatly, without expression. "I am here."

"I've been waiting," she said.

They sat on the riverbank. Rossetti became cold easily now and wore his coat buttoned all the way to his neck and wrapped a blanket around his legs. She thought of the summer before, when he had rowed in his shirtsleeves and performed gymnastics for the children. She wondered if he was thinking of it, too, but his hat was pulled down low over his eyes and she could not see the expression on his face.

"What shall we do today?" she asked, hoping that the old Rossetti would jump up and proclaim that they should mow the hayfields, or that they should go into Oxford and buy bookmaking supplies. But he said nothing. She wondered if he could have fallen asleep sitting up.

"My brother has always hated me, you know," he said at last.

"William?" she said, her heart pounding. "No, Gabriel, that's not true. He's devoted to you."

"Oh, that's what he wants everyone to think. So devoted, everyone says. So kind to lend his brother money all the time, and to arrange things for him when he was unwell. He wants to make a prisoner of me. It's what he's always wanted. If he can have me certified as insane, then he can lock me up and control me forever."

"He's going to have you certified?" said Jane.

"It certainly seems that way," said Rossetti grimly.

"How do you come to know this?" said Jane. "Have you heard something?"

"It's nothing I've heard," said Rossetti. "It's what I've put together. It makes sense, doesn't it? He's always been jealous of me, since we were boys. He's been biding his time, waiting for his moment."

It certainly seemed to Jane that William should have been jealous of Rossetti, who of the two of them had inherited most of the talent, and who had been constantly cosseted. The sacrifices William had made for Gabriel might have made any man resentful. And yet he had never seemed so to her. When she had seen him at Roehampton, he looked haggard and frightened. She had no doubt that removing Rossetti from London had been a good-faith effort on William's part to save his brother's life. And with a sigh she realized that there was no reasoning with the man beside her.

"He seems to be genuinely worried about you," she said, though she knew it would do no good.

"Treachery," said Rossetti, and began to quote from *Othello*. "He's not the only one against me, you know."

"There's someone else?" said Jane.

"I think you know who I'm talking about," said Rossetti darkly. Jane said nothing. She waited instead for the mood to pass and lucidity to return, as it sometimes did. Some days Rossetti seemed almost himself, if less boisterous, and she could tell herself that he was recovering from an illness, like pneumonia.

"Perhaps we should go in and rest," she suggested after a time.

"I am rather tired," he said. "I have such terrible dreams at night that sometimes I'm afraid to go to sleep."

She walked with him to his room, but he did not want her to come in. "I'm perfectly capable of getting myself into bed," he said, shaking her hand off his arm. "I don't need you to nurse me."

Jane remained composed until she was in her room with the door closed. Then she threw herself onto the bed and succumbed to anguished sobs. How could he treat her this way?

Of course, she reflected some time later, after she had spent herself, God could not allow them to be happy, even if her husband could. This was the price she had to pay for the golden summer she had had the year before. She thought she could stand anything if she knew that Rossetti would eventually get well. William Rossetti, guided by the doctor who had treated his brother in Roehampton, was hopeful. They thought a change of air and rest might be all that was necessary.

"Of course he shouldn't drink alcohol," William had told her before he relinquished Rossetti into her care. "No matter how much he teases. It gives him headaches and makes it hard to sleep. I know he thinks he needs it, but the doctor tells me it is actually detrimental to his recovery."

The other rule that William gave her was that he must be weaned from chloral.

"It's terribly difficult," he said to her. "Are you sure you are ready to take on such a task?"

She had no idea what it involved, but she assured him she was. He could not stop taking it all at once, or he would become violently ill and might in fact die from the lack of it. So he must be weaned slowly, a little at a time. When he first arrived at Kelmscott, William Rossetti handed her the case of vials and told her that she must dispense them.

"Start with two in the morning, one at teatime, and two at night," he said. "Then in about a week take away one of the morning ones. Then one of the night ones. Then the one at teatime.

Next to last take away the final morning vial, and then finally the one in the evening. In about six weeks he will be completely free of the stuff."

"What if he asks for more?" she said. "What if he gets sick?"

"You must be strong," said William. "No matter what he says or does or how he tries to manipulate you. And keep that case under lock and key."

She had done exactly as he asked and now Rossetti was down to one vial three times a day. They still had wine with dinner, which Rossetti downed by the bottleful, but he no longer had gin or scotch afterward, and he did seem better for it.

So it was with shock that she entered his room one day with a vaseful of fresh roses to find him dispensing a clear liquid into a glass with an eyedropper. It was ten o'clock in the morning and Rossetti had said he wanted to sleep in.

"Where did you get that?" she asked, more in surprise than in anger.

"You think I'd tell you?" Rossetti snarled. "You, who are in league against me?"

"Gabriel, you know that is not true," she said. "I'm trying to help you."

"Did you know I can no longer sleep at night?" he said. "Did you know that I heave and choke up bile when I wake up in the morning? Did you know that my head aches worse than if I'd been hit in the temple with an anvil, and you take away from me the one thing that will help me?"

"It's killing you," Jane said. "The doctors say so. If you hang on a little longer, it will get better."

"It will be better when I'm dead," said Rossetti.

Jane went cold. "What do you mean by that?" she asked.

"Just what you think," said Rossetti. "Please leave."

She left him there and went to check the cabinet where she kept the supply of chloral. It was all as she had left it. She concluded that Rossetti must have bribed one of the servants to go into town for him, but no one admitted having done it.

In the end she gave up and let him have as much as he wanted. She was too afraid of what he would do if she didn't, and she couldn't bear the thought of losing him, either by death or by his turning against her. She couldn't stand it that he might hate her. When he had as much chloral as he liked, he seemed almost like his old self again, charming and witty. He began to take a notepad on their walks by the river, and to write a little poetry again, which was always about her and which he would read aloud as he worked. Jane loved to hear the adoring words, more for what they symbolized than for the praise they heaped on her: Rossetti was getting better.

One afternoon they were stretched out, as usual, on the bank of the Thames. She lay in his arms as he stroked her hair. He had brought his sketchbook, though he had not opened it. She was reading to him from a new work of Dickens. Then the hunters came tramping through.

It was common enough for hunters to pass by, and she had never thought much about it. They never came in the summer, of course. They had stayed so late at Kelmscott that it was now duck-hunting season. She recognized one as the gentleman who owned the adjoining estate and greeted him politely. But Rossetti stood up, enraged.

"What are you doing?" he screamed. The hunters looked up, startled.

"Excuse me, Mr. Rossetti, just passing," said the leader of the group, their neighbor. They moved as if to go on.

"Stop!" Rossetti shouted. "Thieves! Murderers! Christ killers! Lovers of Satan and of Sodom and Gomorrah!" Before Jane had a chance to stop him, he had advanced on the hunters, who appeared to be frozen to the ground in confusion.

"I will kill you for defiling this land with your sinful feet," he said, and punched one of the men in the face. The man reeled but didn't fall.

"Mr. Rossetti, get hold of yourself," said their neighbor. He attempted to restrain Gabriel but was knocked to the ground.

"Mrs. Morris," cried her neighbor. "Get some servants to help us!"

As she ran toward the house, she watched as the hunters beat Rossetti down and restrained him until she came back with her two gardeners and some ropes. Somehow, though they were seven strapping men, they could not seem to subdue the lone invalid. She tried to help them tie the ropes around Rossetti's wrists, but one of his arms came free and hit her in the face. She fell back, stunned, and stayed out of the fray as they at last held and tied him. She tried not to watch, but his screams and curses were impossible to ignore.

When the doctor came he looked with disgust at the vials next to Rossetti's bed.

"You've been allowing him to ingest this poison?" he said.

"How could I stop him?" she said in anguish. "He said without it he would kill himself."

Now the doctor looked at her with pity instead of anger. "I am sorry," he said. "Mr. Rossetti has had a complete psychotic break."

"What does that mean?" she asked with dread.

The doctor shook his head. "His delusions have become his reality," he said. "He is no longer in the world that we are in. He may return now and then, but it is increasingly unlikely that he will ever be entirely cured."

"What should I do?" she asked.

"Write to his family," the doctor advised. "You cannot care for him alone."

After the doctor had left, she sat by Rossetti's bedside and watched him sleep. The doctor had administered laudanum and it would be hours before Rossetti would awaken. His jaw was bruised from where one of the hunters had elbowed him in an effort to subdue him. His left eye was blackened and he had scratches on his neck and arms. In his drug-induced stupor he no longer strained against the ropes that bound his arms, but she could see that his wrists were red and chafed from his writhings. He was like an animal, without sense or reason.

She thought about the autumn. She had had Rossetti here, but it was Rossetti in body only. His spirit was lost somewhere, and she didn't know if it would ever return. Shall I have a séance for it? she thought to herself. Is he any less dead because his body is still alive? In fact, Rossetti's body only tormented her with what she had lost.

It was foolish to still love him, and yet she did. After all, she thought, it was not his fault. He was very ill. He had not meant to strike her, and none of the hunters had been seriously hurt. He had periods of lucidity where he seemed, if not his old self, then at least someone she enjoyed being with.

The truth was, the doctor was right. The nursing Rossetti required was beyond her abilities. Perhaps it had always been, but it certainly was now. He would have to go back to his brother. Or she could go back to London and William Rossetti could send someone to Kelmscott to stay with him.

Perhaps the breakdown was her fault, as so many people said. The guilt of doing something he knew to be sinful, no matter how hard he tried to rationalize it away, must have been weighing on him. Jane felt that you tried to do your best and God would forgive you the rest, but despite his insouciant air Jane knew Rossetti feared the wrath of a vengeful God.

She could not take care of him. The primary thing that husbands and wives should do for one another, and she could not do it. She had been fooling herself; she was no wife to him. If she had been his wife, perhaps he would have responded to her ministering. Perhaps she could have helped him.

As for herself, she could no longer depend on him for anything, not even affection. He had become an invalid, a dangerous and violent one. The burden she would be asked to assume would be heavy and thankless. And yet, to abandon the man she had pledged herself to was unthinkable. The choices were intolerable.

She stayed at his side until he awoke. The light was fading and in the shadows his expression was hard to read.

"Jane," he said. She was relieved that he knew her. More than once he had called her Lizzie and it had torn out her heart.

"I'm here, darling," she said.

"My head," he said trying to sit up.

"Don't," she said. "You have to rest."

"Did I really attack five gentlemen with rifles?" he asked, feeling his tender jaw.

"Yes, you did," she said.

"I must be truly insane, then," he said. "I don't even remember why I did it. If they passed by the house now, I doubt I would even notice them."

"You were upset," said Jane.

"It defies explanation," Rossetti said, and Jane had to agree.

"I struck you," said Rossetti, looking at her swollen eye.

"Only accidentally," she said. "I was trying to get the ropes around your wrists while the others held you."

He turned his head and she knew that he was crying. "I have been reduced to this?" he said. "I strike you while you're trying to restrain me and then you feed me mugs of broth and bathe me as if I were a child?"

"It won't always be like this," she said. "You will be well again and then things will be as they were before."

"I'm beginning to doubt it," he said. "I think that something inside me is irrevocably broken."

Jane didn't answer, as she was not sure what to say.

"You'll go back to him," Rossetti said.

"Yes," Jane said.

He fell back upon the pillows. "It's probably for the best. It was insanity to think we could live this way, out of time, out of society. We were fools."

That whole, terrible day Jane had not shed a tear, but at last she could stand it no longer. "How can I do it?" she screamed. "How will I stand it?" And she fell upon the bed, shaking with sobs. Her screams brought the servants running, and, though they found no signs that Rossetti had harmed her, they were taking no chances. They forcibly escorted her to her own room, and she offered little resistance as she was led away. A sleeping draft was prepared for her, and, though she hated the stuff more now than before, she obediently drank it. Anything to be away from her own thoughts. Anything to enter a dreamless land of emptiness.

Thirty-one

*J*ANE wrote to William Rossetti, and he came promptly to oversee his brother's care. He did not reproach her for her failure, but he did seem relieved when she told him that she was leaving Kelmscott. She also wrote to her husband to tell him that Rossetti was worse and she was coming back to London. She knew Morris would understand what that meant. Rossetti seemed not to notice, or care, when she came into his room to say goodbye, which was most heartbreaking of all.

On the journey back to London and to Morris, Jane tried to think of what she would say to her husband, but nothing sounded right. "I'm sorry" sounded insincere, because was she really sorry? She was sorry that Rossetti's mind had faltered, she was sorry that his illness necessitated her leaving him, but she was not sorry she had fallen in love with him. She could not say "Forgive me," because what she had done was unforgivable. She would not seek to diminish her treachery by asking her husband to absolve her. "I am home" was completely inadequate. When her carriage pulled up in front of the brick town house, she still had no idea what she was going to say.

He was waiting for her in the parlor, Rossetti's book of verse, *Poems,* in his lap.

"How is he?" Morris asked.

"Not very well, I'm afraid," she said. "He attacked Peter Godrick."

"Attacked him?" Morris did not seem overly concerned. "With a shovel?"

"Flew at him. Hit him. It took seven men to bring him down. The doctor said he has had a complete breakdown."

"My God," said Morris, sounding serious now. "Will he recover?"

"William is there," said Jane. "He will not let Gabriel hurt himself."

"Terrifying, isn't it, how fragile some minds are," said Morris. "Rossetti's mind, it seems, is the thinnest glass. Mine, though, I've been relieved to discover, seems to be fashioned of shoe leather and cannot be more than scuffed."

"Who is to say that the scuffing isn't more painful than the shattering?" said Jane.

"You are the only person in a position to observe who suffers most," said Morris. "Perhaps it is you."

"What is my mind made of?" asked Jane.

"Oh, I think it's a willow basket," said Morris. He put down his pipe and stood up. "Soft and pliable but incredibly resilient. The only way to unravel it would be with great violence and a pair of very sharp scissors."

Jane waited to see if he would embrace her, but instead he picked up her traveling case. "I'll take you up to your room," he said. "There's something I want to show you."

As she climbed the staircase, Jane noticed with dismay how very drab the carpets looked and how dirty the casements were. She had always disliked the house, but the summer at Kelmscott had made its shabbiness seem almost unbearable. When she reached the doorway of her bedroom, however, she halted in surprise. Next to her, Morris watched her face.

"I thought," he said, "that if you were coming home to stay, you might like a change."

He had replaced the garish Victorian wallpaper with Jasmine, one of his newest designs. The fluted white flowers with their gray-green leaves tendriled around pinwheel flowers of pale green. Her bed had been covered with fabric of the same pattern. He had framed and hung some of Rossetti's drawings on the wall, as well as one of his manuscript pages from *Icelandic Stories*. The woodwork had been freshly painted, and a new crewel rug had been laid on the floor.

"William," she said, and touched his arm.

"Shall we plan the menu for the week now?" he asked, but she saw that his eyes were moist. He went to the window to hide his emotion from her.

"I'd like to rest for a moment," said Jane. And then, hesitantly, "Will you sit with me?"

Morris was still watching the street and did not reply. "Jenny and May are back," he observed.

"Mummy's home," shouted May from below, and clambered up the stairs into the room.

"Hello, Mummy," she said, leaping into Jane's arms.

"How was your walk, darling?" Jane asked.

"We saw the most adorable dog," said May. "It had puffs of hair on its tail and around each foot."

"The gentleman said it was a Pomeranian," said Jenny from the doorway. She seemed shy and Jane reflected that it was probably better she was not going to go away again.

"May we have one?" said May, already knowing the answer.

"I'm afraid they're temperamental," said Morris. "But we could shave your head into a little puff and it would be almost the same." He lunged for May and she shrieked in delight.

"What would you like for dinner, sweet?" Jane asked Jenny.

"Turnips," replied Jenny promptly, in a way that made Jane's heart constrict. How she had missed them!

"Just turnips?" she asked.

"With ham," said Jenny. "And potato soup."
"And fried parsnips," said Morris.
"And chocolate cake," said May.

Tudor House, London
January 15, 1873

Dearest Jane,

You must think me terrible for not writing for so long. The truth is, I really was too ill to put pen to paper, but now at last I can write to you and ask how you are. Is your back bothering you terribly in the cold? I hope you are putting the hot compress on it every night, and taking the tablets that Dr. Cook gave you. I cannot have you being unwell.

I am back in London, as you may have heard. My brother has installed himself here to look after me, and despite feeling a little bit like I'm in prison, it hasn't been unpleasant. He is at his office most of the day and in the evenings it's nice to have a little company, even if it is galling to have one's younger brother attend to one so officiously.

I am going to begin painting again, and I need my Proserpine. Will you come next week? I suppose I could understand if you didn't want to, but if you don't come I don't know what I shall do. This painting is really going to be one of my best and it won't work if I don't have you here. Monday morning at eleven?

Your Gabriel

Jane folded up the letter with a sad smile. For a moment she thought of asking Morris what she should do, but then she realized that only she could decide. She went to her desk, pulled out a sheet of her stationery, dipped her pen, and began to write.

London,
January 15, 1873

My Dear Gabriel,

I scarcely know where to begin.

I read your letter with great joy. I knew at once that you had returned to health. Who else can be so ardent, so solicitous, and so demanding all at once?

I miss Kelmscott terribly but am otherwise well. I suppose we will never go there again. The thought fills me with such terror that I can scarcely breathe.

You know, I trust, that I will be your friend until death separates us.

I will be Proserpine Monday morning at eleven, and every day thereafter for as long as you want me.

Your Guinevere

Afterword

Dante Gabriel Rossetti never fully recovered from his breakdown and his addiction continued. He and Jane remained warm friends until the end of his life. He died April 9, 1882. He was only fifty-three.

William Morris was a poet, designer, and social reformer. During his life he was best known as the author of *The Earthly Paradise*, but we know him today as the father of the Arts and Crafts movement, which would inspire designers such as Charles Rennie Mackintosh and continues to inspire today. He died October 3, 1896, age sixty-two. One doctor diagnosed the cause of death as "being William Morris, and having done more work than most ten men."

Jenny Morris was diagnosed with epilepsy, a shameful and untreatable condition at that time. Her condition slowly declined and all hopes for her future were destroyed. She required constant nursing care until her death in 1935.

May Morris was an active Socialist, textile designer, and the editor of her father's *Collected Works*, published in 1915. She died in 1938.

Jane Morris lived quietly until her death in January 1914 at the age of seventy-four.

Author's Note

In historical fiction, a writer begins with the facts. Jane Morris was born in Oxford, married William Morris in 1859, and had two daughters. So far, not very interesting. But here and there, tantalizing details crop up. At the parish school she attended, Jane was required to scour a room every Saturday to prepare for her likely career in domestic service. Dante Gabriel Rossetti kept a menagerie, including a kangaroo and a wombat, at his London house. William Morris often appeared at dinner blue to the elbows from his experiments with natural dyes. Distinct, fascinating personalities begin to emerge, and the desire wells up in me to know these people better. Biography is no longer enough. Since there is no way that I can join William Morris, Jane Morris, and Dante Gabriel Rossetti for dinner at Red House, I have to imagine myself there. Since there is no way that William can pour out his heartache to me, or that Jane can share her doubts and fears about Rossetti's health and their affair, I have to make that imaginative leap.

The novelist Jessamyn West once said, "Fiction reveals truths that reality obscures." I believe that completely. There is a truth beyond the facts, and that is what I am constantly in search of.

Historical fiction transports the reader to another time and place. Granted, it is not Victorian England or Renaissance Florence as the people there experienced it. It is some strange amalgam of the historical record and the author's mind. You may learn things about historical figures that you never knew, and that is part of the fun, but, most important, when you finish reading you feel as if you have met them. You feel that you know them, not just where they were born or when they married or how they died, but their essential self. It may be an illusion, but it is as close as we will ever get.

In imagining *The Wayward Muse,* I have relied on *Jane Morris: The Pre-Raphaelite Model of Beauty,* by Debra N. Mancoff (Rohnert Park, Calif.: Pomegranate, 2000); *Pre-Raphaelites in Love,* by Gay Daly (New York: Ticknor & Fields, 1989); *Pre-Raphaelite Sisterhood,* by Jan Marsh (New York: St. Martin's Press, 1985); *Dante Gabriel Rossetti and Jane Morris: Their Correspondence,* edited and with an introduction by John Bryson (Clarendon Press, 1976); *Dante Gabriel Rossetti,* by Julian Treuherz, Liz Prettejohn, and Edwin Becker (London: Thomas & Hudson, 2003); and *William Morris by Himself,* edited by Gillian Naylor (Little Brown, 2000). The story hews as closely to the facts as possible, though I am sure there are inadvertent inaccuracies, for which I ask your forbearance.

The Wayward Muse

Elizabeth Hickey

A Readers Club Guide

Introduction

Jane Burden is a plain girl, with unremarkable looks and a destitute upbringing. She lives in a run-down house next to the public toilets in the slums of Oxford, England, a daily reminder that her existence is nothing more than waste and filth. Jane's abusive mother rules the house with an iron fist, and her father and brother spend all of their time and the little money they earn at the local pub. But when a band of carousing artists arrives in town to paint the interior of the Oxford Debating Hall, they discover in Jane a beauty she never knew she possessed. Dante Gabriel Rossetti, the leader of the group, is so taken with Jane's somber gray eyes, her slender frame, and her dark hair that he falls immediately in love with her and insists that she sit as the model for his painting of Guinevere. Jane, swept up by Rossetti's attentions and affections, falls for him in turn, and they commence a secretive and passionate affair. When Rossetti disappears without explanation, however, Jane is crushed. In his absence, Rossetti's friend, William Morris, remains in Oxford and asks Jane to model for him. Though his talent and passion cannot compare to Rossetti's, Morris is a polite and thoughtful man, and he gradually wins Jane over by his steadfastness. But Jane hangs on to the memory of Rossetti, and when at last the artists and the lovers are reunited, old flames and friendships are rekindled and new jealousies and secrets emerge.

Discussion Questions

1. When Rossetti inquires about the details of Jane's background he quips, "Poor Jane! All that is needed is three wicked stepsisters and a pumpkin coach." In what ways is *The Wayward Muse* a Cinderella story? Can you think of any other fairy-tale archetypes that Jane Burden embodies?

2. What did you think about Jane before Rossetti discovers her? What was it about her that he thinks is so special? Rossetti nearly convinces her that "she was a princess taken from her royal position at birth and placed with a lowly family for her protection." But Mrs. Burden accuses Jane of condescension and "[getting] above herself." What do you imagine Jane's fate would have been had Rossetti not entered her world?

3. Who determines beauty and how is it measured? It seems that once Rossetti declares Jane a great beauty, everyone else awakens to her charms and agrees with him. How is beauty determined in today's society? Do you see the same effect, in which one person of great influence calls something beautiful and the masses follow suit?

4. In their attempts to seduce Jane, both Rossetti and Morris bring her to places high above the ground—Rossetti to the rafters of the debating hall and Morris to the bell tower of Chartres. She asks Morris: "What is it with you artists and high places?" And he replies, "Perspective. To see things in surprising ways you have to extend yourself a bit." What perspectives or roles does Jane take on in this story? What do you think surprises her? Where do you think she is most comfortable, or true to herself?

5. Both Rossetti and Morris idolize Jane's beauty to the point that she becomes iconic and legendary. Her response to this status ranges from disbelief to flattery to embarrassment to needing the attention. What events or circumstances precipitate these varied reactions? How do you feel about Jane's transformation and her acceptance of her own beauty? Does she use the power of her beauty well?

6. Were you surprised at the friendship between Lizzie and Jane? What do you think about Rossetti's love for both of them—are they equal in his eyes, or different? Rossetti says that, "Neither side of the coin is superior to the other. The dark must have the light, the strong the weak, the sharp angle the soft curve." How is this statement a reflection on these two women? How is it a reflection on his friendship with Morris?

7. Both Morris and Rossetti venture into other art forms, experimenting with poetry, interior design, and artisan-style crafts. Why, if Rossetti has won such acclaim for his painting, is he so destroyed by criticism of his poetry? Was he right to retrieve his work from his wife's grave? How does Morris respond to the praise he receives for his book?

8. What do you make of Morris's "arrangement" for Jane and Rossetti? Is it a noble attempt to gracefully bow out of their marriage, or is it a desperate attempt to maintain involvement in Jane's life?

9. Discuss the title of the book. Is Jane the only muse in the story, or does she have muses of her own? Who, in the novel, could be called "wayward"?

Enhance Your Book Club

1. Print out images of Jane in *The Blue Silk Dress* and *Prosperine* at en.wikipedia.org/wiki/Jane_Burden.

2. Read aloud selected works of Tennyson and Keats, who served as Morris's poetic inspiration.

3. Plan a craft—cover notebooks in William Morris–style wallpaper or buy a stained-glass coloring book!

Questions for the Author

1. How did you discover Jane Burden? What was it about her story that drew you in? How did she come to be the centerpiece of your story, rather than telling it from Rossetti's or Morris's perspective?

I read lots of biographies of artists I like and am interested in and keep a lookout for fascinating stories. I discovered Jane through my reading about William Morris. The most compelling thing for me initially was how someone as charismatic as Rossetti could completely reverse the standard of beauty of the time. I was also interested in how Jane could contemplate leaving an honorable man like Morris for a rogue like Rossetti. Early on I thought about alternating points of view between the three, but I didn't want the architecture to overwhelm the story. And I tend to be drawn to the players in the drama whom history has marginalized, and often they are women.

2. Can you tell us more about the Pre-Raphaelites? Who were they? Who were they reacting to? What did they value aesthetically? How were they received in their day?

The Pre-Raphaelite Brotherhood was a group of English artists and critics, founded by Dante Gabriel Rossetti, John Everett Millais, and William Holman Hunt in 1848. Some consider them the first avant-garde movement in art. They hoped to reform painting by rejecting the conventional and learned-by-rote techniques of Raphael and the subsequent Mannerists. They decried the influence of the Royal Academy of Arts and hoped to return painting to the careful detail, intense color, and complex compositions of fourteenth-century Italian and Flemish art. Ignored at first, the PRB became infamous after the exhibition of Millais's painting *Christ in the House of his Parents,* which many believed to be blasphemous. Critics thought their medievalism was backward-looking and their extreme devotion to detail ugly and jarring to the eye. However, the Brotherhood found support from the critic John Ruskin, both financially and in his writings. The PRB functioned as a group for only a very short period. William Morris and Edward Burne-Jones were really second-generation Pre-Raphaelites, influenced primarily by Rossetti.

3. How did you do the research for this book? Did you either travel, or visit museums and libraries? If so, what was your favorite place? What was the most interesting detail you uncovered in your research?

I visited the Huntington Library in Pasadena, California, which had a lovely show on William Morris a couple of years ago. I also saw a show on the Pre-Raphaelites at the Portland Art Museum in Portland, Oregon, where I live. I read a lot of books on the Pre-Raphaelite group and took a lot of notes. After I'd written the first draft of the book, I went to England. I spent a few days in London at the Victoria and Albert Museum; at Water House, Morris's childhood home that is now a museum devoted to his work and life; and Kelmscott House, which is also a museum and where Morris and Jane lived later in their lives. I went to Red Lion Square, Queen Square, and Tudor House. Then I spent some time in Oxford, at the Ashmolean Museum. I tried to walk out the Iffley Road to the countryside, but the countryside is a lot farther from the center of town than it was 140 years ago. Holywell Street is not a slum anymore, and I had to work to imagine what it would have been like then. I saw St. Michael's Church, Exeter College, and the Oxford Union. My favorite place of all, however, was Canterbury, which I visited because William Morris loved the cathedral there. It made me feel that much closer to him that I responded to it in a similar way.

4. **When did your fascination with art begin? Both** *The Wayward Muse* **and your previous book,** *The Painted Kiss,* **deal with women and their relationships with artists—which figures have piqued your interest most recently?**

When I was twelve I read *The Agony and the Ecstasy* by Irving Stone, about Michelangelo. Perhaps the book changed the course of my life, because I was completely enthralled by it. And it contained all of the elements—the magnificent art, the love affairs, the mixture of history and invention—that I use in my work now. I'm currently reading about the Abstract Expressionists—De Kooning, Pollock, Rothko—and about Francis Bacon. I haven't found a heroine in these stories yet. I may have a fictional protagonist in my next book.

5. What are your feelings about contemporary art? Do you think that there are still stories to be told behind the paintings, or has the prevalence of abstraction made that more difficult?

There are always stories, even in abstraction, I think, though representational painting will always be what I respond to most intensely and viscerally. I love Cecily Brown's hothouse style of semi-representational Abstract Expressionism. Then again, Albert Oehlen, who considers himself a post-nonrepresentational artist and uses his paintings to show the failures of art, makes the most beautiful work.

6. You say in your author's note that going beyond the facts into the stories of these characters was a way to get to know their essential selves. Which character elicited the strongest emotional reactions from you? Who were you most perplexed by?

I adored Morris. I admired him as a person; I was awed by his energy and accomplishment in so many different areas. I think I would have married him myself, if I could! So for Jane to leave him for someone who was so clearly his moral (and artistic, let's be honest) inferior was maddening, just maddening. I had to work very hard to understand her.

7. *The Wayward Muse*, like any work of historical fiction, is a blend of fact and fiction. Can you tell us a little bit about which parts of the story came from history and which parts from your imagination?

Jane spoke very little about her early life, so her relationship with her parents is a subject for conjecture. But her very silence was telling, I thought, and the fact that she did not attend her mother's funeral. Did Jane and Rossetti consummate their relationship before he left Oxford? Was she really in love with him then? Did she marry Morris only as a means for escape? No one knows for sure. I looked at the evidence and came to my own conclusions and tailored those conclusions to the needs of fiction. I compressed the end of Jane and Rossetti's relationship, which dragged on for another couple of years, until 1875. It seemed to me that it was more of the same: his illness and drug addiction, her anguish and uncertainty.

8. **There's a lot of wonderful poetry in the book—are these all original works from Rossetti and Morris or did you create any of the pieces on your own? What about the letters? Do you write poetry?**

A. S. Byatt, genius that she is, can create an entire fictional universe and then write the poetry for the universe and then the criticism about the poetry! But that's beyond me, and so I let Morris and Rossetti write the poetry. I did write poetry when I was young, and I loved Yeats. Maybe someday I'll return to it. I did write the letters, though. I read some of Morris's correspondence. It turned out he had a dryer wit than you might expect.

9. **What is the next project you're working on? Where do you hope it will take you?**

My next book is a departure for me. It is about an artist, of course, but a contemporary one. And it contains elements of history, but it is this character's unraveling of her family history to discover her own provenance, so to speak, that is at the heart of it. It should be a challenge to incorporate the elements I've used successfully in the past with something new.

10. Many historical fiction authors write with the dual purpose of educating and entertaining. What is one thing you hope your readers learn from *The Wayward Muse*? What is one thing you hope your readers feel?

I hope readers glimpse a Victorian era that is perhaps different from what they thought. We imagine that the Victorians were so repressed and proper, but their passions were not so different from ours. I also like to bring to the world's attention figures, particularly women, that time has forgotten. Jane and Lizzie and Georgie were incredible, talented women. Imagine what they could do today!